"Anybody ever tell you that you're packing one hell of an ego, flyboy?"

"I may have heard that once or twice."

"Well, believe it. Thank you for flying us around for the next two weeks, but I'm not interested in filling time in between those flights with convenience sex."

"Whoa! Hold on. Who said anything about sex?" Bo stalked down the step to face Paige. "Last I heard, we were talking about a kiss. One kiss. A kiss where we get to know each other and see if this chemistry we've got going is real."

Were they actually discussing whether or not to kiss? "Some things aren't worth trying. You're leaving soon. You live in a whole different world. My baggage really goes against that world—"

"We're talking about a damn kiss, not a flaming affair."

"I'm at least six years older than you."

His steely blue eyes narrowed with sleepy, sensual intent. "And you're hot as hell, especially when you're fired up."

Dear Reader,

Love is in the air, but the days will certainly be sweeter if you snuggle up with this month's Silhouette Intimate Moments offerings (and a heart-shaped box of decadent chocolates) and let yourself go on the ride of your life! First up, veteran Carla Cassidy dazzles us with *Protecting the Princess*, part of her new miniseries WILD WEST BODYGUARDS. Here, a rugged cowboy rescues a princess and whisks her off to his ranch. What a way to go…!

RITA® Award-winning author Catherine Mann sets our imaginations on fire when she throws together two unlikely lovers in *Explosive Alliance*, the latest book in her popular WINGMEN WARRIORS miniseries. In *Stolen Memory*, the fourth book in her TROUBLE IN EDEN miniseries, stellar storyteller Virginia Kantra tells the tale of a beautiful police officer who sets out to uncover the cause of a powerful man's amnesia. But this supersleuth never expects to fall in love! The second book in her LAST CHANCE HEROES miniseries, *Truly, Madly, Dangerously* by Linda Winstead Jones, plunges us into the lives of a feisty P.I. and protective deputy sheriff who find romance while solving a grisly murder.

Lorna Michaels will touch readers with *Stranger in Her Arms*, in which a caring heroine tends to a rain-battered stranger who shows up on her doorstep. And *Warrior Without a Cause* by Nancy Gideon features a special agent who takes charge when a stalking victim needs his help…and his love.

You won't want to miss this array of roller-coaster reads from Intimate Moments—the line that delivers a charge and a satisfying finish you're sure to savor.

Happy Valentine's Day!

Patience Smith
Associate Senior Editor

Please address questions and book requests to:
Silhouette Reader Service
U.S.: 3010 Walden Ave., P.O. Box 1325, Buffalo, NY 14269
Canadian: P.O. Box 609, Fort Erie, Ont. L2A 5X3

Explosive Alliance
CATHERINE MANN

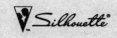

INTIMATE MOMENTS™

Published by Silhouette Books

America's Publisher of Contemporary Romance

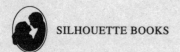 SILHOUETTE BOOKS

ISBN 0-373-27416-5

EXPLOSIVE ALLIANCE

This edition published by arrangement with Harlequin Books S.A.

® and TM are trademarks of Harlequin Books S.A., used under license.
Trademarks indicated with ® are registered in the United States Patent
and Trademark Office, the Canadian Trade Marks Office and in other
countries.

Visit Silhouette Books at www.eHarlequin.com

Printed in U.S.A.

Books by Catherine Mann

Silhouette Intimate Moments   Silhouette Books

Wedding at White Sands #1158   **Anything, Anywhere, Anytime*
*Grayson's Surrender #1175
*Taking Cover #1187
*Under Siege #1198
The Cinderella Mission #1202
*Private Maneuvers #1226
*Strategic Engagement #1257
*Joint Forces #1293
*Explosive Alliance #1346

Silhouette Bombshell

Pursued #18

*Wingmen Warriors

CATHERINE MANN

writes contemporary military romances—a natural fit, since she's married to her very own USAF research source. Prior to publication, Catherine graduated with a B.A. in fine arts: theater from the College of Charleston and received her master's degree in theater from UNC Greensboro. Now a RITA® Award winner, Catherine finds following her aviator husband around the world with four children, a beagle and a tabby in tow offers her endless inspiration for new plots. Learn more about her work, as well as her adventures in military life, by visiting her Web site: www.catherinemann.com. Or contact her at P.O. Box 41433, Dayton, OH 45441.

To my son, Robbie—a charmer, a joy, a blessing.

Chapter 1

"Hey, I thought you said there was a woman behind every tree here." Captain Bo Rokowsky stared through the windscreen of his C-17, broken clouds revealing the barren landscape of Minot Air Force Base, North Dakota.

Not a damn tree in sight.

Laughter rumbled through his headset from the loadmaster "Tag" and the in-flight mechanic "Mako."

"Yes, sir," Mako drawled from the cargo hold. "Suckered you right into working this air show with that one, didn't we?"

"You dudes got me good." Bo gripped the throttle and let them have their victory. Better to take the ribbing over being "tricked" than to admit his real reason for signing on to this mission.

"The clue bird should have hit you like a whole flock smacking the windscreen when old, married Tag told you that Minot joke about the trees." Mako continued to gloat. "His wife would kick his butt if she thought he was checking out the female population. I just tell my girlfriend you keep them all too busy, anyway."

"One at a time, pal." Bo eased back on the throttle, as usual using a casual tone and attitude to mask a deep-seated attention to detail. "Always one at a time."

Stick in hand, Bo guided the craft toward the base, a mere speck ahead in the middle of flat, flat and more flat farmland, where he would spend the weekend at Minot's annual air show—dateless.

Okay, so he had a reputation around the squadron as a player. But he wanted a steady relationship, wife and kids someday as much as the next guy. Maybe even more, since he'd never had a real home of his own.

If that meant he went through a lot of breakups in the search, such was life. It seemed damn shallow to keep dating a woman once he realized she wasn't The One. Some dumped him, too. He figured he was running fifty-fifty when it came to broken hearts given and received.

Painful? Sometimes. All told, though, the journey wasn't a major hardship. He loved women. After growing up in a boys' home, drifting off to sleep every night with sweat and gas hanging in the air, what guy wouldn't prefer to spend the rest of his life pressed up close to a soft, jasmine-smelling woman? Or rose-scented.

Or even spring-flowers-deodorant scented. He wasn't picky.

Still, he was grateful for Minot's treeless state. Now wasn't the time to shuffle those fifty-fifty odds either way. He had more important things to attend to on the ground than his exhaustive and sometimes tantrically exhausting quest for a Mrs. Rokowsky.

He wasn't working the Minot Air Show to meet flyboy groupies, but rather to meet one woman in particular. And no way in hell would *she* be open to sex with *him*.

From the left seat, the squadron commander snapped his critical gaze Bo's way while the boss evaluated. Scowled. "If you boys are done discussing your dating prospects in the Land of Tatanka, let's see about getting this plane on the ground."

Bo clamped his jaw shut. Fun time over, thanks to Lieutenant Colonel Lucas Quade, a gloomy micromanaging pain in the keister kind of leader, better known unofficially around the squadron as "Darth Vader." To be fair, the guy was a solid flier and a technically perfect commander.

Overly perfect.

Loosening his hold on the throttle, Bo flexed the stiffness out of his fingers, already anticipating a couple of hours with his guitar to work out the twinges and frustration. He hadn't "enjoyed" this much supervision since Sister Mary Nic had walked him to the lunchroom in first grade.

Of course he did have a habit of detouring even then.

Under normal circumstances, he wouldn't volunteer to judge the Miss America Contest with Quade, much less spend the weekend under his thumb on a TDY—temporary duty. But nothing had been normal for nearly a year, since the crash landing and capture overseas to be exact. Discovering that drug-running Air Force personnel and civilians in his own community had supported terrorists responsible for the shoot down only rocked his already cockeyed world.

He wasn't even sure he wanted to stay in the Air Force once his commitment was up next month. And wasn't that a kick-in-the-ass life crisis for a guy who'd been certain since the cradle that he would tear up the skies and raise hell with airplanes? He suspected he wouldn't have his answer until he'd put a piece of his past from a year ago to rest by checking on Paige Haugen and her daughter.

The widow and child of the man he'd helped send to jail. The drug-running bastard with terrorist ties.

"Well, Rokowsky?" Quade hissed low through the head-set, punting Bo back into the present. "Are you planning to call for landing weather? Review the approach? Any of this ringing a bell for you, Captain? You're not a lieutenant any-more. How about pulling your weight."

"Roger, sir, I'm on it."

Radioing for the weather report five freaking minutes early, Bo scanned the sky and kept his temper in check. He might question his call to the air these days, but he knew his job and had done everything to the letter on this mission. His check rides attested to his overall nuts-on flying. But wear-ing the uniform dictated no arguing with the big kahuna.

Bo continued to scope the horizon while listening to the all-clear weather report. So what were those dots mutating the sky—

"Birds!" Bo shouted, yanking back the stick.

A flock of birds—geese maybe—swooped into view, funneling below the craft as the C-17 climbed. Somehow Mako's "clue bird" had taken on a life-threatening reality.

His heart drummed in his ears while his hands worked with training-honed instincts. Smacking a goose at this speed would shatter the windscreen, could even kill a pilot.

The plane groaned at the abrupt ascent, then leveled, hummed again. Damn, that had been close. His pulse started to slow—

Whoomp.

His brain barked the answer in sync with Quade's affirmation.

"Bird strike in the number-one engine."

Death for a jet engine. And hopefully only one engine, with no explosion.

Caution lights flooded his control panel, an engine-fire alert. The landing strip grew closer, a stretch in a region as flat as any desert. But was it near enough?

Bo slammed aside memories of last year's desert crash landing quicker than he cut the fuel to the engine with a jerk of the fire handle. "Roger, fuel cut, beginning boldface checklist for engine shutdown."

Voices popped through the headset. Commands. Updates. The cargo plane shuddered through the air with the drag and pull of power adjustments to the remaining engines to compensate for the diminished thrust on the left. Protocol and division of labor was crucial for getting their butts on the ground in one piece. From here on out as copilot he would talk and Quade, in the aircraft commander's seat, would fly. No more evaluation, but plenty more scowling.

"Minot tower," Bo barked into the mike on his headset. "This is Moose zero-one, leveling off, present heading. We just took a bird strike and we've shut down an engine."

"Roger, zero-one," tower answered. "Are you declaring an emergency?"

Bo rocked the microphone button down for private innerphone. "Colonel, are you ready to declare?"

Lean and impassive, Quade hesitated, then nodded. "I think she's flying okay, but yes, let's go ahead and declare."

No surprise. Quade was a conservative aviator to the end. Not a bad thing right now.

Bo thumbed the mike button up for open-air frequency. "Roger, tower, I am declaring an emergency at this time."

"Copy, zero-one, are you able to switch frequencies or are your hands full?"

"Zero-one will accept a frequency change."

Chatter from other aircraft faded as he brought up the new frequency reserved for emergency personnel—the fire chief, command post, flight surgeon's office, maintenance and the supervisor of flying. In spite of his resolve, memories whispered through. During last year's crash landing there'd been no help, no friendly faces waiting for them on the ground as they descended their crippled craft into enemy territory. A missile hit, not a bird, had nailed them because of a flight-plan leak from one of their own.

"Moose zero-one, reporting up, three-two-two-dot-two."

Command Post responded, "Moose zero-one, Minot Command Post. Hotel Conference initiated—" Emergency personnel were up and listening. "Moose zero-one, souls on board and fuel remaining?"

"Four souls and 35,000 pounds."

"Copy four and thirty-five K. What's your plan?"

"We're going to do a controllability check and then a straight-in approach for landing."

Bo continued the radio calls while Quade slowed the cargo plane in midair to ensure it would be controllable at landing speed. At least in the air they could bail out. And there sure as hell was plenty of level, empty and totally treeless countryside for them to ditch.

Tag and Mako thundered up the stairwell into the cockpit and strapped into the two instructor seats behind the pilots, higher in the craft being safer in an emergency-landing situation.

"Gentlemen—" Quade's near-whisper calls had the damnedest way of booming "—everyone locked down tight?"

"Roger," the answer echoed in triplicate.

"Excellent. Once we land, no hesitation, haul ass out and as far away from the plane as possible." In case the plane blew. The unspoken possibility clouded the air with a noxious threat. "Now let's get this baby down in a way that doesn't feature us in the six-o'clock news."

Bo's hands clenched along with his gut. He issued instrumentation updates, keeping himself grounded with his reason for being here in the first place: to check up on Paige Haugen and her daughter. He wasn't sure why he felt so damn responsible for her after what her traitorous bastard husband had done—

Okay, he *did* know why, and it sucked even remembering tagging along with his own teary-eyed mother on her weekly visits to her convict husband. His father. *Father* being a damn loose term for a dirtbag who cared more about jacking cars than hanging out with his wife and son.

Bo rechecked his five-point harness. Not that he'd felt any loss over his father being locked up. He couldn't remember ever having Jackass Dirtbag around the apartment.

Then—surprise, surprise—Jackass had filed for divorce after his release. Teary-eyed Teresa Rokowsky had opened a vein rather than live without him.

As a kid, Bo had blamed himself for not being enough reason for his mama to live. As an adult, he knew where the blame belonged, but that still didn't stop his heart from squeezing at the lost look on Paige Haugen's face when she'd walked into the police station the night of her husband's arrest. The disillusioned expression had multiplied exponentially in newspaper photos after her husband's mob-hit death in prison.

Bo tried to blink away the haunting image even now. Damn it all, he preferred his dreams be filled with visions of luscious babes in bikinis. Instead his sleep was packed with nightmares of a widow with troubled eyes and a kid who was better off without her old man but probably missed him all the same.

Bo braced for landing and closure. Outside the windscreen, the runway waited in the cracked expanse of Dakota soil and cluster of military buildings. Planes dotted the parking area, other craft for the weekend's air show scheduled to start tomorrow.

Lower, lower still they descended. Small clumps of people gathered to watch today's arrivals.

Was *she* there already? Regardless, he would find her.

After he checked on Paige Haugen and her daughter, he would be free to decide his future in or out of the Air Force. He already had his dream custom ordered for that first night of peaceful sleep. By Monday evening he would be snoozing his way into a Caribbean fantasy, his guitar in hand, serenading a coconut-oil-scented blonde with a penchant for skinny-dipping.

A woman without glasses framing pain-filled eyes.

Paige Haugen nudged her glasses straight on her nose again, righting her view of the landing cargo plane. Military fire trucks and security police shrieked onto the runway toward the hulking gray cargo plane touching down, slowing, smoke puffing from the tires and screeching brakes.

Her other hand held firm to the sticky softness of her baby girl's fingers, not so little now. All of six years and nine months, Kirstie proclaimed often enough.

Too young to have hurt so much.

Paige swallowed back bilious memories stirred by the sirens. She wanted to leave. She'd seen enough destruction in her life, thanks to her traitorous bastard husband. But her brother had dropped her off on his way into Minot to restock veterinary supplies, leaving her landlocked at the base for at least another half hour.

The plane jerked to a stop. Seconds later the side hatch dropped open, stairs lowering. The gaping portal filled with flight-suit-clad men pouring out and down the steps. They sprinted away from the craft while the fire trucks swarmed around.

An emergency? Or a part of the air-show events? Surely the crowd would be cleared for a problem with the plane. And not just any plane, but a C-17 from her old hometown. The tail art glinted, afternoon sun showcasing a blue palm tree and half-moon resembling the South Carolina state flag. No matter how far she ran, apparently her past dogged her heels.

Her fingers squeezed protectively around Kirstie's until her daughter squeaked, "Ouch, Mama, you're crunching my hand."

"Sorry, punkin seed." She smiled down, the late-spring sun beaming welcome warmth after a cold Dakota winter, bitter in more ways than one. "I guess I was caught up in the action."

"Those men don't look like they got hurt. So how come there's that amb'lence? Is there a doctor inside? Are they gonna get a shot?" Somber brown eyes peered up from behind Coke-bottle-thick glasses. "I don't like shots much."

Her daughter didn't like doctors, either, suffering a heartbreaking fear of illness and death since her father's murder in prison. Paige's heart pinched. She would do anything to bring back her daughter's smile.

Even face demons from her past by coming to an Air Force base.

"They're as healthy as Waffles's new litter of puppies. See how fast they're running?"

The three men, all her age or maybe slightly older, kept a steady pace away from the craft. She exhaled relief.

Fire trucks circled the plane as a fourth man filled the hatch. The aviator, younger than the others, thundered down the steps and made up the distance in seconds, overtaking, passing.

With a guitar case slung over his shoulder?

How incongruous, yet it broadened her smile and sprinkled relief over her fried nerves. If he'd stopped to retrieve the instrument, then surely this wasn't a real emergency situation. Her gaze tracked the sprinting man abandoning the scene with heart-pounding athleticism.

"It's probably a part of the air-show demonstration, punkin. Or maybe they're practicing for when something really goes wrong." Too bad life didn't offer practice runs. Paige smoothed back her daughter's sweaty blond curls from her forehead. "But if you're scared, we could go look at something else."

"No, please. You promised we could see the planes. You *promised.* What if it rains tomorrow and we can't come back? Then you gotta work Sunday cause Uncle Vic's working Saturday and Uncle Seth hurt his ankle." Kirstie tucked her glasses back up for a better view. "And 'sides, I wanna make sure those men are okay."

"If you're sure." Easy enough to acquiesce when the small crowd blocked the exit, anyway.

"Totally sure." Kirstie stared back with wide eyes devoid of laughter.

Damn Kurt Haugen.

Damn him for dying. Damn him for the many lives he'd destroyed. Damn him most of all for stealing Kirstie's childhood joy. And while she was at it, Paige figured *she* deserved a good swift kick for believing in him right up to the point they'd locked his traitorous butt in jail.

A toxic mix of acid and horror scoured what little of her stomach lining remained. How could he have sold out his country by smuggling terrorist-supplied opium in his restaurant's shrimp trawlers? And how could she have missed that she and her husband were living far better than an up-and-coming restaurateur should?

Paige popped a Tums and bolstered her resolve. She was through being a gullible idiot when it came to charming men. Her daughter needed a strong mama with a good head on her shoulders, straighter than her perpetually crooked glasses.

The four men slowed, gathered, studied their aircraft, chests pumping for air. The oldest, a lumbering man, bent to brace his hands on his knees. Two others swiped their brows with a forearm.

Her gaze skipped last to the lanky guitar-carrying aviator who still stood tall, barely winded in comparison. His coal-black hair reflected the sun's rays, some of the beams lingering to catch along the hint of curl in his close-cropped cut. Why couldn't she look away from him? She definitely wasn't in the market for a man now, if ever again. Kurt had singed her, but good.

She frowned. Did the guy look familiar? Maybe that was what snagged her attention. Except, she couldn't tell for certain from so far away. Maybe they all looked alike in those green flight suits.

Heaven help her if she actually knew him. It was bad enough that her husband had cultivated a couple of young service members with deep debts to help him track military-drug-surveillance flights. But then, he'd threatened others who wouldn't help him.

Coming to an Air Force base and facing so many reminders of her husband's deceit left her longing to dig deep in her purse for the whole roll of antacids. But there was precious little excitement around here to entice her child's playfulness back. The annual air show marked major goings-on in the area, right up there alongside the yearly State Fair and Rodeo.

Not that she was complaining anymore. Unlike during her teenage years, she now embraced the starkness of her home state. Nothing was hidden here. There wasn't even a respectable tree in sight for a good old-fashioned game of hide-and-seek. Definitely different from the verdant marshes of the South that had cloaked so much.

The guitar guy chose that vulnerable moment to glance her way. Dry lightning crackled overhead. Or at least she thought it did because her skin prickled, fine hairs rising with a warning that nature was about to unleash a storm.

What a ridiculously fanciful notion—and a dangerous one. Still her hand sneaked up to check the stretchy band holding back her own hair as blond as Kirstie's.

Her hand fell away. Damn it, she didn't have time for vanity, much less men.

Without breaking eye contact, the guy angled to speak with a grumpy-looking fella next to him, boots already moving forward. Toward her. Ah, geez.

Paige hitched the insulated lunch sack from the ground up onto her shoulder, her heart thumping like thunder answering lightning. "Come on, punkin, let's find somewhere to sit." Far away from here. "We can watch the planes land while we eat."

Kirstie stared up with eyes enlarged by the lenses of tiny kid glasses. "I want to go inside the airplanes."

"And we will. Tomorrow when the show officially starts. Okay? Today the planes are just arriving."

The man ambled closer.

Time was running out. She resorted to desperate measures. "We'll eat cupcakes for lunch."

"I thought I gotta eat protein first so I don't get sick with the flu or new-monia and hafta get a shot."

"I brought peanut butter and jam sandwiches, too," she bartered through clenched teeth. "Blackberry jam. And I'll give you a Rugrats vitamin the minute we get home. Come on."

Kirstie's wide eyes shifted from the lunch sack to the airplanes and back again. Her tongue peeked out of the corner of her mouth.

Yesss. They were seconds away from a sugar high she suddenly craved very much. Paige gave her daughter's hand a gentle tug. "Race ya to that bench over there."

Way over there, far from the man who really, really couldn't be walking toward her.

Kirstie's sneakers smacked asphalt while Paige jogged alongside. The physical labor as a veterinary technician for large farm animals this past year had increased her endurance. Wind and work toughened her up again in more ways than one. Being broke sucked. At least she had a roof over her head, thanks to her brother, and she was trying to pull her own weight by helping his veterinary practice stay afloat.

"Mrs. Haugen?"

The sexy baritone carried on the wind, leaving her no choice but to stop. Paige turned, gasped. Recognition stole her breath faster than any run.

Flyboys didn't all look alike in the uniform, after all. This man resembled no other. She remembered him sure enough, *and* that horrible night she'd first seen him.

Her past came strutting toward her with loose-hipped appeal, guitar slung over his shoulder. He was gorgeous, quite simply a perfectly put-together man with fallen-angel good looks that even an objective observer would note.

And her husband had tried to kill him simply because the man had been in Kurt Haugen's way. She fought back tears and shame.

"I didn't mean to startle you, ma'am."

Ma'am? Paige winced. Now didn't that put her in her old-lady place?

Bo Rokowsky would probably be shocked to hear about the whole lightning sensation. God, he was likely all of about twenty-six or seven. Too young for her.

Her thirty-three wasn't ancient, but she suffered no delusions about her looks. Sure, she didn't crack mirrors, but she would never be mistaken for a supermodel even with an overhaul.

She was comfortable in her own skin now, far more so than during her weekly manicure life. But she wore jeans for working with animals these days, rather than sundresses for pampered-wife dinners. Her glasses never stayed straight. And carting around an extra twenty pounds on her body that couldn't be called baby weight anymore didn't exactly engender rubbernecking stares from men.

"Mrs. Haugen?" The young god's forehead furrowed. "Are you okay?"

"Mom," Kirstie jerked her hand, whispering, "aren't you gonna answer?"

"Hello." Wow, what a conversational gymnast.

"You probably don't remember me."

Could she bluff her way out by pretending she didn't know him? Except she'd never been a good liar, unlike her husband. "I remember you. It was a…memorable…time, Lieutenant Rokowsky."

"It's 'Captain' now."

Had that much time passed since Kurt's arrest and death soon after? Nearly twelve months. Why was this man here?

Kirstie clung to Paige's leg, silent and trembling. Her little girl who used to turn fearless cartwheels now approached the world with more wary feet.

Hugging an arm around Kirstie, Paige wrapped her in as much security as possible. She couldn't imagine this man would deliberately hurt a child. But even an unwitting mention of Kurt left Kirstie searching for hives on her legs, convinced she'd contracted a deadly disease that would require an injection.

"That was quite a show your crew put on, Captain."

"Show? Oh, you mean the sirens."

"And the sprint."

"We flew into a flock of birds, took one in an engine and had to call for an emergency landing."

"So that wasn't a performance for our benefit?"

"Afraid not."

Why wasn't he leaving? Working? What did he want from her? "Don't you need to do…*something* after a landing that frightening?"

"Stuff like that happens in the air—birds, engine fires, rapid decompressions. All in a day's work." His fingers flexed inside his flight gloves. "At least nobody's shooting at us."

She winced at images of Kurt's arrest the night he'd held this man and another family hostage in hopes of finding a ticket out of the country.

"I meant in a war zone," he amended gently.

She tried to smile. And failed. "Oh."

He stepped closer. Man and musk and a masculine protectiveness emanated from him, wobbling her knees.

Bo brushed her elbow. "How are you?"

Scared. Afraid she couldn't feed her daughter. Terrified one of her husband's connections would come after them. She was also mortified. Decimated.

Lonely. And really, really enjoying the hot strength of this man's touch against her elbow. Ah, geez, was he actually leaning closer, his nostrils flaring as if catching her scent like a stallion choosing a mate?

No problem, then, unless he got worked up over the smell of Hawaiian Tropic sunscreen.

She eased her arm free. "We're building a new life. I appreciate your taking the time to say hello—" Now wasn't that a whopper lie? "But my daughter and I are about to eat lunch."

"Cupcakes," Kirstie whispered from around Paige's leg.

Resting his guitar on the cement, he lowered to one knee in front of Kirstie. "Sounds like my kind of meal."

Was he angling for an invitation? For what possible reason? She hated being suspicious, but when someone you loved betrayed you so totally, trusting strangers was all but impossible.

"Well, goodbye, Captain, we need to get mov—"

Kirstie released her death grip on Paige's thigh and inched forward. "Will you show me the airplanes? I'll give you half my cupcake."

"Kirstie," Paige shushed low. "Captain Rokowsky probably has—"

"Bo." He tapped the name tag on his flight suit. "My name's Bo."

"He has other things to do."

Bo glanced over at the three men and then back. "I'm afraid your mom's right."

Kirstie's disappointed sigh huffed up to rustle sweaty bangs. Then her spine straightened with her old spunk. "What if I gave you my whole cupcake? It's chocolate with sprinkles."

"Sprinkles, huh?" He scratched his square jaw. "That's a tempting offer, but my boss is going to come looking for me soon, and he gets cranky when we're not on time. I just wanted to say hello before debrief."

"De-what?" Kirstie's curiosity about all things flying overtook her shyness. As much as Paige wanted to run, she couldn't bear to stomp on the spark returning to her daughter.

"Debrief. That's when we talk about the flight so we can learn how to do things better the next time," he explained with surprising patience for a young bachelor with "player" stamped all over his godlike body and confident strut.

"Oh, kinda like how I hafta go to school."

"Exactly. But are you coming back tomorrow? I could work around those other things to spend an afternoon with two pretty ladies. If it's okay with your mama, of course."

He grinned up with unrepentant mischief, as if he knew darn well he'd maneuvered her by offering in front of Kirstie. Yet why offer at all? Didn't he have better things to do? It wasn't *that* deserted in Minot.

"Are you always this *accommodating?*" And full of bull, she silently added.

"I aim to please." His smile kicked up a notch, his perfect face somehow enhanced all the more by his ever-so-slightly crooked teeth. "What do you say, ladies? Are you going to stand me up tomorrow?"

"No way." Kirstie's curls bounced with her shaking head. "You betcha boots we're coming back. Mama promised."

Whoa. Somebody stop the Mack truck force of this guy and her daughter. "Hello? I'm here, too."

"Mama always keeps her promise." Kirstie rolled right on. "'Course sometimes she says 'maybe,' but that means she's not sure and she never promises 'less she knows for sure, 'cause it's important not to lie."

"She's right." Bo nodded sagely. "Sounds like you've got a good mama, Cupcake."

"Kirstie. My name's Kirstie Adella Haugen and my mama's name is Paige."

"Well Miss Kirstie Adella Haugen…" Scooping up his guitar, he stood, killer grin rising in wattage along with him. "I'll meet you and your mama at noon tomorrow over by the Thunderbirds' booth. All right, Paige?"

Her stomach flipped like one of those planes in flight. She wanted to say no, no and hell, no.

But Kirstie smiled.

Paige sighed, defeated by a hip-high six-year-old, no less. "Yes, thank you."

Kirstie's squeal was ample reward. "I'll see you tomorrow, Captain Bo."

"Looking forward to it, Cupcake." Winking, he pivoted away, swinging his guitar back over his shoulder.

Watching him swagger off, a glint of sunlight dancing through the hint of curl in his hair, Paige reminded herself that the veneer of charm dulled all too quickly without substance beneath. And since she had no intention of going deep with this man, she would be able to keep her daughter safe for the span of one afternoon outing.

As he tossed a wave over his shoulder, and flashed her a perfect smile with charmingly imperfect teeth, she couldn't help but wonder who would protect her from the likes of him?

Chapter 2

He hadn't packed protection for this TDY.

Protection?

Bo almost startled back a step on the tarmac at the unexpected thought. Still, he kept right on watching the soft sway of Paige Haugen's even softer looking hips as she hunted down a bench for the cupcake lunch with her kid.

Why was he worrying about condoms today? The emergency landing must have rattled his brain. He'd known full well when leaving Charleston this morning that he wouldn't need birth control since he would only be seeing Paige Haugen. She was the *last* woman he would choose to sleep with, given the mess a year ago, and no doubt *he* would be last place on her list.

Now didn't that sting more than it should while at the same time firing up testosterone at the challenge?

Like he needed more firing up. The singsong melody of

her Dakota accent still strummed his raw senses. Her tangy
sunscreen scent clung to the dry air. And damned if sunscreen
didn't smell like coconut oil and tropical fantasies.

Her shoulder-length locks offered an enticing bonus of
softness. His hands itched to discover just how silky her hair
might be gliding through his fingers. And suddenly he thought
of another Minot saying to go along with Mako and Tag's
"tree" discussion.

Why not Minot?

Freezin's the reason.

Yeah, she'd given him the cold shoulder all right when he
was near burning after a glimpse of her generous breasts straining against her 4-H T-shirt. He could have been standing in a
winter snowdrift and melted that sucker in five seconds flat.

Gusting wind whipped the eighty-degree May weather
around him along with rat-size mosquitoes, itching him out
of his sensual haze. The pesky insects bred and hatched in the
piles of melting snow, thriving, big like everything else in this
wide-open landscape.

He slapped his neck. Paige Haugen would certainly rather
swim naked through a pool of these monster mosquitoes
swarming the flight line than spend more time with him.

Paige Haugen.

Naked.

The image threatened to take root with a tenacity he knew
better than to allow. She was an attractive woman—smelled
damned good. But his goal here was to get her out of his head,
not plant her more firmly in his thoughts.

She and her daughter emerged from the other side of the
small crowd, making their way toward a metal bench. She
swung the insulated sack between them and started doling out
food. His mouth watered at the thought of tasting a cupcake,
followed by a patch of Paige's skin.

As if she felt his gaze, she glanced over—and away just

as quickly. He couldn't blame her for wanting to avoid him after the way things had shaken down with her husband's murder in prison. Reminders of that had to suck, regardless of whether or not she'd loved the dirtbag.

And speaking of another Jackass Dirtbag, he knew from his mother that love wasn't logical.

"Rokowsky?" The commanding tone of Quade's voice rode the wind and prickled at him like those mutant mosquitoes.

"Yes, sir?"

Bo turned to his squadron commander, prepping himself for the butt ripping undoubtedly on its way for something or other. Some days, proving his boss wrong was all that kept him in the service.

Lean and lethal, Quade stopped nose-to-nose, cold anger icing the air between them. "What the hell were you thinking wasting time to pick up your guitar?"

That if I got myself blown up you would celebrate over being short a smart-ass captain? Bo kept his yap shut and let the commander have his say. Open defiance never won the day, a lesson he'd learned well overseas in Rubistan.

"When I order you to abandon the aircraft, you damn well haul out. Is that understood, Captain?"

"Yes, sir." Definitely understood, but he would do the same again in a heartbeat.

Bo hitched his guitar up on his shoulder. The six-string acoustic had been a gift from Sister Mary Nic when he'd graduated from high school. Purchased with a nun's poverty-level salary, the guitar was golden in his eyes. He would die before losing it.

The commander's rigid stance relaxed minutely. "I guess we can call this day a wash since you saved our bacon by spotting the bird strike and pulling up in time. That was an excellent job of maintaining focus in the face of distraction. Well done, Captain."

Quade rarely dispensed praise, so it always stunned the fight right out of a guy's gut. "Thank you, sir."

"Close your slack jaw, Captain." Aloof steely eyes assessed. "You think I'm being a hard-ass because it's fun? I'm not here to be your friend. I'm here to make sure that at the end of my tour, we have as many airplanes and aircrew as when I started."

And they both knew that was already impossible. Their unit had lost two planes to man-portable missiles, but, thank God, with no fatalities. Barely. A year ago when Bo's plane had been shot down over the Middle East, his crew had been captured by warlords before the Rubistanian government intervened with a rescue.

Bo's fingers flexed inside his flight gloves. He'd been so full of himself and confidence. Open defiance. He'd ended up with two broken hands, totally useless to his crew, marking the beginning of his doubts.

He wasn't afraid of dying. He wasn't even afraid of another beating, no more than a normal fear. But he was scared as hell of someone dying because of him.

Knowing he wasn't directly at fault for his mother's suicide didn't squelch the notion that he should have done something. And in the middle of his doubts had fallen this woman with her haunted eyes behind funky, black-framed retro glasses.

His gaze cruised back to Paige on the bench with her daughter. Kirstie licked the top off her cupcake. The mother mirrored her daughter, clearing half the frosting with one swirl of her tongue. Paige's lashes fluttered closed in ecstasy, flaming visceral heat to life while his defenses were down.

A shadow fell ahead of him as Quade shifted closer. "Someone has to stay with Mako and the plane for the next couple of weeks until it's repaired. Obviously I can't be that someone because of my duties back at the squadron."

Bo straightened as the implication—and prospect—sunk in. Any other time he might have chafed at what promised to be two, even three weeks of inactivity. But fate had just thrown open his window of opportunity with Paige Haugen.

"I'm the logical choice to stay, sir." Gaze magnet-stuck, Bo watched Paige thumb chocolate frosting off the corner of her mouth.

"Strange running into her here today, and you two talking," the boss noted quietly.

"Yes, Colonel, it is." Could Quade see inside his head? Probably. The man was everywhere, all the time.

He wanted to like the commander, certainly respected his airmanship. But Quade went out of his way to be unlikable.

Quade cleared his throat and backed up a step. "Well, Captain? Don't you have some paperwork to file before these damn mosquitoes make lunch out of us both?"

Before Bo could answer, Quade pivoted toward Tag and Mako a few yards away. "And you two, what are you gabbing about? The flight's not over until the weight of the paperwork equals the weight of the plane, even if we had to make an emergency landing."

The big kahuna punctuated his orders with precise marching steps of his boots on asphalt. "Tag, unload your gear off the airplane and let's head over to base ops. Mako, park this baby correctly and bring me a maintenance status ASAP, then meet us over in base ops so we can coordinate with home to ship the parts and people here to patch her up…."

Quade's voice droned into that *Peanuts* cartoon teacher blur of "mwah, mwah, mwah" while Bo followed, studying Paige from a growing distance. A man stopped beside her, a burly guy in jeans and a plaid shirt. The dude snitched the rest of her cupcake with unmistakable familiarity.

Talk about a splash of cold water that still didn't wash away coconut-scented fantasies. He'd never considered she might have moved on with her life. But her husband had been dead for nearly a year—arrested and held without bond last May, murdered in prison the following month.

Bo forced his eyes off her and onto his crew. He should be happy for her. Yippee, whoo-hoo and all that. He was off the hook.

So why the kick in his gut?

He had until tomorrow at noon to figure it out. Too bad he couldn't think about anything except Paige Haugen on a beach towel, setting aside her quirky glasses and swimsuit for a skinny-dip.

"What's the skinny on this guy Kirstie says will be showing you around the air show tomorrow?"

Sliding out of her brother's truck, Paige stifled a wince at Vic's overprotective tone. He slammed the driver's side door on the blue Ford, boots smacking perpetually dusty earth in their patchy front lawn. No sculpted southern gardens and potted ferns for her here.

"Back down, Vic." The last thing she needed was Vic joining forces with their cousin Seth to track Bo Rokowsky, much like they'd done to her first prom date. At least Seth would be slowed by his currently busted ankle. "Bo and I met in Charleston, and he remembered us."

It was a…memorable…time.

What an understatement. She reached into the back seat and unbuckled her sleeping daughter, careful not to bump her baby girl's head on the rack full of fishing poles across the window. "Kirstie's such a charmer, he offered to take off for a couple of hours tomorrow to give her a guided tour."

Brotherly eyes all-knowing under the brim of his John Deere trucker hat, Vic circled around the hood to the passenger side and leaned to scoop the snoozing kid from her arms. "Offered for Kirstie, huh?"

Overprotective tones shifted into a higher gear than the straining generator behind their white clapboard house/clinic. Some things never changed. Her older blond brother reminded her of their looming two-story home—weathered, starkly attractive and so very loyal no matter what nature threw their way.

Of course, Vic had been right about Kurt, and she thanked God every day this past year that her brother had never lorded it over her. He'd welcomed her home without question, given her a job and worked like crazy to fill the void in Kirstie's life left by Kurt's death.

With a sleepy sigh, Kirstie sagged against Vic's plaid-covered chest. His devotion was all the more heartbreaking since he'd lost his own daughter in a drowning accident four years ago. His wife had blamed him—the heartless witch—and filed for divorce, the breakup so bitter he'd dug in his bachelor heels deep.

Still, he hadn't winced once when Kirstie had hauled Little Tykes Central through his wide bar gate and into his yard. He swore their arrival was an answer to a prayer, that giving Paige room and board in exchange for a lower salary saved him the pinch of hiring someone at full price.

He'd rescued her pride as well as her butt. She owed him big-time. "Kirstie failed to mention I'm easily six years—" or more, *ouch* "—older than the guy."

"Doesn't matter to a man. And it's not like you're ancient or, uh…" His gaze landed on the stacked bags of feed in the back of the truck. "Or dog food."

"Where do you get your charm?" She elbowed him in the side.

She didn't want this discussion, and she sure didn't want to remember that lightning-crackle moment with Bo Rokowsky. Must be lack of sex messing with her head. Yet if she thought overlong about Kurt touching her, her stomach lurched like the brush tumbling past her feet. How could she have made love with a man so devoid of decency and not sensed something?

Forget about sex. Numb was better. Or it had been, until one lightning look from a cocky flyboy shocked her nerve endings to life again.

"Captain Rokowsky was charmed by *Kirstie.*" Paige hooked her lunch sack over her shoulder. "I should probably check on Seth manning the reception desk and see if he needs ice for his ankle—"

"Captain, huh? He must not be too young."

"Still too young for me, since regardless of my actual age I feel a hundred these days." She smoothed a hand over her sleeping daughter's head resting on Vic's shoulder. "How about you put Kirstie down on the sofa inside and I'll get a head start unloading the supplies?"

"Damn sweet deal for me."

"Just make sure to click on the intercoms so I can keep an ear out for her."

His smile faded. "I won't let anything happen to her."

She squeezed his sturdy forearm. "I know. Thank you."

A long swallow and curt nod later, he thudded up the steps to the circa 1920s farmhouse.

Paige circled around to the back of the truck and lowered the tailgate. Bending at the knees, she hefted a fifty-pound bag of Mrs. Svenson's rice-fortified dog food for her aging collie. Paige adjusted the weight on her shoulder and started toward the vet offices spoking off the house, a five-by-five clinic sign flapping in the wind, hinges creaking.

Muscle ache offered a healthy, welcome reminder that she held her own now. She trudged up the four side steps, her eyes drawn to the lonely landing strip out back where their cousin's Cessna Skyhawk was parked, stirring images of a certain guitar-toting pilot.

That plane would be better served reminding her of their precarious financial position. They stayed solvent by Seth flying them out to remote locales for emergency calls. Ranchers paid through the nose for that service. But mad cow disease and lower beef prices had hit the plains states hard, leaving ranchers panicking over every sick animal, yet short of funds to pay the doctor bill.

Their cousin's sprained ankle would take at least two to three weeks to heal before he could fly again. What a long time to pay a stand-in pilot, even the crappy one Seth had scrounged up who was working for bargain-basement rates.

"Maybe I should invest in a parachute," she mumbled, leaning a hip against the wooden door frame to bear some weight while she slid one hand to the knob.

She reminded herself the substitute was licensed. His finesse factor in the air wasn't great, but they didn't need pretty flying.

Bo Rokowsky was all about finesse and charm—

Ah, for Pete's sake.

The bell tinkled as the door swung wide to reveal her cousin manning the reception desk. Resembling a blond beach bum more than a meticulous pilot, he lounged back in the office chair with his foot propped on the counter. Baggy cargo shorts and a faded fishing hat made for eclectic receptionist garb. "Have fun today?"

"A blast." Paige kicked the door closed behind her, the scent of ammonia-washed tile greeting her with antiseptic reality. No flowery, insubstantial fantasies here.

Would she be doomed to think of Bo every time she saw a plane? You'd figure she would have enough jammed in her head. She was a working, single mother with a floundering family business to keep alive and a life to rebuild. She would not allow some player flyboy with his charming swagger and killer smile to derail her. "How's the pain today?"

Seth shrugged in that guy manner indicating that to admit pain would be considered wussy. "I'll be ready to kick Vic's ass in a couple of weeks."

"I'll be sure to warn him." Paige flung the sack of dog food onto the counter, her muscles screaming "thank you" in relief.

Not exactly dog food in the looks department, huh? She glanced down at her ragged fingernails and chapped hands, flipped them over to reveal more calluses. Damn it, she was proud of these hands, and she wouldn't let silly vanity steal the joy of accomplishment.

Closing her fingers into a fist, Paige knuckle-nudged her glasses so her unsteady world would tip right again, only to find they were already straight. And she had no choice but to attribute the off-kilter feeling to something—or someone—else.

Given a choice, Bo knew Paige Haugen wouldn't have joined him at the air show for their tour today. So he'd left her no choice by offering in front of her daughter.

Lounging against the Thunderbirds booth, Bo searched the milling crowds for Paige. Wind battered the inflated toy planes dangling from the wooden crossbar. He swatted one from in front of his face for a clearer view. Would she blow him off and not show up? She was already—he shoved his flight-suit sleeve away from his watch—three minutes and forty-seven seconds late.

Irritation nipped, along with more of those atomic mosquitoes. He might not have the best dating record in the world, but he never stood anyone up.

Dating?

This was *not* a date. They were just going to crawl around in a few jets and helicopters, watch the aerial acrobatics, down some of those hot dogs steaming the air. Besides, there was that other guy who stole her cupcakes.

Bo rolled his sleeve back over his watch. Sure he was attracted to her, but the last thing he needed was to tangle up her life with his. Even if she didn't live clear across country, even if her husband hadn't pointed a gun at his head, he would not risk upsetting Kirstie's world. The kid had enough to handle without getting attached to a string of her mama's boyfriends only to watch them walk away.

All moot points because he would only be around for two weeks, three tops. He would keep this and further meetings light, uncomplicated and definitely with no sexual undertones. If she even showed up.

He checked his watch again, trying to ignore his grumbling stomach only made worse by those steaming hot dogs two booths over. And the turkey legs.

And coconut?

His nose twitched. Bo turned to find Paige weaving her way toward him and, oh, yeah, this day would be a torturous exercise in self-control, if he could smell her even from this far away. His hands might not be able to take her, but he allowed his eyes to feast their fill for a few indulgent seconds. Jeans never looked so good as they did riding low on Paige's luscious hips, right where his hands itched to hook. Would the heat of her skin warm the perpetual ache in his reconstructed fingers?

Whoa. Danger zone.

Back off those thoughts pronto, pal, and just keep enjoying the view. Instead of a hair band, today she swept away blond strands with one of those small bandannas tied behind her head, sort of a peasant-handkerchief style with tiny yellow flowers to match her shirt pattern. She sure made the pale color come alive.

Lifting a foot, he shined the top of his boot against the back of his calf. He caught himself midpolish. Not a date, damn it. He slammed his boot to the ground just as Paige dodged another tourist to stop in front of him. Kirstie tucked against her mama's leg like an unshakable wingman.

Bo shoved away from the booth. "Ready for your tour, ladies?"

"Yes, thank you." Paige folded her arms over her breasts.

Only looking, he reminded himself. No harm there. Or was there?

He shifted his attention to Kirstie and tousled the kid's hair. "Good afternoon, Cupcake. Have you eaten lunch yet?"

"Nope." She eyed the hot-dog booth with longing.

Paige knelt to tie her daughter's pink-and-red tennis shoes. "You ate a second breakfast at eleven."

"Not lunch, though, and maybe he didn't get to eat yet, neither."

"Right you are." He extended his hand for Kirstie to take. "How about a hot dog?"

The kid eyed his hand warily. Because he was a stranger? Or because of the thin scars lining his skin? They provided him with constant reminders of the day his fingers had been crushed by a Rubistanian warlord who didn't appreciate attitude from a prisoner.

Paige's gaze skimmed down to his hand, bare of a flight glove today. A whisper of a puzzled frown slipped across her face, gone as fast as it appeared.

Bo let his arm fall to his side. "How about you hold on to your mama. Wouldn't want to lose you in the crowd."

Four hot dogs, two bags of chips and three lemonades later, Bo wadded up their trash and pitched it into the barrel garbage can while Kirstie peppered him with questions. Paige seemed beyond eager to let her daughter carry the conversational load. Somehow her silence made him far more aware of her than if they'd fallen into easy banter.

"Well, ladies, now that my stomach isn't growling out a whale song anymore, how about we look around? The aerial displays don't begin for another two hours, so we should be able to work our way through everything on the flight line."

He started to palm Paige's back. She sidestepped without even looking his way.

Well, hell, Prickly Paige. It wasn't like he planned to haul her behind a booth for a quickie. Although that sounded appealing.

For his own sanity, he kept a safe twelve inches between them while they strolled past booths packed with hats, shirts and more inflatable airplanes, like countless other air shows he'd attended. They wove around a recruiting table toward the rows of parked aircraft.

"I wanna start with that." Kirstie pointed to the Thunderbird on display.

"You got it, Cupcake." He hefted Kirstie up onto the ladder, while the pilot in attendance helped her into the cockpit.

Bo backed away, dipping his head to lower his voice—and hey, if that gave him a quick whiff of Paige, well then, no harm no foul. "They always want to start with the flashy planes."

"Very different from your C-17." She shaded her eyes to study the rows of parked planes—cargos, bombers, fighters, from current day and years past. "A lot smaller."

"Are you insinuating my big plane's a compensation?" Ah, hell. So much for no banter.

Paige's fair complexion pinkened.

He let them both off the hook before things got even more heated. "I also flew a T-37 and T-38 in pilot training."

A polite smile flickered while she kept her eyes fixed on her daughter tucking her tiny head into a helmet. "You enjoy flying."

"A plane's like no other toy out there." He'd spent hundreds of hours at St. Elizabeth's orphanage dreaming of a job with endless toys and trips around the world.

He'd never considered warlords.

What had Paige dreamed of as a child? Certainly not ending up the wife of a drug dealer who pumped terrorist-generated opium into the U.S. He studied her for a long, silent moment. Maybe it was time to acknowledge the big pink elephant she seemed determined to ignore. "North Dakota's a long way from South Carolina."

She stayed quiet for so long he thought she would ignore him, anyway. Finally her gaze slid down from her daughter and landed square on him without flinching.

"Apparently not far enough because here you are."

Her spunk reached out and grabbed him by the libido.

He liked a woman who held her own. "What brought you here?"

Her spine went so straight he expected her to just snatch up her kid and leave. Good God, the woman couldn't build walls any higher if she had a forklift and team of construction workers to help. "I wasn't referring to your husband. I meant what made you choose here to settle?"

Her rigid stance relented. "I'm from the area. My brother and cousin offered me a job." She tucked a stray strand under the scrap of a scarf and nudged her glasses straight again. "So much for independence, huh? But I feel safer here."

Safer? The back of his neck prickled a warning. Why hadn't he considered her husband's past might pose a threat to her future? There hadn't been witness-protection offers since she had nothing to offer up on Haugen's dealings. A mixed blessing. "Has there been any cause to worry?"

She gave a tiny, not at all reassuring, negative shake of her head. "Most important, my daughter's happier here. It's been difficult for her, losing her father. My brother and cousin can't replace…him. But they love her."

"Your brother and cousin?" Like maybe a cupcake-stealing brother or cousin?

"I live with them. We run a business together."

"What kind of business?"

"My brother's a veterinarian. I'm a licensed veterinary technician." She skirted the roped-off area around a fighter plane. "We fly out to remote locations to treat farm animals."

"What about your cousin?" He braced her back as a crowd of teens jostled past. His hand fell away fast.

"He's our pilot and owns the plane. Or at least he was flying until he busted his ankle falling through a loft while we were out on a call. We've hired a temporary pilot—" She stopped short. "I'm tired of talking about me. Why don't we talk about you for a while? Something other than the size of your plane, of course."

A laugh caught him as unaware as her humor. She smiled back, crinkling the corners of pretty brown eyes behind those funky black glasses, and damned if he didn't forget what they were talking about altogether. Who needed chitchat? This was a day when he could only enjoy the view, anyway.

"Hey?" Kirstie called, climbing down and halting conversation. "You guys are lookin' awful red. Are you feelin' hot?"

"Uh-huh." Bo registered the little girl's words but stayed focused on the mother staring right back at him with a frozen smile.

Kirstie hopped to a stop between them. "Want some sunblock? Mama packed it in her bag. SPF 45. That's the best so you don't get skin cancer. My daddy died of cancer, don'tcha know."

Huh? Bo jerked his eyes from Paige and looked down at Kirstie who was already distracted by the MH-53 Pave Low helicopter on display.

Paige's jaw tightened. "She's been told the truth even if she says otherwise. She's coping the best she can."

She set off after her daughter, leaving Bo in their wake. Realization dawned. Even if there wasn't some lurking threat from Kurt Haugen's past dealings, these two ladies might well have problems brewing that he couldn't fix in a few short weeks.

But with Paige's brown eyes planted even more firmly in his conscience, he also now knew he was a hundred percent committed to trying.

Two hours later Paige worked up another smile to cover her jittering heart rate, her facial muscles tuckered out from pretending that this wasn't a bizarre day. She stood silently beside Bo in the late-afternoon sun while Kirstie enjoyed a simulator ride.

Why was he spending so much time with them?

He'd been charming, respectful—and sexy as hell. But he couldn't really want to spend all day with a single mother and her kid. Heaven knew there were plenty of women checking him out with definite interest. Still he kept his attention on Kirstie and her.

Even now he maintained his steady stream of military anecdotes, pointing to a hulking B-52, then to a smaller Canadian CF-18. He shared real life stories she would enjoy rather than only dry technical talk or the printed information on the display stands in front of each craft.

She didn't want him to be likeable. And she definitely didn't want the suspicions crowding her head, but Kurt had broken her ability to trust.

Did Bo suspect she knew something about Kurt's activities? The authorities had cleared her, but that didn't mean the public agreed. She'd lain with a downright dirty dog of a man, therefore she must have fleas.

Kirstie stumbled out of the simulator. She paused long enough to tug her new overlong Thunderbird T-shirt covering her shorts before racing ahead with dizzy steps past a WWII plane. Heading for the inflated kiddie moonwalk, Kirstie zipped past an A-26 Invader's risqué nose art of "Miss Murphy"—a woman riding a bomb.

Definitely un-PC, but rife with an implication that upped Paige's jittering pulse. She needed to focus elsewhere, maybe with thoughts of lancing bovine boils.

Instead she kept remembering that her daughter had gone a whole hour without checking herself for hives. "Thank you for making this such a special day for Kirstie."

"My pleasure. You've done a great job with her in spite of everything."

A few yards away, Kirstie plunked down in front of the moonwalk. She kicked off her Strawberry Shortcake tennis shoes, jammed them into an empty cubby and disappeared inside the red, green and blue inflated cavern.

Paige sagged on a nearby bench. Muffled childish squeals echoed happiness through the canvas walls—such a simple sound of joy she no longer took for granted.

Bo hitched a boot up on the edge of the bench, resting his elbow on his knee. "And what about you? Have you enjoyed yourself?"

Too much. She stared at his black leather boot, inches from her hip, suddenly aware of how alone they were in the odd anonymity of faceless people massing and moving. She tore her gaze upward, so far up until she stared into ocean-blue eyes full of concern.

Go away. Please. "Why are you really here?"

"The air show."

"Seems like a strange coincidence."

"All right. I confess," He shrugged broad shoulders under the stretch of green flight suit. "Not so much of a coincidence. I'd heard you moved here, so I traded up with my buddy Scorch who was scheduled to fly with the commander." He stared down at his scarred hands, then back up at her. "I wanted to see how you're doing. Like you said earlier, what happened last year was memorable—life changing. I don't regret the role I played in helping the cops catch your husband, but I am sorry you were hurt."

Sympathy hurt more than scorn. "I'm the one who married the son of a bitch. Some would say I got what I deserved."

"I'm not some people."

"Thank you." Was that husky voice hers?

He leaned closer over his knee, his draped hand perilously close to her shoulder, only a short reach from her breasts. The healer in her longed to soothe the white lines of scar tissue.

The woman in her just longed to touch him.

His deep blue eyes drew her in without either of them moving. "Some would say—maybe *you* might even say—I helped put him in jail where he died."

"I'm not some."

"I'm glad."

The loudspeaker squawked updates, filling a silence between them too heavy with memories, pain and a need born of loneliness. She dimly registered the five-minute warning for the start of the biplane demonstration. She didn't know why she was so drawn to this man, but she was smart enough to recognize the time for a healthy retreat.

"Of course, I understand you only did what you had to that day. But, Bo, that doesn't mean it's easy for me to be around you. You've been wonderfully patient with Kirstie, and I can't thank you enough—"

"I don't want your thanks—"

"You have it, anyway. But I need a breather from memories."

"So we'll put off the rest of the show until tomorrow."

"I can't. I'm on call for emergencies tomorrow since my brother's on call today." Thank God for logical excuses that wouldn't make her admit she was afraid of her attraction to this man.

"Then let's find a time to meet after." A slow, wicked smile lit his eyes.

She wanted to smile back. Hell, she wanted to lean into his hand and let him fill his palm with the weight of her breast even though they were in the middle of a crowd.

She really did need to get out of here. "You're a good man to worry about us. But you can go back to Charleston with a clear conscience. We're doing better every day. Any leftover wounds are his fault not yours."

The moonwalk entrance flapped open and kids began pouring out. Paige shot from the bench, not even bothering to hide her haste. "My brother can bring her to see the flights tomorrow. I think Kirstie's had enough excitement for one day."

"You mean her mother has," he muttered.

Better to ignore him than launch into more dangerous-ground conversation.

"Kirstie," she called into the crowd of children retrieving their shoes. "It's time for us to go home. Kirstie?"

She searched the mass of kids, most of whom were wearing oversize white Thunderbird T-shirts, doggone it. Her stomach tightened with the first hints of apprehension. "Bo? Do you see her?"

"She's here. There's no other way out. Just stay calm. Kirstie?"

"Kirstie Adella Haugen." Paige rolled out her best maternal-mad tone, betrayed by a shaky quiver.

The last of the children dispersed, the storage cubbies holding only a lone pair of Strawberry Shortcake shoes, specialty laces sporting little green Ks.

Chapter 3

Kirstie plopped onto the grass behind the Moonwalk, scratching the sore spot on her head. Those stupid big kids sure did stomp the little kids. She'd gotten knocked over four times and nobody even said sorry or excuse me.

So she'd found a hole in the back to slip through. That was a lot easier than getting her hair stepped on again if she pushed out the front door with everybody else. Now she just had to find a way back to her mama and Captain Bo without getting her favorite Strawberry Shortcake socks dirty on all the greasy cords and junk.

"Do you need some help?"

Her tummy bumped. She looked over her shoulder. A man stood behind her.

And he was a stranger.

She squinted through her glasses. He was old, really old. Probably as old as her mama. But he wore a uniform, kinda like a policeman, so he must be okay.

"Nope. I'm not lost." She pushed to her feet and dusted off her bottom. "My mama's out front resting her tired pups."

"Good girl." He crouched in front of her. "You shouldn't wander off from your mother."

She didn't like him getting so close. She backed up and— ewww—stepped in the mud. "I'm not supposed to talk to strangers."

"That's right." He nodded. His big bushy eyebrows made him look kinda spooky, and kinda goofy, too. "But I'm not a stranger, Kirstie Adella Haugen."

Surprised, she stopped inching away. "How do you know my name?"

"I'm a friend of your daddy's."

Her tummy bumped again, harder this time. "I don't got a daddy anymore. He died of the polio."

"Polio, huh?"

"Yep. He got shots," she winced at the word *shots,* too close to a truth she didn't want to think about because it made her stomach hurt more. "But the medicine didn't help so he went to live in heaven. Hey, wait, if you knew him like you said then you would already know he got dead."

"I knew him a long time ago."

That made sense, sorta. And her mama didn't talk about it much, except for that one time she'd told her about what happened when her daddy got shot.

The kids in first grade talked about it though. A bunch. And they didn't think he went to heaven at all like Uncle Vic said.

She scratched her belly right over her tummy ache and backed all the way to the corner of the moonwalk. "I gotta go before my mama gets mad. Uncle Vic says she's a real pill when she gets her knickers in a knot."

Kirstie looked around into the crowd and aw, geez, Mama sure did look mad already. "I really gotta go."

"Who's that with her?" He pointed to Bo pushing through the people with his shoulder.

"That's Captain Bo. He flies airplanes."

"He's your mama's new boyfriend?"

Boyfriend? Kirstie's tummy stopped bumping and started rolling. She swallowed down her hot dog and the chips—and cotton candy Mama didn't know she'd shared with Bo while her mother had gone to the Porta Potti. Was he really a boyfriend? Emily at school said her mother's boyfriends always pretended to be nice then left her with a baby-sitter.

The thought of being alone made it tough to breathe.

She shook her head. "Nu-uh. It's just me and mama and Uncle Vic and Uncle Seth, 'cept Uncle Seth hurt his foot." That was more people than she used to have before her daddy died, but she was still scared at night. "You really knew my daddy before he died of the polio?"

"We used to race dirt bikes out there in the fields when we were supposed to be picking up rocks."

"Kirstie?" Her mother's mad voice reached her seconds before Mama raced over to her. "Kirstie, honey, you were supposed to be out front."

Not a mad voice like she'd thought after all, but a scared voice. Her mother picked her up and backed away real fast from the man.

Bo stepped between them, and he *was* mad. "Would you like to explain what's going on here?"

"No harm meant." The man held up his hands. "I just wanted to make sure the little girl wasn't lost." The guy with bushy brows ran into the crowd so fast she already couldn't see him anymore.

Kirstie risked a quick peek at her mama. Uh-oh. She had that sucking-lemons look on her face.

It would probably be better not to say the man knew Daddy since talking about him made her mother even more sad. "I was watching you the whole time, Mama. I know to holler really loud if somebody tries to snatch me. I'm s'posed to shout 'No! You're not my parents.' Right?"

Bo tugged a curl on her head, his face not so mad anymore. "That's right, Cupcake. You sure scared your mom, though, running off and all."

She thought about hollering that he was hurting her hair, even though he wasn't. Then maybe he would go away and not be her mama's boyfriend.

Her mother hugged her tight. "We need to leave now, punkin."

Rats. She didn't want to go. She just didn't want Bo smiling at her mother anymore.

"I'm sorry." Kirstie thrust out her bottom lip and made it wiggle a little.

"I'm sure you are," she said in that you're-in-trouble-anyway voice, "and we can talk about it more in the truck."

No luck with boo-boo lip. Her daddy would have given her a candy bar if she did boo-boo lip.

Before he died of the shots.

She held her eyes wide without blinking until she worked up a big, fat tear. Not too tough to do, all of a sudden. She felt it trickle down her cheek, cold and wet.

Mama's mad look went away, and she hugged tight again, her heart going *thump, thump, thump* against Kirstie's side. "Love you, punkin. I just want you to be safe."

"I know."

Mama kept squeezing extra tight until it even hurt a little. She did that a lot since Daddy died. It was hard being good all the time so her mother wouldn't get scared and stuff.

Kirstie tried not to wriggle even though she wanted down. Sometimes she wanted to run outside and keep running while she shouted and got really messy. And then maybe she'd make it all the way back to her house in South Carolina with the swing set and the merry-golds she and Mama planted. Her daddy would still be there and her tummy would stop hurting every day.

Her mother gave Bo a wobbly smile. "Thank you for being here. I wouldn't have wanted to look for her alone."

"No problem at all. I'm just glad everything turned out okay."

He smiled back—at Mama.

Kirstie's stomach rolled with hot dogs and cotton candy and lemonade and those chips. She clapped a hand to her mouth—

And upchucked all over Captain Bo's shiny boots.

Ah, geez, the joys of motherhood.

Paige hefted her wailing daughter in front of her and raced for the nearest trash can by a looming helicopter. Kirstie seemed finished puking, but experience taught a mom not to count on lucking into a solitary spew.

Her glasses jostled down as she ran. She tried to juggle Kirstie and nudge them back up, but darn, her baby girl was getting heavy. "Hang on. We're almost to the trash barrel."

"Do you think I got the chicken pox?" She glanced back with horror-stricken eyes. "Or maybe I gots that mosquito disease."

Sigh. "You don't have malaria." Paige screeched to a stop in front of the garbage bin, positioning Kirstie over the open top. "How do you feel now?"

"Better." She groaned. "Or maybe not."

Paige leaned farther. Her glasses slipped, fell—*plop, ching*—into a pile of cans and half-eaten hot dogs. Great. "I think you just ate too much."

Paige's hot dog churned in her stomach, as well, from fear more than indigestion. Her hands still shook after seeing Kirstie with that man. Had it been her imagination that he was too careful in keeping his face averted? She couldn't remember anything more than a big man with blond hair—a description that fit much of the male population in this area packed with folks of Swedish and German descent.

So what if he was a guard of some sort? He could have been anyone. Kurt's connections were so scummy her teeth clattered in fear over the possibility that any of it might come near her daughter.

What could they want from her? Kurt had been in debt up to his lying eyeballs. She'd sold off everything for a fresh start in a place that had one of the lowest crime rates in the country, a great big plus for moving home to North Dakota.

Kirstie straightened and sagged back against Paige's chest. "All done, punkin?"

She nodded. Paige set her on her feet and rifled through her backpack for wet wipes, most everything in the distance a blur, but retrieving her glasses would have to wait. She swiped around the tiny pink mouth.

Kirstie hiccupped. "How do you know it's not malaria?"

"You don't have a fever." She smoothed a second wipe over her daughter's cool forehead then along her hands.

"But I feel hot, really hot. How do you know for sure?"

"I'm the mama." She wadded up the wipes and pitched them in the trash—aw, hell, where her glasses were. "I know everything."

What a joke.

"But you said yesterday you don't know how one kid can go through five outfits in a day. So see? You might not know this, neither," she whispered. "I'm gonna hafta go to the doctor."

Patience, she reminded herself. As difficult as this was for her, it was worse for Kirstie. "I'll take your temperature when we get home. I *promise.*"

Hiccup. "'Kay."

A lanky shadow stretched over them. Bo. Heat prickled up her neck until she longed to soothe a wet wipe over her skin, too.

"Wanna pass me one of those for my boots?"

She winced and gave him the whole travel container. "Oh, sure. I'm so sorry about this."

"No problem." He knelt, swiping a clean sheen back to black leather. "It wasn't like she could help it. And this isn't the first time my boots have been thrown up on."

"You're only saying that to make me feel better."

"No way." He stood, tall, taller still until his shadow engulfed her. "I was in Guam a couple of years ago, and we had this great luau that left one of the flyers green the next morning."

Kirstie looked up from Paige's leg. "Did he have malaria?"

"No, Cupcake." He chucked her chin. "Bad swordfish."

Bo leaned past into the trash can, presenting a blurry-but-dog-gone-well-clear-enough image of long legs, lean hips and a perfect butt. Must be the flight suit. It *had* to be the flight suit making him so appealing. Surely he wouldn't look as incredible out of it.

Out of the flight suit? Now there was an image she did not need, since visions in her head were crystal clear.

He straightened, her shattered glasses dangling from between his fingers. "I hope you have a spare set with you."

She stared at her last pair of glasses. It would cost her a hundred bucks she couldn't afford to get new ones. "No spare set, here or at home."

He looked from her to the useless lenses and back to her again. "How blind are you without them?"

"As a bat." Even though she could see him close up, the rest of the flight-line activity faded to fuzzy until his face was *all* she could see. "I'll call my brother to come get us after he lands from his rounds—"

"I'll drive you," he interrupted. "Your brother can give me a ride back to base at his convenience."

An hour together in the truck? She could barely stem her starved hormones on a crowded flight line. An hour alone with him and she would be toast. "I thought you only had the afternoon off."

"I can wrangle more time. The loadmaster and I are good friends. He'll trade shifts for me to give tours of the plane tomorrow."

"Please, don't go to any more trouble." An unwelcome excitement stirred. She would just have to pray her daughter stayed awake in the truck. Fat chance. "I'm sure I'll find someone around here I know."

"Do you really want to drag malaria-girl all around the flight line until you find a ride?"

Did he have to be funny as well as drop-dead hot?

But he had a point. She needed to get Kirstie home. Being a parent meant putting her child's needs first. And she couldn't shake the shivery fear of seeing her daughter talking with that stranger.

Truth be told, standing next to Bo Rokowsky with his overconfident smile warmed those chills of fear right off her for a blessed moment. She would be independent again in an hour. For now, Kirstie needed Bo Rokowsky.

Paige thrust her keys into his hand and tried to ignore tantalizing, oh-so-adult thoughts of all the different ways *she* could need him.

Bo gripped the steering wheel on the Ford F-250, speeding farther into Dakota farmland. He needed to get Paige and Kirstie settled back at her place before he returned to base and started digging deeper for info about Paige's life here in Minot.

He didn't like it one damned bit how fast that dude behind

the moonwalk had faded into the crowd when confronted. Nothing overt, nothing concrete, but still…just wrong. Instincts were there for a reason.

Add in the fact that he was certain Kirstie's pouty-lip act had been covering up something, and he had concerns. After all those years at St. Elizabeth's, he knew kids and their maneuverings inside out.

Kirstie had a secret.

Said secretive kid was now tuckered out and snoozing in the back seat while her mama hugged the passenger door as far away from him as possible. The truck jarred in a pothole, rattling fishing poles in the racks across the back window and rocking Paige closer to the middle. For two seconds, before she scooted back.

How many times would she pretend to keep herself busy with shoving a strand of hair into her bandanna? He wanted to kick Kurt Haugen's sorry ass all over again for making this woman so wary of men.

Maybe he could put her at ease with conversation. Bo hitched his elbow on the open window, breeze heavy with hints of fresh-mown hay and country hits from the radio.

His fingers tapped along the steering wheel in a tuneless match to the piano in the country ballad. "I'm glad she's okay."

"I hope so."

"Looks to me like she overdosed on hot dogs and fun."

Her hold on the door loosened. She studied him through slightly squinting eyes. "How does a bachelor get to be such an expert on kids?"

"I grew up in an orphanage."

"Oh, my. I'm sorry." A blond lock slithered free again, whipping across her face.

"It was better than home." He looked back to the road, not that he needed much attention keeping the truck lined up on the straight band of two-lane highway. "My parents are dead."

Of course, his father hadn't died until ten years after he'd dumped his burdensome son at St. Elizabeth's, but Paige didn't need to know that part.

"I lost my parents a couple of years ago, heart attack for Dad, stroke for Mom. They were older, since they had their kids later in life, but it still hurt losing them." Her hand inched across the bench seat as if flat out itching to offer him a sympathetic touch. "I can only imagine how tough it must have been for you so young. I'm sorry."

"Don't be. The nuns made great surrogate moms to all of us. And there sure were a lot of nuns. No one lacked for attention. The whole experience gives me some insight to where your kid's coming from though."

Enough of that. The conversation was getting heavier than he preferred, and he definitely did *not* want her looking at him with sympathy.

Staring through the windshield at the stretch of rocky farmland, he searched for a subject change. Not much to pick from, just rows of wheat beside bare fields of rock, grain towers, a couple of barns and endless telephone poles.

He'd have to go with the rocks. "What's up with those piles of stones?"

"Sodbusters pile them up as they plow the fields." Her pretty brown eyes went dreamy. "I used to spend weeks following my dad and brother out in the fields after school and in the summer."

"A hard life?"

Dreaminess fled. "A wholesome one I didn't appreciate near enough."

"Sure would be nice if we could learn those life lessons the easy way, but some of us have to be kicked in the head."

She smiled, a helluva lot better than sympathy.

A tousled blond strand caught on her damp lip. Paige finally gave up restraining her hair and reached behind her head to untie the small bandanna. She shook her blond hair free in a satiny curtain.

Blood slugged through his veins. His grip tightened on the wheel in sync with a tightening farther south. Pure lust pumped through him. No dodging or denying.

He inhaled three deep breaths of barley-laden air.

She leaned against the door, hair streaming forward unfettered. "I'm sorry about Kirstie's fit back at the base. You didn't sign on for puke-and-tantrum duties with the tour guide gig."

Think about hurling kids. That would help. Right? "No big thing. Like I said before, I've seen worse fits. Hell, I've pitched worse. And I've definitely hurled on a friend's shoes back in my misspent youth."

Her low laugh whispered over him in the fresh countryside air. "Like you're ancient now?"

So she was evaluating his age. Interesting. "Not any more 'ancient' than you."

"Think again." Her laugh turned to a snort. "I'm certain I have a good six or seven years on you. Besides, in here," she tapped her chest, "I'm over a hundred in life experiences."

Ditto, lady. A great big ditto.

Memories of the crash, capture, later discovering people from his own country had sold him out palled the humor if not the desire right out of him. "Then we're running even."

She glanced at his scarred hands holding the wheel. Still she didn't ask. Respectful of boundaries? Or just afraid he'd take it as an invitation to cross hers?

Her eyes skated away, fixing on the nothing-filled horizon that she undoubtedly couldn't see, anyway, without her glasses. "Kirstie's a smart kid, already reads at a third-grade level. She's been checking out library books on illnesses. She knows how Kurt died—the basics anyway. But she tells everyone he died of this or that disease. I'm taking her to the school psychologist, who insists that other than an occasional case of the bubonic plague and self-denial, she's a perfectly normal kid."

"You're both handling some heavy crap."

She folded her hands in her lap, scarf bunched in her fists. "Please don't take this the wrong way. I appreciate that you're being nice in checking up on us. And I understand you probably have some 'heavy crap' of your own to deal with after what…my husband—" two hitched breaths later she continued "—did to you. I wish I could reassure you, but honest to God I'm barely keeping my sanity here, and having you around is not helping."

"It's easier for you to run from me, then?"

"You're mighty judgmental for a man who hasn't walked in my shoes."

He plowed ahead with the conversation as well as the miles. "I'm going to be here for at least a couple of weeks with the broken plane."

Her eyes went wide, big pools of wary brown. "Bo—"

"I'd like to spend time with you and learn more about the treads life put on those shoes of yours."

"Because you're worried about Kirstie losing a parent?"

"Maybe I'm just attracted to you." Where had that come from? What a dumb-ass thing to say guaranteed to spook her. At least she couldn't jump out of the truck, since he had her kid in the back seat.

Her eyes went wider, damn near filling her face. "I'd rather you felt sorry for me."

Now didn't that smack him right down?

But he wasn't giving up. He steered along the narrowing road, her two-story white house breaking the monotony of flat road and fields. A speck appeared beyond and above. A small plane, a Cessna Skyhawk, also known as a Cessna 172. Four-person seating capacity, all-metal single-piston engine. High-wing monoplane—one long wing over the top of the plane.

His fingers clutched the steering wheel, and he could all but feel the plane's yoke in his grip. His hands and feet yearned to pilot that craft to the ground and adjust the pilot's approach. God, he loved to fly.

Paige's sigh gusted through the truck cab. "There's my brother and my house."

Conversation and day over. Yeah, he heard her.

She was that wary of being alone together? In a good or bad way? Before he could follow the thought through to a possibly sensual conclusion, his attention snagged on the tiny craft descending, too fast. The Cessna's nose flared up, too high too soon. Who the hell was flying the plane? A five-year-old? Obviously some newbie looking to log hours for free. "That's your temporary pilot?"

"Yes." She crossed her arms defensively.

The nose gear hammered the landing strip. No damn surprise. His teeth ached in sympathy for the passenger. The plane bounced back up off the ground before nailing the asphalt twice more. Thank God the plane held together. This time. His determination to see more of Paige, to reassure himself, to find answers jelled into a simple answer that actually promised to be fun.

Purpose set, he threw the truck into Park and his determination into overdrive. "You climb in the plane with him and you'll make your daughter an orphan before long."

"He has his license—"

"For a Moped maybe."

Hooking his arm over the steering wheel with a relaxed air, at odds with the anticipation knotting his gut, he shot a smile her way that had won over far tougher cookies than Paige Haugen. And he did *not* need to think about just how soft this tough cookie was, or he could forget about appearing casual. "I'm stuck here for at least two weeks baby-sitting the busted C-17 while they wait for replacement parts, then for

Mako to complete the repairs. That will leave me with more than enough time."

Her hitched breath pushed her full breasts tighter against the pretty yellow fabric. "Enough time for what?"

"Time for *me* to be your temporary pilot."

Chapter 4

"Whoa. Hold on just one minute. We already have a pilot, but thanks for the generous offer." Paige gripped the truck door in search of some control and steadiness. Bo Rokowsky couldn't actually be proposing he spend two weeks flying her around North Dakota?

"Calling that guy—" Bo stabbed a finger toward the blur of the plane fishtailing down the landing strip "—a pilot constitutes aviation blasphemy."

"Well, he's licensed." She paused, picking at the frayed knee of her jeans. She glanced back up at the fuzzy image of the plane, the whole yard hazy, thanks to her broken glasses, the world narrowing in focus to just her and this man. "And he's, uh, reasonably priced."

"Nah? Really? I never would have guessed."

"No need to be snarky." She slumped back into her seat amid a symphony of hello-barks from the dogs in the boarding kennels.

"Lady, I'm actually complimenting you, here, because I figure you had to be smart enough to know *that*—" he nodded toward the air-hack again "—isn't worth top dollar."

"And you are?" She couldn't resist jabbing defensively.

"You bet your fine ass I am."

Damn his arrogance and—

Fine ass?

Hers?

Heat tingled along her skin, then cooled. He must have some agenda here for dishing outrageous compliments. She'd barely understood why he would want to spend an afternoon with her. But two weeks? That went beyond logical. Something was up, and she hated that she didn't know what. There had been enough secrets over the past years. She studied him through narrowed eyes until he frowned.

"What?"

"I can't figure you out."

"Quit trying. It's been my experience that women spend a lot of time searching for something in a guy when the obvious answer was right there in front of her face."

Great. She was darn near blind.

"How about clueing me in to the obvious, then?" Not that she intended to take him up on his absurdly generous—and suspicious—offer. However, it would be reassuring to know why he'd made it.

He stared out over the runway as if gathering fuel for his argument. God, he really was too handsome—strong cheekbones and jaw set in a classic face that belonged on some Renaissance statue. And how ironic was it that her crummy vision even gave him a sort of halo effect?

"Well, Captain? What's your reason for this altruistic offer to help a couple of strangers in North Dakota?"

He shifted in the seat to face her, square jaw set. "I feel bad about what happened to you because of your husband.

I'm here and I want to help you if I can, add in the fact that I really like to fly and now have a couple of weeks off. Let me tell you, time off's a rarity in the military these days, with everything that's been going on overseas."

His flexing hands over the steering wheel drew her attention from his face. The sinking sun cast a rosy hue along the scars until they appeared angry and fresh instead of faded with time. Those hands held a story, and somehow she sensed it would make him more human—more intriguing—than even those slightly crooked teeth.

"If you need to unwind, why not go to Mt. Rushmore? Or you could check out the Badlands and some of their casinos."

"Thanks, Madame Tour Guide. Been there. Done that. And lucky for you, I have a private pilot's license and would rather hang out with you. Must be your charm and gratitude." His eyes flicked with sarcasm.

Contrition itched. "Sorry. But you're being rather pushy here."

He shrugged. She bit back a sigh. Heaven help her, she was surrounded by Alpha males determined to lead the pack. "You have to admit this sounds rather suspicious. Why would you help us for nothing, because, trust me, the pay's next to nothing."

"You can lower the defensiveness. I do want something out of this bargain that has nothing to do with money."

Uh-oh. Dry-lightning alert. The hairs on her arms rose while the rest of her tingled with thoughts of want and need and fulfillment. "Like what?"

"Flight hours."

Huh? "Flight hours?"

"I'll get free civilian flight hours, and that actually is worth more than you would expect outside the military world." With his wrist draped over the steering wheel, he drummed his fingers along the dash as if picking out a tune. "Here's my pitch,

I'll hang out to fly you and your brother on your rounds in exchange for using your plane to log in some hours on my own when you're off duty. The Cessna's a different plane, different challenge than the C-17, and it *does* cost to fly. A lot."

And didn't she know it? She'd about choked when she saw the appraisal for Seth's plane. Even used, it was priced at about the same as a decent-size house.

Bo's logic made sense, and it wasn't his fault her husband had been dishonest. Bo didn't deserve her defensiveness, and he most especially didn't deserve her anger, but where was she supposed to put it all?

"You're only offering to save my pride," she said with a feeble last attempt at self-preservation.

"I'm offering to save your fine ass from a crash." He angled closer over the bench seat. Not that anything would happen with Kirstie asleep in the back, but sheesh he was in her space big-time. "What did I say a second ago? Don't go looking for a hidden agenda. And you do have a fine—"

"Stop. Please." Laughter tickled her raw stomach lining. God, it was fun to be lighthearted in the middle of the mess her life had become. "No more ass discussions, if you don't mind."

"I'm a man. I enjoyed the view. So sue me." He smiled, showing off those too-cute, slightly crooked front teeth again. His smile faded to seriousness. "But don't do something stupid like turn down my offer."

He had such a way of making things sound logical. Or was that cute smile of his addling her brain? "If you go around helping everyone this much, it's a wonder you have time to work."

"Don't make me out to be some altar boy who searches for needy folks to help. Believe me, the picture doesn't fit."

"So you weren't an altar server?"

Red stained his skin just above his collar. Who'd have thought bad boys blushed?

Boy?

All man.

"Okay, so I was an altar server. But I was a very bad one."

That, she believed. "So why does this bad man want to help me?"

"I can't just stand by doing nothing when there's a problem and I have the means to solve it."

Spoken like a true Alpha, which actually brought some peace and understanding. There might be more to his agenda and she should probably keep digging, but bottom line, she had to accept. There wasn't really any other choice. Vic was probably already firing the temporary pilot, anyway.

Maybe she could resurrect her economy-size bottle of Tums for a couple of weeks, not a crutch, but more of a survival ration around this man. "You're right. It's an incredibly generous offer that I can't afford to turn down."

That wits-addling smile began to creep over his face again.

Paige held up a pointer finger. "I still have to talk to my brother and cousin, though." She gestured out toward the thin strip of runway where the blurry pilot leaped from the craft while a big blond blob she assumed was her brother slumped against the side. Uh-oh. That awful, huh? "It's Vic's vet practice and Seth's plane. And they would also have to deal with firing the other guy, who happens to be a student of Seth's from his stint teaching at a flight school before he joined up with Vic."

Although even Seth admitted the guy was rock bottom of his class.

"Fair enough."

"Might as well do that now. Vic will be walking over in a second."

She reached for the door handle, already wondering what her overprotective lug of a brother would have to say about this turn of events.

"Christ on a crutch, Paige." Bo's low whistle turned her around before she reached in to retrieve her snoozing daughter. "That walking mountain is your brother? I thought the mosquitoes were monster big. What about your cousin Seth?"

"Seth's even bigger, lumberjack material with a beach bum facade, and how strange is that since there aren't any beaches here? He wanted to fly for the Air Force, even started ROTC at the University of Miami. But then he grew again and was too tall. All the farm feeding and fresh air, I guess."

"Poor dude. That sucks for him."

She looked at her brother—the blond blur ambling her way. Hmm. He *was* tall. Funny how she just thought of him as the pest who'd cut her favorite Barbie's hair off. She turned back and found Bo already unbuckling Kirstie with ease. Accepting his help could become a habit even in two short weeks. She needed to establish boundaries, and for once she might not mind her hulking relatives' help with that. "And, Bo?"

"Yeah, Paige?"

"They really don't like it when anyone checks out my ass."

Don't be an ass, Bo reminded himself, not for the first time. Charm always won the day, hands down.

Hefting Kirstie the rest of the way out of her seat for Paige, he slammed the passenger door closed and started toward her behemoth blond brother who was saying goodbye to the inept pilot. Good thing the temp was getting into his car to leave so they could get right to the discussion of a replacement, something that had to happen pronto. The guy hadn't even tied down the plane, for God's sake.

Bo kept his steps slow but purposeful, giving himself a few extra seconds to think—and assess her brother. Making sure Paige didn't climb into the Cessna with that joke of a pilot was too damn important to screw up because his libido wanted to think for him.

Hitching Kirstie over against his shoulder, Bo thrust out his other hand. "Good afternoon. Rokowsky. Bo."

"Vic Jansen, Paige's brother," Jansen answered with a heavier lilt to his Dakota accent than his sister. The overgrown veterinarian in a John Deere hat and blood-caked jeans gripped back, firm and hard in that unspoken male measuring ritual.

Bones once crushed groaned in protest. Bo kept his face clear and returned the shake without a flinch. "Nice to meet you."

Maybe.

"So you're the Air Force captain Kirstie was telling me about." Without elaborating further, Vic Jansen pulled his hand free and turned to his sister. "How did the air show go today? You're home early."

"We had a wonderful time. Bo showed us around and shared details about the aircraft we wouldn't have gotten on our own. It was great, right up until Kirstie ate too much and—" Paige swirled her hand in front of her mouth "—you know. Then my glasses slipped off and broke when I held her over the nearest trash can, so I couldn't drive."

"Sounds like a full day." He nodded to Bo. "Thanks for seeing them home safely."

"No problem at all, dude. It gave me a chance to check out—"

Paige's face blanched.

"—some of the countryside." He subdued a smile. He might be reckless enough to razz her about her excellent back view, but he wasn't stupid enough to announce it to her brother. Especially when he needed to win this man over to his side, something he couldn't do with Prickly Paige around.

Bo passed Kirstie, leaving Paige no alternative but to take the kid. "You probably want to put her down."

"Bo—"

"What?" He flashed his best earnest look her way. "I just want to talk to your brother about our discussion."

"Fine, but I'll be right out in a few minutes. Don't wander off without me." Backing away, she met him gaze-for-gaze with a look that said she wasn't letting him steamroll her by joining forces with her brother.

Damn. He liked her more by the second. And she really was easy on the eyes with all those soft curves he sure wouldn't mind explor—

"Rokowsky," the behemoth rumbled.

Crap. She hadn't been joking about the big guy's radar when it came to his sister and men. Bo jerked his gaze off the fine view of her striding past the kennels of yipping dogs. "Jansen."

"My sister moves fast." He gestured toward Paige already charging around the clinic entrance toward the front porch. "I expect she'll have Kirstie down and settled in two minutes flat. So say your piece quick."

Bo lounged against the quarter panel of the truck, keeping his body language laid-back. "Paige tells me you're in a tight financial spot with your cousin's bashed-up ankle keeping him out of the cockpit for a couple of weeks."

"Prideful Paige told you?" Jansen shook his head. "I don't think so."

Prideful Paige. Prickly Paige. Pretty Paige. Yeah, all three made her too interesting by half. "She told me some, and I read between the lines well."

Jansen stayed silent. Waiting? A man of few words? The guy didn't give off any hints.

Except…wait. He looked like Kirstie right before she'd blasted his boots.

The guy had a weak stomach.

Bingo. Achilles heel identified, Bo launched his attack. "I take it from your green tinge you didn't enjoy that landing much."

Jansen swallowed hard without answering.

"No need to be embarrassed. I saw the whole thing and shee-it. I'd have been tempted to grab an airsickness bag. Guy flared the nose up too soon. I figure he's either a rookie or only used to flying the big planes."

"Rookie. Graduated a while back, but he's low on hours."

Time to go for the pitch. "I have two weeks off and I'd like to help."

"How come?"

Straight up would work best with this guy. "Flying's easy for me. I enjoy it. You need a pilot. I have plenty of hours in smaller planes and I'm glad to show you my logbook."

Time for more truth, well, except for the part about how the scent of Paige slathered in coconut oil twisted his libido inside out. "And, yeah, I met your sister back in Charleston. I'd like some reassurance that everything's okay for her now. No logical reason other than the fact that I can't leave a problem unresolved. Guy thing, I guess."

Bo waited for the verdict, already planning a counterattack if Jansen said no. And waited. Good God, this dude took his time making up his mind.

Finally Jansen swept off his hat, swiped his brow and settled the cap back in place again. "I'd be a fool not to consider it. Let's go for a spin in the Cessna and see if those hotshot wings on your flight suit are genuine."

Yes! He could nail that landing with his eyes closed. Who'd have thought the behemoth would be easier to wrangle than his five-foot-four sister?

Now that he and Jansen were on the same team, he would mention the man who'd been speaking to Kirstie, so Jansen could keep watch without further upsetting Paige. "A flight sounds perfect, and if we move fast we can take off before Paige returns. There's something I'd like to talk to you about alone once we're airborne."

* * *

Now that was a real landing. Even with her vision seriously compromised, she could tell the difference between Bo's smooth landing and the halting hatchet job the other pilot managed.

Absently swinging open the chain-link gate on the kennel's grass run, Paige studied the airstrip through the wire mesh while puppies scampered to greet her. The Cessna cruised to a stop, a Dakota sunset splashing the last hints of lilac and magenta to colorize rocks and wheat fields. Great heavens, the guy was a damn good pilot, and they were lucky to have his help.

Labrador-beagle-mix puppies pranced around her ankles, yipping and nipping, begging for attention. She lowered to sit on the grassy ground with Waffles's litter of pups. Her hands drifted to stroke floppy ears while she watched, her memory filling in details currently fuzzy.

Across the field, the airplane hatch swung open. Déjà vu whipped over her faster than the evening wind carrying the scent of barley and the earthy fertility of spring. Just like the day before, Bo Rokowsky's body filled the open portal, green flight suit stretching across broad shoulders as he leaped to the ground. He walked around the plane with confidence, securing tie-downs and setting chocks on the bare landing strip beside the small metal hangar.

There was something fascinating about those zipper-suited sky gods, and yeah, something intriguing about this one in particular. She allowed herself a Paige-of-the-Past moment where she sagged against the chain-link kennel and daydreamed. Puppies clambered willy-nilly over her lap while fantasies kept an equally frolicking pace. In her mind she could be eighteen again. She would be twenty pounds lighter in looks and a million pounds lighter in concerns. Free to flirt.

Except, if she was eighteen that would make Bo Rokowsky all of eleven or twelve. Ugh. And bottom line, she wouldn't trade her daughter for a million do-overs with guaranteed happy endings.

Paige angled herself away from visions of the plane and its pilot. Five-week-old Brownie collapsed against her thigh with huffy exhaustion. Draping him over her leg, she stroked the tired puppy to sleep while two more chewed on each other's ears. The remaining four settled against Waffles for supper.

Nice. Normal. Exactly the sort of grass-roots-values life she wanted for her daughter.

A double shadow stretched, easy to distinguish the two even without glasses, her hulking brother and a certain lanky pilot.

Vic strode past to scoop up a puppy scampering close to the exit. "Baby sister, I don't know what you did to convince this guy to help out, but we'd be idiots not to pounce on his offer." He thrust the squirming mutt toward Bo. "Let me wash off. Then I'll drive you back out to base so we can discuss scheduling." He thumped Bo on the back. "And thanks for the heads-up."

Without another word, her brother lumbered away. Leaving her alone with Bo? What was up with that?

Great. The only thing worse than Vic in overprotective mode was Vic in megaconsent mode. And wasn't she quite the contrary brat today? Darn Bo Rokowsky for making her all itchy.

She patted the snoozing puppy in her lap. "So we're all set?"

Bo dropped down beside her, cradling his mutt in one hand and rubbing it with the other. "I'll make the arrangements with my commander to take leave while I'm here. I'll still be on call if Mako needs me to fire up the plane for a test, but otherwise, I'm free. I'll start after the paperwork's filed Monday."

Paige watched his big, scarred hand rub over the downy fur. She swallowed hard to erase the visions of how painful the injury must have been to require such intricate incisions. "You like dogs?"

"Who couldn't like this dog?" He lifted the puppy eye level.

"It's not a purebred."

"Neither am I."

He said it to be funny, but she wasn't sure he thought so. "What kind of dog do you have back home in Charleston?"

Bo rested the animal on his thigh again, shadows masking his expression as the sinking sun brought the anonymity of night. "I'm gone too much to have a pet. Wouldn't be fair to an animal, boarding him for months at a time."

An insightful statement, which made the guy hot and funny *and* sensitive. Man, she really needed him to say something jerklike soon or she'd be sagging in his hand like that happy puppy. "You're gone that much?"

"Over half the year on a regular basis, even more lately with all the commitments overseas."

"Wow, that's rough."

"I'm seeing the world, playing with the coolest toys the U.S. Government has to offer. Retirement comes around fast enough. I'll have a dog then." He nodded to the sleeping pup on her leg. "Although it looks like the animals boarded here aren't lacking in attention."

"We try to play with them and let them out as much as pos-sible. Cuts down on the cage cleaning, too. Kirstie helps with the walks and treats."

"Seems she's looking to follow in her mama's footsteps."

"Maybe she will." Paige toyed with the dog's ear. "Better than following in her father's, I guess."

Oh, God, why had she said that? She wanted to gobble the words back down and let the acid in her stomach burn them away along with so many painful memories. She forced her eyes to stay on the puppy and hoped Bo would ignore her slip.

"What does a person do to become a veterinary technician?"

Thank you. "I have an associate's degree in veterinary technology. It's a two-year degree, much like a two-year nursing degree. I can do lab work, testing, start and maintain IVs, catheters, take X-rays, perform anesthesia on animals, and such. I can give injections even pick up some emergency calls if Vic is out, but can't prescribe medicine or diagnose. And I can't do surgeries." She leaned toward him with a wicked smile of her own. "Although Vic has let me neuter cats on occasion."

"Neutering, huh?" He grimaced.

"Uh-huh."

"You're one tough lady."

"I'm getting tougher." Her hands curved protectively around the pup while words bubbled up in spite of acid and good sense. "I was going to attend vet school like my brother, but I met Kurt and didn't want to leave the area. We got married and started moving around so much it was difficult to enroll again. Once we settled in Charleston, Kirstie came along. I always figured after she went to kindergarten… But then…"

He turned his head along the fence to look at her in the dark. "Things fell apart."

"Pretty much."

Overhead, halogen lights flickered, sensors kicking in with nighttime. "How did you meet him?"

His question jolted her more than the lights stuttering to life. She should have expected him to continue the conversational thread that she started not just once but twice. Subconsciously trying to scare him off? "Um, we were taking a chemistry class together at Minot State University. We'd both lived in the area all our lives, but went to different high schools."

"Does Kirstie have other relatives here, then, from her father's side?"

God, he made it easy to talk, and even though the memories hurt they just kept flowing right out of her mouth, so many stored words. "No. He was an only child of older parents, like mine. His parents are dead now, too, thank heavens, because it would have broken their hearts to see what he became."

Like it broke yours.

He didn't say the words but she could almost hear them, anyway. Certainly she could see them in his expressive eyes now crystal-clear blue in the blazing security lights that showed far too much for her to feel at all secure. Still she searched, wondering what more she would read, and found the last thing she expected...

Understanding.

Then his face smoothed back into the charmer smile, and he lifted the puppy to eye level again. "What's this fella's name?"

"Fella? You'd better brush up on your male-female anatomy lessons, pal, because that's a girl."

"Ahh. I should have guessed. Girls always are much more fun to hang around with than guys, anyway."

She rolled her eyes. "Do you always lay it on this thick?"

"Pretty much."

Honesty again. She liked that. She let herself lean back against the chain fence and enjoy the moment, sitting alone in the dark with a handsome man who thought she had a nice ass and was worth the effort to charm. She'd spent so many hours as a teenager sitting in this same yard dreaming of a man who would wine and dine her as a break from shoveling manure out of stalls.

She'd been a fool in the making even then. "I really didn't know what he was doing."

Nightmares still woke her in a cold sweat, horrific dreams where people pointed accusatory fingers at her. Kurt Haugen had been her husband, the man she'd chosen to give her body and life to, and he'd become scum. There must be something bent or twisted within her since she'd chosen him. She must have known and just turned a blind eye. Surely she knew something more even now, since he'd died without fingering all his connections.

Her only defense? She truly had been a blind idiot. "I was stupid and too trusting, but I swear to God, I didn't know," she vowed again.

"I never thought you did."

An exhale rattled from her, and she wondered why it mattered so much that he believe her, this man who would mean nothing to her, a man who would be gone in a couple of short weeks. But she needed to hear the words and hope maybe tonight she could sleep with the peaceful assurance that somebody other than her family really believed her. She didn't bother to say thank you. The words probably would have slammed to a halt against the lump clogging her throat, anyway.

Bo's hand slowed along the sleeping dog's back. "You never did say what her name is?"

Paige started to tell him the dog's name was Butterscotch, but stopped, tugged by the way he cradled the puppy and talked about someday having a pet when he could give it the attention it deserved. "We haven't named her yet. How about you decide on something before you come back Monday?"

She braced for another of his killer smiles—a smile that never came. He just returned her stare with somber intensity that stirred more of that dry lightning inside before he set the soon-to-be-renamed dog on the ground beside her and stood.

"Yes, ma'am. I'll see you then."

And for some scary reason when he said ma'am this time, she didn't feel at all old.

Chapter 5

Bo felt the music soak into him, resonating through the strings into his fingers. Playing the guitar—or the piano, drums, even some saxophone when the mood called— brought the world back into focus for him by paring everything down. Only notes at his command remained.

Sprawling back on the lumpy sofa at the Minot AFB temporary lodging facility, he propped his tennis shoe against the coffee table, flight suit exchanged for jeans and a T-shirt. His right hand plucked while his left fingered along the frets in routine scales that somehow became a song of their own in the rhythmic musicality of warming up. His buddies didn't seem to object to his tunes, so he kept picking away, scales shifting to Bach on the guitar.

Rather than separating the crew into officer and enlisted quarters, they'd been bunked together in a suite with four rooms attached to a common room, as per the flight orders:

maintain crew integrity. Not that Quade's closed door invited much camaraderie or bonding as called for in the orders.

Tag's door, however, stayed open while he sprawled on his bed talking to his wife on the phone. Mako perched on the edge of the sofa, his boots and polishing kit spread out over the coffee table in front of him. Bo let his fingers find their way along the strings until Bach morphed into a calypso beat that sounded a little too much like a tropical tune ready-made to serenade a luscious lady sunbather.

Nu-uh. Not gonna go there.

He forced his fingers to hammer out some Rolling Stones. Damn straight he wasn't getting much satisfaction these days. Sexual or practical.

Jansen was keeping an eye out for suspicious strangers around his sister, but didn't have any helpful insights. Bo's computer search on his laptop about Paige's dead husband hadn't brought any new info other than the standard questions about identifying the rest of the man's contacts, which shouldn't have surprised him. He'd spent countless hours over the past year researching the bastard.

And Paige.

Damn. He forced his strumming to segue into vintage Carlos Santana. A guitarist for the ages.

His soul settled.

At least something was going his way. He'd already spoken to Quade about taking leave while he waited around for the plane to be repaired. The commander had glowered and nodded, then headed into his room. Door closed. No chitchat.

Mako unwrapped the torn T-shirt rag from around two fingers. He tossed aside the polish-stained cotton cloth along with the small round tin. "Figures you would find the lone tree here in North Dakota."

"Tree?"

"You know—woman behind every tree." He swiped the

buffing brush along the sides of his boot. "Apparently from what I saw at the air show, you found that tree."

It took Bo a second to remember that Mako wouldn't have recognized her. While they'd partied together on TDYs over the years, the jokester tech sergeant was new to Charleston Air Force Base, a recent transfer into the maintenance squadron from McChord AFB in Washington.

"I already knew her from when she used to live in Charleston." Enough on the subject to cover his butt if someone filled in Mako, but not so much as to offer up more about Paige's past than she would want out there.

"Cute kid she's got," Mako pressed, awful damn nosy all of the sudden. Buff, buff with the brush along one side. Buff, buff along the toe with a reminder of puked-on boots that needed polishing. "Single mother, I assume?"

"Uh-huh. Widowed." His thumb slipped on a string.

"Pretty lady."

"Uh-huh." Understatement. Blond and lush even in jeans and no makeup, Paige resembled one of those WWII pinup posters he'd once seen in an Air Force museum.

"Are she and her kid the reason you're asking for leave while you're here?"

Bo set aside his guitar. "Something wrong with sightseeing? God knows we've all got leave time coming out of our ass since they keep us too busy to use it."

"So you're planning a trip down to Mt. Rushmore with that leave you asked the colonel about."

Why the hell was everyone pushing him to Rushmore? "Are you looking to start a travel agency? Next thing we know, you'll be passing out leis and discount booklets."

Mako tossed down the buffing brush, with a smirk. "That's a lot of defensive bad attitude over just hanging out with an old friend. I smell a story here."

Evading would of course prove the guy's point. "I'm taking time off to do a favor for a friend by flying her around some. Yes, it's the woman who was at the air show. She works with a vet clinic that makes emergency calls to remote locales."

"Ah, I get it." Mako snagged the lighter from his polishing kit and flicked once, twice, again until a flame shot free. Slowly he glided it along the top to heighten the sheen. "Doctors Without Borders for cows."

"Pretty much. Beats hanging out watching my nose hairs grow while we wait for those shipped parts to arrive."

The flame snaked a blue path over the boot, reminding him of fire from the engine when he'd crash-landed in Rubistan. Fire that could have engulfed them after the bird strike. Fire that *did* engulf him every time he looked at Paige Haugen.

And that was the core of his frustration.

Yeah, he enjoyed women, but he was always in control, like with his music or in the plane. He called the shots right up to the time either he walked or they did. He didn't like one damned bit how much he'd wanted to stay with her—in a dog kennel for crying out loud—just to hear the Dakota melody of her voice while mosquitoes chewed his hide.

Mako set aside the boot and lighter. "If she's just an old friend, how come you didn't give her a tour of our plane?"

"Because I knew you'd smirk just like you're doing right now."

Laughing low, Mako scooped up his shining kit and boots. "Fair enough. And on that note, I'm ready to rack. See ya in the morning, sir."

Snagging his guitar by the neck, Bo stood. He meant to stride right past and stow his guitar in his room. So why was he stopped outside Tag's door? The guy was busy talking with his wife, Rena, about their new baby, anyway.

Bo started to move on. Tag held up a hand signaling for him to wait.

Swinging his legs to the side of the bed as he sat up, Tag waved Bo in while still talking on the phone. "Hey, babe, it's time for me to head over to the gym. I'll call tomorrow and let you know details of how they're getting the colonel and me home on Monday."

Tag smiled at whatever she said in response. "Great. Yeah, babe, love you, too."

And the guy did. No question, Tag and Rena Price had something special, that sort of something Bo had thought maybe he'd find some day.

Yet even rock-solid Tag had experienced marital troubles a year ago. The loadmaster had been in the process of a divorce at the time of their shoot down in Rubistan. After their release and return, a surprise pregnancy—and the threat of Kurt Haugen—had brought Tag and his wife back together again.

Bo waited in the open doorway. He and Tag shared some hellish memories, bonding crap that took them past normal officer and enlisted boundaries. Tag had been there for him right after the shoot down and during their capture. The older man had taken a boot to the ribs to deflect more blows after Bo's hands were broken.

He didn't know what he expected to gain from talking to Tag now. Some fatherly advice maybe? About what? He wasn't even sure.

"You okay?" Tag set the phone on the bedside table.

Was he referring to the emergency landing? Or Paige Haugen? Damn but Tag had a way of fishing with those short questions that left the field wide-open for interpretation.

"Just hanging out, nothing to do. I'm fine. Why wouldn't I be?"

Duh. Because he couldn't stop thinking about how Kurt Haugen had held them all hostage in Tag's home until Tag had risked tackling the man while Bo shielded Tag's pregnant wife.

Haugen had hoped to find information about military drug-surveillance flights to offer his mob boss in exchange for a ticket out of organized crime and safe passage to another country. The guy had been obsessed with starting a new life with his wife and daughter, had even discussed how he would trick them into leaving under the guise of a "surprise" vacation.

His fists clenched at how close Paige had come to a fugitive lifestyle, or an arrest in a foreign country where she could have been left to rot in a hellhole cell. He knew firsthand how much hellhole cells sucked. Relaxing his fists, he worked his wrist back and forth, thankful for the modern technology of surgically inserted metal pins and screws.

"So you're all right." Tag shoved a hand through his salt-and-pepper buzz cut. "Kudos to you then, my friend, because seeing that blast from the past on the flight line had me racing for the phone last night to hear my wife's voice and make sure she's okay. Crazy, huh?"

"Nah, not at all." He slumped against the door frame, one tennis shoe up and flat against the molding.

"Exactly my point. So, I'll say it again. You okay?"

"I'm fine enough. Haugen deserved to go to jail. We weren't the ones who killed him." Ah, hell, and there was a part of his problem, because he'd wanted to dig Haugen up and kill him again, the father of that somber-eyed little girl. "Even if he'd died that day in the takedown instead of later in jail, we would have been justified. He held a pregnant woman hostage, for crying out loud." Tag, Bo and Tag's son, as well.

Tag's jaw flexed. Hard. "Yes, he did."

Logical, but still hard as hell to reconcile. "A crime's a crime, but somehow it feels worse when women and kids are hurt."

Tag's wife. Their baby.

Kirstie.

Paige.

Damn. His eyes fell away to Tag's latest paperback splayed open on the bed. "Why the hell do I feel so responsible for her and her kid?"

Tag didn't bother asking what woman and which kid. He didn't say anything at all, his knack with silence always prompting more words than a dozen questions.

"I could be spending the next couple of weeks on easy duty baby-sitting the plane while Mako finishes his repairs. Instead I'm going to be humping my butt around in a beat-up Cessna making house calls on sick cows."

Tag studied his clasped hands for long silent moments before words finally rumbled up. "My wife says one of the fundamental reasons for arguments between men and women is that sometimes women just want to vent. But when men hear about a problem, we start listing ways to fix it and cut short her rant."

"Yeah, so?"

"A woman doesn't necessarily want fixing. Sometimes she just wants to vent so she feels better about what can't be changed."

"And that helps me how?"

"I don't know. You tell me."

"Good God, now you really sound like your counselor wife." He thought of all those mandatory psych evals he and the rest of the crew had been required to attend after the shoot down. Damn but he resented anyone getting too close, crawling inside his head and making him discuss crap that didn't matter anymore.

Tag's weathered face creased with a slow grin. "Counselor? Me? You're lucky I can't punch an officer, *sir.*"

Bo let his return smile answer. "You chiefs have a helluva way of making that sir sound like a put-down."

"Hey, at least I don't have to worry about you sniffing after my daughter, Nikki."

"Jesus, Tag, I was just helping her out with some advice on university courses."

"Just so it stays that way."

"Yeah, yeah, we all hear you loud and clear around the squadron. No crewdogs for your baby girl."

They shared a laugh at the familiar routine of razzing.

Sure, he didn't have any answers. But at least he now knew he wasn't a nutcase for wanting to fix things that weren't his concern. But hadn't he already made progress? He'd taken care of her pilot problem and alerted her brother about the stranger encounter at the air show. That should have brought satisfaction, resolution.

It didn't.

Tag's words shuffled around in Bo's head about men searching for ways to act. There were still problems. She needed more than a temporary pilot. Any idiot would recognize that, and he liked to think he was at least slightly above idiot level. Logic told him the rage he felt must be nothing compared to what roared inside of her with no place to go.

She needed relief from that pain.

He couldn't erase the heartbreak her scumbag husband had brought, but he had a talent for making women laugh. If ever he'd seen a woman in need of laughter, it was Paige Haugen. So he would play it laid-back, tease a smile from her, lighten her load until he pinpointed the rest of the problem. Damn straight. He'd come up with a solid transitional plan.

Not a convenient excuse to play with a flame hotter than any shooting out of Mako's lighter.

Sipping flaming-hot coffee from her travel mug, Paige stared out at the Cessna wing slicing low-lying clouds in a morning sky while Bo piloted beside her. Okay, so she was actually checking out his reflection in the window with her new glasses, but hey, she was being covert and cool about it.

His left hand on the yoke, his right rested on the throttle. The steering yoke in front of her mirrored his movements until it somehow seemed he sat in her seat, as well. What a strange thought she'd never entertained when Seth flew—or that awful substitute pilot who'd pitched an unholy fit over being given the heave-ho.

Radio chatter echoed from the headsets they both wore even though they could talk across the console over the low drone of the engine. The man was in complete command here among the dials, controls and clouds. His self-assurance inspired confidence that she could drink her coffee without fear of scalding.

Chicory-scented steam wafted from her mug up to fog the new glasses she'd bought Sunday at the mall. She set aside her mug and tugged the thin gold frames down and off, a more conservative choice than the funky retro glasses she'd bought in defiance right after she arrived in Minot. The glasses would offer a constant reminder that she needed to squelch impulses brought on by this man.

Hitching up the edge of her T-shirt, she swiped washed-soft cotton along the condensation. Coffee, a good night's sleep and a new clear vision of the world—manna for her soul. Sure the coffee stung her raw stomach, but the caffeine and warmth stole through her with a much-needed boost. The weekend attraction must have been a fluke.

A tingle of awareness prickled to life, and she paused cleaning her lenses. Her gaze skated left and…yep. Bo was watching her. Actually, he was watching her clean her glasses, which hitched her T-shirt up to bare a band of skin.

She dropped her shirt and jammed her glasses back on her face. Coffee. Now.

Ahhh. She gripped the mug and glued her gaze outside.

Talk about having her head in the clouds. Jeez. He was just a man, for Pete's sake. The whole dry-lightning melodrama moment from Friday and Saturday must be just that. Melodrama, not reality. She'd been a victim of overemotionalism during a vulnerable moment brought on from visiting the base. There could be no other explanation for why sitting in a stinky dog kennel with a man seemed bittersweetly romantic.

Paige checked her watch again. Four minutes since takeoff. Chuck Anderson's farm was only a twenty-minute ride by plane, cutting the travel time in more than half by soaring straight rather than contending with slow-moving farm machinery blocking bumpy and narrow roadways. And every minute counted for the horse hit by a car. Luckily she was qualified to take this call since her brother was already out.

Bo's legs flexed inside snug jeans as his tennis-shoe-clad feet rested on the rudder pedals. How come she'd never noticed the tight confines inside this plane before? She could smell the leather of his brown aviator jacket worn with jeans and a white T-shirt, transforming him into something that could have been straight out of *Top Gun*.

Of course, he was probably too young to remember that movie since he would have been about ten or eleven at the time. She'd seen it on a high school date. Yet watching Bo pilot the plane through the low-lying clouds with such confidence, she began to question her guess on his age, even knowing his recent promotion to captain meant he was likely less than thirty.

"How old are you?" The words tumbled out of her mouth ahead of rational restraint.

"Twenty-seven." He cut a quick look her way, a telling glance with a slight smile that acknowledged there was really only one reason she would ask.

"I'm thirty-three." Only a month away from thirty-four, actually, her conscience prodded her. She tipped the travel mug for another sip.

"Guess that means you're at your sexual peak."

She scalded her tongue and throat with a choked gulp. "I can't believe you said that. Are you always this—"

"Blunt?"

"Audacious."

"Audacious? Hell, no. That's a sissy word."

"Fine, then. No sissy words for the big warrior man." Even while she struggled to be somber, laughter tickled her aching stomach. "Let me rephrase to more manly terms. Are you always this frank?"

He tossed her a laid-back grin. "Nah. I usually try for more charm, but you looked so darn prickly, I couldn't resist teasing a smile out of you."

Pressing back into the leather bucket seat, she wrapped her hands around the warmth of her cup, still stunned and even more tempted to laugh. "Well, please try to contain yourself next time."

"There you go being prickly again." He thumped his forehead. "Better put down your coffee because I can already feel the urge to say something frank like—"

"Bo!"

"—how it's a damn shame *I'm* too old for *you* since I'm a good seven years past my sexual prime." He held up a forestalling hand. "If we were to have a relationship at all. Which I'm totally clear that you aren't interested in with me, so the whole subject is just on a theoretical level. I'm only talking about basic biology. Surely you're at ease with physiological discussions, given your medical background."

Past his prime? Her eyes snapped right to his muscled thighs, broad chest with shoulders filling leather to perfection. Gulp. He looked mighty toned to her, fit enough to more than keep up during—

She brought her mug to her mouth and studied the wing again only to find the cerulean sky reminded her of his eyes. "Basic biology, huh? Interesting discussion you've chosen for today."

"Hey, I wasn't the one who asked about ages." His face blanked with an innocence so at odds with the fallen-angel twinkle in his eyes that she had to laugh again, which encouraged the glint even brighter. "I've always thought it was one of nature's greatest jokes, that men and women peak at different times. Although it lends credence to the argument for a younger-man and older-woman relationship."

"Basic biology, my butt." She put her mug on her knee. "Are you flirting with me?"

"Yes, ma'am, I sure am. Just good old-fashioned fun that doesn't have to lead to a damn thing."

"Do you talk about sexual peaks with all your friends?"

"Now couldn't you just see my old loadmaster pal's face if I did?"

A snort splattered coffee against the topper on her mug. "I'm going to choke to death if you keep this up."

"I don't think so." He adjusted the altimeter setting. "You have the most incredible laugh, almost like a song, but it's a little hoarse, as if you haven't used it enough lately."

His words stole the laugh right out of her. Hadn't she thought the very same thing about her daughter's lack of smiles and laughter just a couple of days ago? Could Kirstie's sad little eyes be as much her mother's fault as her father's? Had she depressed her daughter with her own morose mood?

"Ah, hell, Paige. What'd I do now?"

"Nothing—" she forced a smile "—nothing at all. I'm just not a morning person."

She shrugged and worked on finishing her java as if it were a monumental task requiring all her attention. She needed to recoup after this new insight. Thank God, he got the message and stayed quiet for the whopping three minutes more it took to reach Chuck Anderson's family farm.

What was she thinking by bringing it up, anyway? Flirting was all well and good, but sheesh, she needed to keep herself grounded in reality, not pickup fantasies. She was a single mom in jeans and a T-shirt, her only cologne a hefty slathering of Avon's Skin So Soft to keep the mosquitoes away.

He decreased the throttle and lowered the flaps. The ground grew closer, the sprawling spread enlarging by the second, the landing steps familiar to her after so many flights with Seth. Bo pointed the craft toward the dirt strip runway, notched the flaps down again. Leveling the wings, he flared, raising the nose, all accomplished so smoothly she kept watching him—until she startled in surprise when the gear touched down without so much as a jolt.

His feet tipped the tops of the rudder pedals where the brakes were located, then flexed back down to guide the nose wheel as they taxied to the end of the grass strip. He pulled the throttle all the way out and turned the key. The engine shuddered off.

Bo whistled low through his teeth as he unstrapped. "The guy's got quite a spread here. I wonder how many hands it takes to help run this place? If those rows of bunkhouses are any indication, he's got quite a payroll."

Twisting back for her bag, she glanced over her shoulder. "What makes you think a guy owns it?"

"Get your PC knickers unknotted. You told me the guy's name earlier when we loaded up."

"Oh."

"Prickly Paige is in need of a smile again." He waggled his brows.

"Don't say another word." She held up her hand, totally unable to stop the smile.

He tapped the upward tilt of her lips. "I don't need to now."

The heat of his touch lingered far longer than her smile. Vaulting out of the door to the dusty ground, she clutched her black leather bag and started toward the waiting Suburban. She didn't want to depend on any man for her happiness ever again, even for so much as a few short weeks.

Chuck Anderson waited by the hangar with his idling vehicle—a member of the big blond lug club like her brother and Seth. "Thank heavens you're here. Even my stable head is having trouble keeping old Buck still."

"We'll have him patched up soon," she assured, careful to keep her distance from Chuck.

He'd asked her out last Valentine's Day, even included Kirstie in the invitation to make it seem less threatening, less like a date, even though the spark of interest in his eyes told them both it was. She'd said no, just as she'd done when he'd asked during their college days. She'd chosen Kurt over him because Chuck looked like a player.

What a joke in retrospect.

Objectively speaking, he was an attractive guy. Exactly the sort she should be with, given her love of animals and that Kirstie would have a wholesome environment. There just wasn't a spark.

Much less dry lightning.

Damn it, she'd gone for romance the first time and been so very wrong. She needed to be Practical Paige, even if that meant she was prickly, too.

She glanced at Bo threading ropes through the metal eyelets on the wings and tail, completing the tie-down. She kept backing—and just about walked slam into the side of the Suburban. Ah, for Pete's sake. She grabbed for the truck handle.

Her eyes met Chuck's as he slid behind the wheel. He looked from her to Bo and at her again, regret flicking through his hazel eyes before they blanked.

Was her attraction to Bo that obvious, even when she was at her prickly best? What a wake-up call. She refused to be the kind of woman who ran around with her tongue hanging out over some man.

Maybe she needed to get to know more about Bo beyond just the charmer flyboy facade. Then this obnoxious obsession with smelling his leather jacket would go away.

Yanking the seat belt down and around her, Paige set her eyes forward on the overlarge red barn in the distance by the pastures and bunkhouses. She definitely needed to learn more about Bo Rokowsky, discover the man's inner pig—and please, God, let him have one.

She didn't have time for teenage fantasies or even single-woman romances. She had a daughter to raise, a life to re-build and an ailing horse to patch.

Plopping onto the swing, Kirstie scuffed her red tennis shoe through the sand and wondered if she could get away with telling the school nurse she was sick. Again.

Then maybe she could go home. Uncle Seth would have to come get her since her mama was off with *him*. Bo. Yuck. But Uncle Seth could drive the car instead of the truck—and he would call Mom to come home 'cause he didn't do puke stuff too good.

Might work.

Except the school nurse was getting kinda smart about how much Kirstie showed up. Most of the time now she just got a paper cup of water and a pass back to class.

A pack of shouting kids playing tag ran past. Kirstie tugged the chains and jerked the swing into motion. It wasn't fair. Her mom got to ride around in the plane all day while she was stuck at school.

She pumped her legs harder and harder, higher and higher until she could just about see over the roof of the school. She was the one who liked airplanes, not her mom. Her mom didn't even really enjoy flying. Maybe she would hurl on Bo's boots, too, and then he wouldn't want to be their pilot anymore.

Except she really didn't want her mama to feel sick. She just wanted Bo to go away and her daddy to come back.

A hand settled against her back and shoved her higher. Kirstie almost jolted off on her face into the dirt. Holding tighter to the chains, she looked back over her shoulder.

"Hello, Kirstie Adella." It was the man with the bushy eyebrows from the air show again.

"What are you doing here?" She stopped pumping her legs.

"Just helping out at school, which means I can say hi to you again." He had one of those visitor passes clipped on that people picked up at the office.

Her swish took her closer and she double-checked. Yep, it was shaped like an apple and it said Visitor. She got a little less scared and started swinging again. It must be okay for him to be around. The man with bushy brows and a visitor pass kept pushing her.

Like her daddy used to do. "What did you and my daddy do around here when you was kids?"

"Well, we went to school together, although we liked the monkey bars more than the swings. And we always went to the county fair and ate lots of candy apples."

"My daddy did like candy apples, lots. Caramel ones, too."

"We would ride the roller coaster over and over again."

"I like roller coasters." And so did her dad, even if she didn't know that before. All this meant he'd been a regular kid. Her father wasn't a big bad monster who deserved to get shots like all the kids at school said. He couldn't be.

'Cause if he was, what did that make her?

Kirstie swallowed hard. If she started crying, the teacher

might make her go inside and then she couldn't talk to the guy with bushy eyebrows anymore. She blinked back her tears and kept her face forward so she could pretend her dad was pushing her.

"What's your mother doing today?"

She wanted to talk about her father, not her mother. "Working."

"At the house?"

"Nuh-uh. She's flyin' today."

"So your Uncle Vic's at the house?"

Okay, she could kinda pretend these were questions her dad would ask. "Nope. He's gotta fix a cow or bull or something somewhere else. Uncle Seth's gonna take care of me today."

"You don't seem happy about that."

"He's no fun since he can't play ball or nothing. He just sits in front of the TV with his foot up while he makes me do my homework." Her stomach started hurting again. It wasn't very nice to bad-mouth Uncle Seth. "But he says if I get all my homework done, we'll drive to McDonald's for supper."

"He can drive with his busted foot?"

"Yep. As long as he takes the car and not the truck 'cause the car doesn't have a—" She moved her right hand where that stick thing was in the truck, then grabbed hold of the chain again real quick.

"I get what you mean."

"Yeah."

Push. Swoosh. Push. Swoosh. "You'd better do all your homework so you can go."

"I don't like math much." Even her Uncle Seth said fractions were too hard for first grade, but he almost made it fun the night they'd practiced halves and quarters with a pizza.

"But you like McDonald's."

"Yeah."

"Your daddy liked math," the man rumbled from behind her. "He would be proud if you finished up all your math homework so you could go to McDonald's with your uncle. He would probably be happy to know you're getting out of the house and having fun."

"I guess he would." Maybe fractions would work with a cheeseburger.

The pushing stopped and he stepped around in front of her. "I should go now."

"Do you hafta?" She dragged her feet through the sand to slow the swing.

He knelt in front of her, real nice like. "I'm afraid I do. I have to get the sound system working right in the auditorium for the school board meeting this evening."

"Guess that's important. We won't be there, though."

He stood. "Your mom and uncle aren't going to make it back in time?"

She shrugged, wondering if maybe she should try to play sick after all. "Probably not."

"Hmm. I guess there will be no one to keep all your animals company for supper." He backed away with a real nice nod and wink. "Enjoy your McDonald's."

Chapter 6

"Seth took Kirstie to McDonald's," Paige announced, tucking her cell phone into her purse.

Bo tied down the plane after their return trip from treating the horse and wondered how one woman could pack so much musicality into so few words. Apparently his teasing had set her at ease after all. He hadn't realized how really pretty those North Dakota loops in her tones sounded until she'd rolled them out nonstop in the small confines of the Cessna, questioning him about favorite color, foods, movies.

Red.

Chili dogs.

Twelve O'Clock High. But yeah, he liked *Top Gun,* too, which seemed important to her for some reason.

This light-and-easy flirting thing was beginning to backfire on him, because he was starting to like her, which made him want her more. Too much.

He needed to finish up for the day, get back to his room and regroup before he did some dumb-ass thing like flatten her to the plane for a thorough kiss. No woman should smell this good after working with a horse, for God's sake. Still, he kept catching a whiff of her scent—aloe today instead of tropical sunscreen.

Bo bent and snagged the tie-down rope attached to the ground and reached up to loop it through the metal eyelet on top of the left wing strut. "McDonald's, huh? Lucky kid."

"He didn't expect us back so soon." She tapped her new glasses back in place, thin gold frames glinting the same color as her hair in the late-day sun. "So he took her out for a Happy Meal as a reward for finishing up her math homework."

"She'll enjoy that." He fashioned a slipknot and tightened. Wind stirred a fine mist of dirt at foot level.

"There was a message on my voice mail. One from my brother, too." She fidgeted with the strap to her vet bag, strands of blond hair sneaking free from her ponytail after the long day.

Why didn't she just go into the house and prop up her feet? She'd certainly put in a long enough day. Another thing to like about Paige, along with her steely spine, was her obvious gift in treating animals.

She'd checked out the horse and wrapped his cracked ribs in short order, declaring the animal fit with no punctured organs.

He strode to the right wing and connected another tie-down. "Is your brother back?"

"Not yet." She scraped her hair from her face only to have the wind streak it forward again. "He's still working with the bull out at Tom Walking Eagle's."

Bo's eyes shot straight over to the two-story house—a sprawling place with empty rooms and beds begging to be occupied. No problem. He would just leave. Their flight agreement only covered day calls. Another vet was picking up nighttime emergencies and one of the weekends. Even if Vic didn't mind him being around Paige, apparently he didn't plan to risk any overnighters.

Smart man.

He had no business starting anything with her. He'd told her that friends could flirt without it going anywhere, and he'd meant it. Yeah, she turned him on, but there were plenty of women he'd been attracted to and never pursued.

Except, he couldn't remember being this tempted.

So go for it, his libido urged. His conscience, however, told him to leave this wounded woman the hell alone. Let her rebuild her life with some steady guy like Anderson rather than settle for sex with a scarred rebel who wasn't even sure what he wanted to do with his life anymore.

Bo cinched the rope from the ground to the plane's tail. The action down south in his jeans must be seriously draining the blood supply from his brain. He definitely needed distance ASAP. "You can go on up to the house now if you want. I'm almost finished here."

"Thank you." She didn't move from her perch by the plane.

"I still have to set the chocks and then I'll stop in to say goodbye." Quickly, no hanging around in that house alone. "But then I'd better hit the road."

Unless somebody asked him to stay for supper in the big empty house with all those beds. They could use each other's bodies for plates.

"You really are an amazing pilot."

"Huh?" He was thinking about how to resist having sex with her—sex that she wouldn't offer anyway—and she wanted to talk about the Cessna? Usually he enjoyed the hell out of discussing planes. But right now he wanted to plan a seven-course meal savored off the creamy skin of Paige's stomach, which he'd seen when she cleaned her new glasses with the edge of her T-shirt.

He'd thought the funky retro glasses were fun, but he liked these, too, the way they gave her more of a preppy, prissy air in spite of the jeans and mud-stained T-shirt. Her glasses issued an undeniable invitation of, "Take me off and kiss this lady until the starch melts from her spine."

For some reason the notion of stripping her of those glasses tempted him as much as the thought of bunching and inching up her washed-thin T-shirt.

He turned away before he got harder and popped the snap on his jeans. He probably already had a zipper imprint.

"You're an amazing pilot," she repeated. "I'm making small talk here, getting to know you, like with the favorite foods and movie discussion."

Talk was good. He needed to engage his brain with something other than X-rated fantasies. Since she seemed chatty today, that could work as long as they stayed outside.

He opened the small aft cargo door and pulled out the chocks. "And you're a damn good animal doctor."

"I'm not a doctor, remember?"

"Whatever. Although I'm not sure how much of a compliment you've given me if you're comparing me to that hack."

"Seth's a great pilot, too, but even he's not as smooth as you are—and if you tell him I said that, I'll have to deny it."

"No problem." He knelt to set a chock in front of the nose gear. "And thanks."

"No problem," she repeated.

She studied him through narrowed eyes as if she couldn't see him clearly, when he knew full well her new glasses should be working fine.

Leave. Leave. Leave, he nudged himself. Drop your sorry, horny ass into the rental car and stay away from this woman.

Wasn't Seth due back sometime soon? How long did it take to drive to McDonald's, feed a kid and drive back?

Hours, out here.

He definitely needed to finish up and hit the road. He'd made Paige smile more than once. Her job obviously brought her happiness. The way she'd calmed the horse had been a mesmerizing sight. After securing the plane at Anderson's place, he'd jogged the mile over to the barn and found her…gentle voice soothing the spooked horse while she listened to the heart, lungs, stomach for punctured organs, like an EMS tech for animals. All the while handling an animal that could crush her with one stray kick.

This confident woman could take care of herself. No doubt she had baggage to deal with from her husband, but who wouldn't? And she had more help handling it than many single mothers, thanks to her brother and cousin. So what was up with the restlessness chewing his hide?

She followed him around the nose of the plane, gripped the wing overhead and leaned, stretching her T-shirt taut across generous breasts. "Have you always wanted to be in the Air Force?"

In need of an outlet, he kicked a chock secure under a rear wheel with extra force. "I didn't know what I wanted to do growing up, other than I wanted to fly planes and buy myself some kick-ass toys."

"You mentioned growing up in an orphanage."

"From the time I was five. Yeah."

"The same age Kirstie was when she lost her father." She trailed him to the other side. "That must have been difficult for—"

"Yeah. I guess so." He didn't want to discuss those days. He'd rather talk about the scars on his hands than the morning he'd walked into his mother's room to ask for a bowl of Frosted Flakes and found her— "After I got to St. Elizabeth's,

I had it good, safe, was well fed and got lots of hugs from the nuns."

Last wheel secured. He was done. Time to leave. But his feet wouldn't move.

He leaned against the side of the Cessna and stared into pretty brown eyes that invited him to share. "But when you're seven and ten, even twelve, you don't recognize how important those things are. You want dumb-ass things like a bike no one else has ridden. A batting helmet with your name stenciled on it. To make sure I could have everything on my list—and the list was long—I figured I had to go to college."

"Which is why you took an ROTC scholarship." She nudged her glasses straight with one pointer finger.

"There were other offers on the table, but the ROTC deal came with money, a chance to fly *and* the most kick-butt toys I'd ever imagined."

"How many years do you owe the Air Force for the scholarship?"

"I'm coming up on the end of my commitment to the Air Force."

"Are you staying in?"

"I don't know yet."

That stunned her quiet for a full five seconds of silence filled only with dogs barking in their kennels. "What would you do if you left the Air Force?"

"It's tough to imagine being grounded. I could fly for the airlines, or any number of other things like doctors without borders, FedEx even."

His mind winged to the looming deadline for deciding whether to stay in the military and take off the uniform for good. He'd met his commitment, given something back to society like the nuns had taught him. He'd enjoyed flying Paige around today, but he wasn't sure how he would feel about going a lifetime without any more high-stakes missions. Except, he also couldn't face seeing another military brother like Tag take a boot in the ribs for him.

He slammed the aft cargo door and reminded himself he didn't have to decide jack right now.

"What did you study in college? Have you considered a job in that field and just enjoy your flying as a hobby? I hear most pilots study engineering, maybe? Or military history."

"Education."

"Excuse me?"

"Hey, I even know a bomber guy who majored in jewelry technology. Something wrong with that?"

"No! Of course not."

"Because I would find it very un-PC if you don't get that shocked gawk off your face."

"Consider it erased." Her shock shifted into a grin that crinkled her nose.

Yeah, making this woman smile gave him one helluva charge. All that talk of sexual peaks was backfiring on him with a vengeance. "Do you ever think about going back to finish up veterinarian school like you originally planned?"

Longing chased through her eyes, then faded. "I have a daughter to raise."

"You could do both."

"If I won the lottery along with eight more hours in the day."

"Valid point. And speaking of more hours in the day, I should probably let you put your feet up or something." He shoved away from the Cessna. "Time for me to hit the road, anyway. I'll walk you up to the house before I go."

Confusion flickered in her eyes behind the new glasses. Had she expected him to hit on her once they landed in spite of his insistence that friends could just flirt? He searched deeper in her eyes and definitely saw confusion—and undeniable wariness. He'd never expected her to be this swayed by the flirtation between them, especially given all the crap she was still going through.

Jamming his hands into his jeans pockets to keep from touching her, he started toward the house. Paige followed, her steps brisk to keep up, so he slowed. She'd worked hard, in fact worked hard every day, and suddenly he wanted to slip her glasses off for her to sleep.

A much more disturbing thought.

Sidestepping the vet sign swinging in the yard, he strode up the walkway toward the clinic door. The sun set late in the spring here, so the halo of the fading day still lit the yard. But the clinic was empty. Like the house.

An uneasy itch crept along his instincts. She shouldn't enter into an empty house alone. He scanned the yard, found nothing out of the ordinary. The house, barn and hangar loomed quiet, unlit with doors closed. Sure, the dogs were causing a ruckus in the kennel, but he assumed the plane had riled them or they were shouting to Paige for food and attention. No cars were in sight along the flat expanse of land other than his rental. Which meant Paige would have no way to leave if something happened.

He wasn't going anywhere.

"What grades?"

Bo dragged his eyes off the deserted road. "Pardon me?"

"What grades and subject did you focus on?"

Resting a tennis shoe on the step, he leaned back on the porch post. Outside would be safer for talking until her brother or cousin returned. "I have a double major in education and music."

"You could be a band teacher?"

"Or chorus, even elementary music."

"Now there's an image." She sagged against the opposite porch post, eyes lighting with whimsy. "A really nice image, actually. What made you declare that as a major, especially since you planned to fly?"

"I have to admit that at first I chose it because I figured it would be an easy program to get the degree I needed for an Air Force commission. I know all about kids, and music is a breeze for me."

Damn but she was easy to talk to. Sure, he liked women's company, enjoyed charming them and watching them smile, but Paige cut through his BS and just talked to the man. No games, but still plenty of fun.

"And teaching the kids wasn't so simple after all?"

"Hell, no." He spoke on autopilot, mostly still enjoying the way her full lips formed words or pursed when she listened, lips devoid of any gloss. The dampness would taste of pure her. "I worked my ass off with child-psych classes and testing-statistic courses. Then there was music theory. And the first day of student teaching was a bi— Uh, particularly challenging."

She leaned back against her hands. "There are women who would plant a big kiss on your face for recognizing that working with kids is a tough job."

Her eyes crinkled at the corners, her laughter ringing like a song he might try to write someday. The tune, totally and uniquely Paige, swirled in his head, scaling back life and concerns until he said to hell with it all and just felt the music. He was only going to kiss her, after all, not start some steaming affair.

Bo stepped closer. "Are you one of those women?"

No, every rational bone in her body screamed. No, she wasn't the sort of woman who would throw her arms around this gorgeous, oh-so-young and too-charming man standing across from her on the porch steps.

But right now she sure wanted to be. "You're smooth, Rokowsky."

"Not smooth enough, apparently, because you're still standing over there." He tapped the toe of her shoe with his.

All of about twenty-four inches away. Close enough to catch the scent of leather. "You want to kiss me?"

"I was thinking *you* would kiss *me* in light of the whole 'Bo rocks because he knows kids can run you ragged as hell' revelation." He straightened from the porch post, closer without touching. "And then I would kiss you back."

Her fingers dug into the splintery wood behind her. "Do you hit on every woman in your path?"

Closing in on her, he hitched a foot up one step higher, the heat of his thigh brushing hers as he effectively blocked her way. "No need to be insulting."

Her fingers held tighter to the wooden post behind her until splinters stung. "Glad you realize that would constitute smarmy behavior."

She'd only dated a couple of men—boys really—before Kurt, but she wasn't a total innocent, and she had been married for ten years. Ten? Paige shuddered. She didn't want to think about her dead husband, especially not now.

Something was drawing her to this man in spite of all the logic telling her to keep her hormones sealed up tight for two weeks. A full day of undiluted Bo Rokowsky made for a heady brew to a woman who'd been a damn long time without a drink.

A persistent inner voice that sounded remarkably like her practical big brother reminded her she hadn't been tempted to drink even lemonade with Chuck Anderson, much less taste *him*. And, man, now that Bo had placed the image in her head of the two of them, legs tangled…

Hello? Like the vision wasn't already there.

"I'm a one-at-a-time guy, thank you very much. Whatever I'm doing, I give it my complete and undivided attention."

"Is that so?"

"Yeah, and I really want to give my undivided attention to kissing you." A furrow tucked between his brows. "No, wait.

I would more than kiss you. I'd touch your hair and let it slide through my fingers. I'd smell your neck and wonder what that aloe scent is—"

"Avon's Skin So Soft, a mosquito repellant."

"And a mighty sexy bug repellant it is, suddenly the most erotic scent ever."

Damn, he was hypnotic even when he was funny.

Step away!

Step away from the bad boy, her mind blared like a recorded warning that people too often ignored and vaulted right over the restricted-area rope into forbidden territory.

Fishing the house key out of her pocket, she eased down a stair, farther from the heat of his thigh and the scent of leather. "Well, thanks for the compliment, but I believe I'll pass."

The furrow trenched deeper. "You'll pass?" he growled. "That's all you have to say?"

He did confident just right, self-assurance without arrogance. Although she couldn't resist jabbing, "I guess you don't hear that very often."

The furrow between his brows smoothed as the killer smile returned. "Ah, okay, now I get it. You want to make me work for it. Cool. I can do that. I'll enjoy charming you."

Charming.

One word smacked her right back into stark reality. She had a weakness when it came to charming men. "Anybody ever tell you that you're packing a helluva an ego, flyboy?"

"I may have heard that once or twice."

"Well, believe it. Thank you for flying us around for the next two weeks, but I'm not interested in filling time in between those flights with convenience sex."

"Whoa! Hold on. Who said anything about sex?" He stalked down the step to face her. "Last I heard we were talking about a kiss. One kiss. A kiss where we get to know each other and see if the chemistry we've got going is real."

He thought they had chemistry, too?

Argh. She was such an idiot. She slapped the key down on the railing. "So you just want to make out for two weeks?"

"Um, well…" He scratched his head. "I didn't think we'd necessarily hop right into a haystack or something today. But if the kiss is as good as I'm certain it's going to be, we could have dinner, see how the next kiss goes."

"And if we land in the haystack later… Yeah, I get it. I'm not a fling sort."

"Neither am I. Believe it or not, I actually enjoy talking to you. So if all we end up with is conversation and a few kisses, no harm no foul."

Were they actually discussing whether or not to kiss? "Some things aren't worth trying. You're leaving soon. You live in a whole different world. My baggage really goes against that world—"

"We're talking about a damn kiss, not a flaming af—"

"I'm at least six years—" almost more, as of next month "—older than you are!"

His steely blue eyes narrowed with sleepy, sensual intent. "And you're hot as hell, especially when you're fired up."

He slid off her glasses.

Oh.

His mouth covered hers.

Double oh.

Dry lightning didn't just crackle overhead, it snapped through her veins and along her skin until even the roots of her hair tingled from pure sensation. She wanted to attribute it to his incredible technique so she could distance herself by labeling him a player. But he wasn't even moving. Neither was she. They just stood for a frozen second, lips brushing, holding.

Then he reached, fingers banding around her arms—good thing or she would have fallen smack on her butt. And, oh my, he moved, slanting his mouth over hers and drawing her flush against him, leather and muscle and man imprinted against her. She'd been so long without a man, without comfort and kisses, she hadn't even realized how much she'd missed until seeing a certain flyboy strut toward her on a crowded flight line. She'd been dead inside.

Not anymore.

Nerve endings fired back to life with a near-painful intensity. Touching lightning hurt. And enthralled.

Her hands flew up to grip his jacket, fingers twisting in leather while her mouth parted under his. His low growl shivered through her, emboldening her to meet the bold sweep of his tongue. Right now she couldn't seem to scrounge for reasons to worry about age differences, past problems and current concerns. Her fingers inched up leather to his shoulders, farther still into his hair, caressing along the bristly short cut at the nape of his neck.

So much for self-control and restraint.

She eased back to whisper against his mouth, "Did you kiss me first or did I kiss you?"

"I don't know." The hot breath of his answer steamed along oversensitized nerves. "But I'm damn sure going to kiss you first now."

His face lowered toward her as she arched up on her toes for more. Much more. Yeah, maybe they could spend the next two weeks necking on her front porch, in the plane and the barn, too. And, hey, the swing hanging from their lone oak tree even sounded fun when she thought about draping herself over his lap and swaying through the air while her senses soared. Of course she would probably incinerate in two days, but what a way to go.

He eased back, staring down with such intensity and not even a hint of arrogant victory, which would have made it easy to punt him off her property pronto. Unless he was a consummate actor, he was shaken, affected, on fire as much as she.

"What do we do next?" She dipped her fingers under his collar along the strong column of his neck, already regretting what she *should* do next, half hoping he could persuade her, anyway.

"Unless you tell me very clearly otherwise, you go inside and I return to base alone."

He wasn't going to push. That helped, and didn't all at once.

"I wish…" She could be different, impulsive, less afraid and more daring, that she could indulge in carefree sex. "I wish."

He tucked her glasses in place again. "Me, too."

Backing away, he slid the key from the railing as her hand trailed down his arm to let the moment linger just a little while longer. Bo angled past her, up the steps and jammed the key into the bolt. Before he could twist the lock, the door swung wide.

What?

The door should be locked. Seth couldn't have forgotten.

Tension radiated from Bo for one foreshadowing second before his arm shot out to bar her from entering. "Get back, Paige. Now."

Foreboding scoured her gut. She tucked to the side of the porch post, a quick glance over his shoulders revealing…

Destruction.

Glass glinted on the floor amid overturned cabinets, scattered papers and busted bags of dog food. A cat streaked through the open portal and between porch spindles.

Someone had broken into the clinic.

Chapter 7

Bo's focus narrowed to the havoc smashed and strewn through the clinic, his muscles tensing, ready to spring into action. Survival instincts shifted into high gear, shutting down all thoughts except securing the area and protecting Paige. They were out in the middle of nowhere, no neighbors close enough to provide a safe haven for her, and no way of knowing if inside or outside would be better.

Reaching into his leather jacket, he pulled free his cell phone and passed it back to her. "Here," he whispered low, quick. "Call 911."

He listened, ear tuned for any noise from an intruder still lurking. Nothing. Silence echoed from inside, leaving outdoor sounds all the louder. Paige's panting gasps of air. The thud of his own heart. A cat purring as it twined around his ankles in a figure eight while Paige whispered into the phone.

Leaning, he grabbed a wrist-thick log off the top of the

small woodpile near the wood stove. He'd rather have his 9mm, but something was better than nothing. Scooting the tabby aside gently with his tennis shoe, Bo reached to affirm Paige was still following. "Stay behind me, but stay close, keep a watch out behind us."

Her body heat and low breaths warmed his back, reassuring him that for now she was fine. Deeper into the clinic, he sidestepped file folders splayed across the floor. Dog chow and shards of glass crunched under his slow treads.

Still no one. He scanned the interior. Exam room doors gaped open, seemingly undisturbed.

A light shone from the back office. He gestured for Paige to tuck behind the reception desk while he crept closer to find… An empty room.

Papers littered the floor, a window gaping open. Bo charged across, tossing down the log and hefting himself up on the high sill to look out. Dusty footsteps marked the ground, ending when tire tracks started, their culprit obviously long gone. Someone had likely heard the plane return and beat a hasty retreat. At least the cops could take molds of the tracks and shoe prints for clues.

Relief that Paige was safe mixed with frustration because he couldn't confront the enemy. Adrenaline pumping overtime, he dropped back flatfooted into the office.

"We're clear," he called, needing to see her, *now,* and reassure himself she was okay. "Did you get through to the cops?"

"They're on their way." Her voice preceded her into the office. Phone clutched to her chest, she sagged against the door. "Uncle."

"What?" Was she losing it? Concern carried his feet a couple of steps closer in spite of his brain shouting for him to stay back when they were both overrevved, raw.

Hungry.

"I give." She swept a hand over the mess. "I'm crying uncle. I've had enough excitement for one lifetime, thanks. Where can I go to order one of those nice, regular boring lives where I get to bring up my child in peace?" Her shaky laugh and crooked glasses damn near broke his heart.

Screw wise decisions. He strode over a toppled potted cactus to hook an arm around her shoulder and draw her in close, for himself as much as to comfort her. She melted against him, no tears, but so soft and sweet smelling his arms held tighter. He breathed in the aloe scent of her the way he soaked in a song to soothe his soul until his world steadied.

Finally, his adrenaline-pumped instincts took a breather and let his brain kick back into high gear—with a vengeance. What if he'd let her walk in here alone? He'd tried to send her to the house while he'd been tying down the plane and working even harder to harness his libido. Who the hell knew when the break-in occurred? He assumed the vandals had left when the plane approached, but they could have slipped through the back while he and Paige had been making out. A herd of cattle could have thundered by and he never would have noticed.

He had to get hold of himself around this woman and quit sniffing her hair like some horny adolescent. But first, maybe he would hold her a while longer.

Sirens whined low in the distance.

"Bo?"

"Yeah?"

"Look."

He turned to follow her pointed finger to the clinic's medicine cabinet—bashed and open.

Four hours later Paige scooted a box across the office floor with the toe of her tennis shoe as she collected papers. Vic was restoring order to the patient files out in the lobby, while

Bo hammered plywood over the shattered glass on the medicine supply cabinet, unspeaking, steady. It would be easy to get used to his help, a fact she'd remembered in time to pull herself out of his arms and greet the police on her own.

Was anything in her life not a total mess? Much like her feelings about the kiss she and Bo had shared. At least they couldn't talk with Vic to overhear in the next room, which would give her more time to gather her thoughts—and will-power.

She tore her eyes off Bo's broad shoulders stretching his white concert T-shirt, back to the current clutter littering her life. Thank God Kirstie had finally fallen asleep upstairs, and Seth was on hand to watch over her. Paige shivered. She couldn't imagine letting her child go anywhere now without one of them glued to her side.

The police had already come and gone, declaring it drug-related vandalism. She just wished Seth had taken longer at McDonald's so Kirstie didn't have to arrive home to find five cop cars in her yard.

Yep, five.

Back in Charleston, a break-in would have warranted one car, but crime was so low in North Dakota, they received plenty of department attention, for which she was eternally grateful. All the more reason to plant her roots deep in this stark but fertile region.

Hopefully, the police would have answers soon to this break-in anomaly. Molds had been made of the footprints and tire tracks—a truck. Great. There were only about a kajillion of those around here.

Ah, hell. When had she become so defeatist? Right about the time she'd cried uncle and turned into a noodle-spine against Bo's chest. Enough of the self-pity garbage. She wasn't the confused, duped fool of a year ago.

She kicked the box to the side and knelt, sliding her hand

under the office desk, searching by touch to fish out two more letters. She glanced over them. A credit card offer. Another letter from Kurt's lawyer. Two hefty reminders of her sucky financial state.

Jamming them into a drawer, she refused to think about the problems Kurt left behind. She had enough of her own to sort through without more of his grief.

Bo lined up another nail. "Anything missing from the meds?"

The hammer landed home with a smack hard enough to make her wince.

Sheesh, she was strung tight from too much roller coaster in the past few hours. Discussing practical details would be so much safer than addressing what really hung in the air between them right now—a killer kiss.

She fell back onto her butt and tossed papers into the cardboard box to be sorted later. How dare someone invade her life like this, threaten her family? "I can't be sure what's here until I take inventory."

"Are veterinary drugs usable for humans?" He stuck three more nails between his teeth.

"Sure, some of them are major targets for the black market, two drugs in particular. Ketamine and diazepam—or Valium as it's more commonly known."

He pulled the last nail from between his teeth. "What's Ketamine?"

"Ketamine is used for human burn victims. We use it for temporary, quick procedures." She settled into the comfort zone of her career. Here, at least, she was in control. "It's effective on cats when we declaw them, also works as an injectible preanesthetic on dogs and cats when mixed with diazepam. Ketamine is a strong hallucinogenic, and wow can you ever tell it when those poor kitties wake up."

"I imagine that has a high street value." He tapped the last nail head flat and dropped the hammer back into the toolbox, along with the fist full of nails *clink, clink, clinking* into the tray.

"You're right." Rising, she hefted the box up onto the corner of the desk.

He leaned back against the patched cabinet, hands tucked away in his jeans pockets. "Can you think of another explanation for why someone would break in?"

"Besides looking for drugs?" Plenty of reasons, all so scary they made her want to grab the Aztec blanket off the back of the office sofa and ward off the oncoming chill of premonition. "You mean because of Kurt."

"He died before he fingered all of his connections."

"He and his attorney were working to cut deals with the D.A. for a better sentence." And signed his own death warrant by giving those connections time to shut him up permanently.

"If those connections think you have information, they might come after you."

"I don't have a clue about his—" She plopped onto the sofa and forced herself to consider his words. "But of course they don't know that. Why wait a year to come after me?"

"If we knew, we'd have the answer to who did this."

"So we're back to square one and a messy office." *We.* Ooops. She'd been right to fear leaning on him, because it was beyond easy to think in *we* terms when Bo Rokowsky strutted into her life with all his quick answers and help.

Would he notice her *we* slip?

If he did, at least he stayed silent. He just kept those sexy baby blues pinned on her with slow blinking assessment that reminded her of the moment he'd pulled off her glasses to give her a kiss she couldn't afford to remember—but didn't stand a chance of forgetting. Her lips parted, her lungs suddenly hungry for more air to relieve the building pressure in her breasts tingling with the phantom sensation of pressing against the hard wall of his chest.

Footsteps sounded outside the office, halting footsteps that brought a welcome reminder she had bigger concerns than sexual frustration.

Seth poked his head around the door, leaning on his cane. "Hey, Paige, Kirstie woke up, nightmares from all this garbage going on. She needs you to tuck her in again."

Paige bolted to her feet. "Thanks, Seth." She shot a glance at Bo on her way out the door. "And thank you for your help."

The thought of her child's cries squeezed maternal instincts hard with the reminder of the main reason she couldn't afford to shout uncle for even one weak second. Turning her back on Bo and temptation, Paige sprinted down the hall and up the back stairs toward her daughter.

Paige's speeding footsteps echoed in the empty office. Bo shoved away from the boarded-up medicine cabinet, righting a chair on his way to the door out into the reception area.

Who would want drugs and why? In spite of any other theories, the obvious answer was teenage vandalism. Connecting it to Kurt Haugen as they'd discussed was a stretch, although a part of him wouldn't mind laying blame at that bastard's feet. His mind also niggled with possibilities closer to home. He wanted to trust the people in Paige's life, but he'd learned long ago that sometimes folks hurt the ones they loved.

His eyes landed on the two Jansen men behind the reception counter, Vic shuffling loose papers back into files while Seth shoved them into the drawers. The two lumberjack-size guys wore the same face with way different personalities. Vic with his John Deere hat and stoic grief. Seth with his battered fishing cap, cargo shorts and don't-give-a-crap air.

What if the break-in was a cover up for someone closer to

home? Seth was in a helluva lot of pain. Could he have helped himself to some relief? Even if he'd been off with Kirstie, he could have tipped off a friend about when the place would be vacant.

His hands ached with memories of his own recovery. There had been more than one moment when he might have sold his soul for an extra shot of morphine to get through physical therapy.

Bo studied the man's eyes. The pupils were a hint larger, but it was nighttime.

He shifted his focus back to Vic. It was his practice, so why trash the place if he needed something? And the guy seemed earnest in wanting to help his sister, in which case he wouldn't have stressed her with something like this.

The veterinarian stopped to study one of the folders, cross-referencing with computer data. "I keep thinking about that guy who approached Kirstie at the air show."

Was Vic trying to throw him off the trail by mentioning the air-show guy to him—and to the cops earlier? "Have you spoken to Kirstie about it?"

"Paige and I both talked to her even before this, but the kid's not coughing up any new info other than what you two saw—the back of a blond guy in some kind of repairman's uniform. The discussion seemed to scare her even more until she clammed up. We're walking a fine line here with a kid who's already on shaky ground, given what's happened over the past year." He slapped manila folders in a steady rhythm, the counter slowly reappearing from under the mess of the break-in.

"It's a reach connecting the guy." Although, the encounter still set off more than a few warning bells in his mind.

"That it is. But then, as much as I didn't like Kurt Haugen, I would have considered it a reach that he would ever sink so low." His hands slowed, his shoulder dropping. "Maybe I should have, so I could have saved my sister a load of heartache."

"He fooled people who saw him every day." Bo knelt to rake trash back into a wastebasket, not sure he wanted to follow this conversational path.

Seth snorted. "The guy was in debt up to his ass with his restaurant business. He was ripe for the picking when the mob approached him. Not that it justifies anything."

"Just trying to make sense of it all."

Seth swept off his ratty fishing hat and Frisbee-tossed it across the counter. "It sucks not knowing when the boom might smack or which direction it'll come from, a lot like falling through a barn loft at the Anderson place and busting this damn ankle of mine. Out of the blue. I wish I could be more help in holding my own and watching out for Paige and the munchkin."

Vic clapped him on the back. "Hang in there, man. Not much longer until you're in the air again."

And Bo would be out. His life would be back on track, and he would never see Paige or her kid again. Just like he wanted it. "I can bunk here, too, starting tomorrow."

Hey? Where the hell had that come from?

Duh. From a deep well of testosterone and protective urges that he didn't see any chance of ditching.

Vic shoved aside the stack of restored files and gave Bo his undivided attention. "Another generous offer for my sister."

Seth smirked, jingling change in the bottomless pockets of his cargo shorts. "Purely altruistic, I'm sure."

Bo knew when to keep his trap shut.

Vic blinked slowly. "Thanks, but we have friends we can call."

"I'm sure you do," Bo acknowledged without backing down. A key to savvy aviation involved making fast, smart decisions in a crisis, and not flinching from a set path.

Seth nudged a couple of stacks under his propped foot for higher elevation. "No friends with his military training, though, and I'm not particularly ferocious looking hobbling around."

"Thanks for helping him, Judas." Vic snagged Seth's fishing hat and swatted his shoulder.

"My pleasure." Seth snatched his cap back and folded it into one of his pockets.

A lengthy sigh of defeat ruffled prescription slips in front of the pissed-off vet. "Makes sense for you to sleep here rather than commute all the way out here every day and back at night." He pinned him with a piercing glare. "But you'll be staying in your own damn room."

"Of course."

"Alone." Vic rocked back on two chair legs with a casualness totally negated by the vein throbbing just below the brim of his John Deere cap.

"Dude, I'm here to help your sister, not hurt her. And she is an adult. You'll just have to trust her to know what's good for her."

"Your answer's not reassuring me, Rokowsky." Vic's vein throbbed faster along his temple.

Nothing he could say would reassure any overprotective brother. So he didn't bother spelling out that while he found Paige hot as hell, he intended to keep his hands to himself. He settled on spelling out a piece of the truth. "I'm not here for you. I'm here for her."

"For how long?" Vic shot back with unerring aim at Bo's own doubts.

"Long day." Paige arched the kink out of her back as she strode toward Bo's rental sedan parked under the boughs of the lone sprawling oak. The swelling wind twisted the dangling swing in a lazy figure eight dance.

Security lights blazed to create a halogen halo around the house, clinic and kennels. At least the animals would bark if anyone approached, small reassurance after her home had been violated.

Those lights also showcased well Bo in jeans and his concert T-shirt, leather jacket hooked on his finger over one shoulder. His eyes flickered over her chest, lingered for two hammering heartbeats, then jerked back up to her face.

He shrugged into his flight jacket. "Is Kirstie okay?"

Paige straightened, fast. She would work out the kinks later, maybe in about two weeks when this guy hopped on his plane for a return to South Carolina. She might *wish*, but she couldn't afford the temptation of more mind-blowing kisses or warm strong hugs from this man who carried so many memories of the past. And her daughter needed stability.

But a selfish part of her insisted she deserved comfort, even the two-week variety, except another part of her balked at that kind of relationship. Maybe she should start dating again. She couldn't imagine spending the rest of her life alone and, oh my God, celibate.

It had been a year since Kurt's arrest, nearly a year since his murder. She was a woman as well as a mother. Somebody like Chuck Anderson would be perfect, uncomplicated and she didn't want him.

She wanted this man. And, sheesh, she sure did have a history of wanting unwisely.

Paige strolled closer, stopping by the lonely tree, a safe two feet away from Bo beside his sedan rental. "She's asleep for now, just scared and trying not to show it. I can relate to that."

Memories of being held by him earlier in the office tormented her with the sweet gift of sharing her burdens. A person could get used to that, a person should have that, but she hadn't just made a simple mistake in judgment in her relationship with Kurt. She'd screwed up in mammoth proportions.

Bo's blue eyes darkened with concern even if he didn't move toward her. "Are you okay?"

"I'm fine." Sorta. Enough to get through the night if she kept a tight rein on herself. She clenched her hands into fists, digging her nails into her palms, the slight pinch a slow but sure reminder of how falling for a Bo sort of guy would one day hurt like hell. "Thank you for the support earlier, but I'm almost certain I'll crumble if I get any more sympathy. Does that make sense?"

"Not really. But then we all cope in different ways, and I have to respect your boundaries."

"Thank you." Holy cow, this guy knew the right words to slip right past her defenses.

Kurt had encouraged her to count on him for everything, financial as well as emotional, insisting there would be plenty of time for her to spread her wings once Kirstie grew up. But this man talked about healthy boundaries. He even discussed and supported her dreams of returning to college.

The circle of light warmed into a close bubble of privacy against the dark countryside. She dug those fingernails harder into her palms.

Bo scratched the back of his head. "This may not be the best time to bring it up, but, well, the guys and I were talking and it really is a helluva drive back into Minot after a full work load of flying. So when I return in the morning, I'm going to start bunking here."

She forgot all about digging in her nails, surprise making her hands go slack. She didn't buy his excuse for a second. "You're staying out here because of the break-in."

"Doesn't hurt to have an extra guy around." His easy shrug shifted the leather jacket around his shoulders, a whispered slide of heavy, smooth fabric.

"And that's your only reason?" She braced her sagging spine against the tree, better than leaning on a man again. "I thought you said you were respecting my boundaries?"

"You think I'm moving here to get lucky? Lady, I'd have to be an idiot to try that with your watchdog brother on hand."

He had a point and now she felt foolish. "Then why are you doing this?"

"Make no mistake, I would still follow you inside in a heartbeat—if your brother was on Mars and the past evaporated for a day or two. But I heard you earlier about not letting this—" he gestured between them "—tug we feel go anywhere. I like to think I have enough self-control to keep my hands to myself." A wicked smile tucked in his cheek. "No matter how enticing the woman."

Heat crawled up her neck even as she resisted the urge to roll her eyes at his blatant flattery.

His smile faded. "What happened with the break-in puts a new spin on things. This is about the business of keeping your practice afloat and a roof over your head. Most of all this is about keeping you and Kirstie safe. Even on testosterone overload, I recognize everything else has to take a back seat."

He sure did have a way of taking the sting out of saying he could live in the same house with her and not do a thing about it. "And you've already talked this over with my brother."

Bo nodded. "He's not happy about it, but sees the logic. He puts your safety first."

"Then it's settled." As much as she wanted to stand on her own two feet, only a moron would turn down the extra security of his presence. For her daughter. "I'm sorry for sounding ungrateful, but the thought of having you here makes me feel this tug between us all the more. Frankly, that scares me as much as vandals prowling the town."

"You sure don't pull punches, lady, or make it any easier for a guy. I like that about you. But no worries." He held his hands in front of him. "I meant what I said about keeping these to myself."

"Fair enough." Her hands behind her, she splayed her fingers along the roughened bark, the tree's gnarled sturdiness offering a welcome support that demanded nothing in return. "Thank you for making me smile today. I needed that."

"No problem." He fished his keys out of his pocket. "I'm going to head out now. Mako's waiting to catch supper together."

How silly that she didn't want him to touch her but she didn't want him to leave. Soon enough he would be around 24/7, and wasn't that a scary and exciting thought all at once?

"Mako?" she called out, shoving away from the tree. "That's his nickname, right?"

Pausing, he propped his elbows over the open sedan door, bronzed wrists contrasting to white paint. "His call sign. Yeah."

"What's your call sign?" She edged round the oak and slid down to sit on Kirstie's swing.

"Bo."

Her fingers wrapped around the hemp rope, her toe dragging the dusty ground while the rope creaked with each gentle sway. "But I thought your real name was Bo."

"It's what I go by." He tapped the name tag on his brown leather jacket. "But it's not my legal name."

"Why do they call you Bo?"

"Kind of like 'Bo is for beau, can I be yours?'" His half-cocked grin suggested he was joking. Or not.

Great. He really did have a player reputation. A good thing or bad since he was staying in her house now? "Really."

"Actually, no."

"Then what does it mean?"

His cobalt-blue eyes glinted with the twinkle of stars overhead. "Everybody's got a theory they like to torment me with by threatening to spread it around."

"Such as?"

He studied her for four slow creaks of the swing before stepping around the sedan door, closer to her. "Tag insists it's because of the Rokowsky—cow—in my name. Bovine. Bo."

"Ewww. Guys can be so gross. Is that the truth?"

"Maybe. Maybe not." He leaned one shoulder against the tree. "Then there are those who say it's a package reference."

"Package?" Oh, my. He couldn't actually mean... She forced her eyes not to drop lower.

"As in, I'm the total package with a bow."

Those slightly crooked teeth sure did charm her as much as his smile. "Uh-huh. So which is correct?"

"All of them around the squadron. None of them in reality. It's a takeoff from my real first name."

"What is it?"

"I've gone by Bo for so long, nobody even remembers my real name."

"And it is?" She needed to know. Because he'd kissed her? Or because she wanted to be different from everyone else?

His jaw flexed in time with a low roll of thunder in the distance. "I was named for my father, and my call sign grew from that long before I joined the Air Force."

Her heart ached for him and the pain he still obviously carried over losing his parents.

"And his name was?" she asked gently.

Winds encircled in a band somehow far more intimate than the halo of light, the gusting growing stronger until it seemed to create a vortex with them at the epicenter.

Finally he shrugged with a no-big-deal air. "Boyd, which I shortened to Bo. I'm not much into the junior gig."

"Okay, Bo it is then." Thunder cracked again, followed by a distant snap of more lightning.

He straightened from the tree and stopped her swing with one hand. "We should probably get away from this hundred-year-old lightning rod."

"I guess so." She stood, bringing their faces close again, much like when they'd kissed on the porch.

Thunder pounded. Or was that her pulse hammering? Another second and she would hop into the car with him to search out the nearest hotel. Good God, what was wrong with her? She considered herself a healthy woman with normal urges, but she didn't like the prickly heat stinging her skin with an out-of-control need.

She sidestepped him. "Good night."

Her feet beat a hasty retreat through the dusty yard thirsty for the rain. By morning she would have her head on straight again.

"Honey." Bo's voice rode the wind to stop her.

Huh? He couldn't mean… She turned on the bottom step. "What?"

He stood by the open door of his white rental. "You asked me to name the puppy, and I chose Honey because of the color of her fur."

Bo ducked into the sedan and slammed the door.

Honey. She rested her cheek against the porch post while taillights faded into the night. A raindrop splatted on her nose. He'd remembered their conversation, thought of her, wanted to name the puppy, and that stirred an unwelcome warmth in her heart. The burgeoning wind creaked the swing faster, thunder increasing to announce the impending storm to a woman too weak-kneed to dash inside even though rain dampened her hair.

If she expected to survive the next two weeks with her sanity intact, she needed to clear the air about this explosive attraction attacking their hormones. And definitely no more moonlit conversations.

Because who'd have thought his sensitive words would be as tempting as his kisses?

Chapter 8

"Crap!" Bo smacked a mosquito on his arm, striding out of the hangar storing his damaged C-17.

Too bad the Base Exchange wasn't open yet so he could pick up some Off spray before he headed to Paige's for the day. He scratched the rising bite bump. The mosquitoes were having a field day with the muggy aftermath of the rare rain providing new puddles to nest and multiply, generally making his crummy mood worse.

Another sleepless night would do that to a guy. No dreams but plenty of wakeful images to torment him, such as Paige's quivering chin when he'd done a simple thing like name a puppy. This was not the kind of woman a guy boffed in a haystack.

Blinking against the bright sunlight outside the shadowy hangar, he slapped his neck. Mako's singing taunt followed him as the guy launched into a second chorus of the old seventies tune, "Tie a Yellow Ribbon," the oak tree reference catching him square on with more memories of Paige on the swing, pretty and tempting and so strong he wanted to protect her all the more.

He turned back, calling inside to Mako, "Hey, dude, have you ever considered voice lessons?"

Jet engine parts littering the concrete floor around him, Mako patted the side of the looming cargo plane. "This old gal likes my singing well enough as it is."

"Then she needs a new hearing aid," Bo razzed right back on his way across the tarmac and back to his rental car.

The in-flight mechanic had laughed his ass off over Bo explaining he would be bunking out at Paige's place. With her brothers. And a kid under the roof. Sheesh. Talk about chaperones out the wazoo.

Hadn't made a bit of difference to Mako, but then, flight crews lived to razz each other. They played hard, joked hard, lived hard, because you never knew when the missile hit was a second away. A reality he understood well from that flight in Rubistan—a subject guaranteed to sink his mood into opaque territory.

And he still didn't know what he planned to do with the rest of his life. At least he had a firm plan for the next two weeks. Albeit, an increasingly frustrating one.

The kiss the night before only proved the obvious. He was weak as hell around this woman. A vulnerable look from her, combined with honest to God caring questions and he was ready to jump her bones. He'd barely made it into the car.

An hour later, gear stowed in the trunk, he pulled off onto the two-lane road leading to Paige's house. At least he would be flying with her brother today, making rounds and taking any emergency calls.

He slowed behind the mail carrier as the school bus

chugged past, clearing the driveway—where Kirstie still stood holding her mother's hand. What was up with that?

Bo turned onto the dirt driveway, cruising to a stop under what was quickly becoming his least favorite tree in the state. He stepped out of the car and popped the trunk to unload his gear. "No school for you today, Cupcake? Are you sick?"

Kirstie stayed mute and stepped closer to her mother's leg.

Paige tugged her around in front and looped both arms around Kirstie, mother and daughter a mirror image of blond hair, glasses and wide eyes. "We thought it might be better if one of us drives her for a while."

Safer.

What was wrong with the world that the kid couldn't ride the bus with her friends? "Going with Mom's cool. You probably get to sleep later, huh?"

"Nope." Kirstie watched him unload with obvious resentment.

Hey, kids always liked him. He was a pal. Tossing aside his military-green duffel, he knelt in front of her. "How about I take you up for a ride in the plane after we're done with work today?"

Kirstie squinted, her resentment double blaring. Yeah, kid, you're gonna have to pick. Carry the grudge—whatever the hell the reason—or get your flight. Standing, he backed up to give her space, the seed planted. "Think about it while you're at school and we can talk more later."

Paige's pretty lips mouthed, "Thank you." Then she leaned to face her daughter. "Run and get your lunch box off the counter, punkin, or we're going to be late."

After the kid sprinted up the stairs and out of sight, Paige turned back toward him, the muggy wind playing with her hair that refused to stay constrained in a red rubber band. Memories of their kiss from the day before, a kiss they'd

never been alone long enough to discuss, hung in the air between them. Better to face it head-on and get the subject past.

Paige toyed with a drooping branch overhead. "About
that kiss—"

"—that we shouldn't—" He stopped. "What?"

She waved for him to continue. "You first."

"No, you go ahead."

"Really, I'd rather hear what you have to say."

She deserved his honesty. Bo flattened a hand to the roughened bark. "I was going to say that we shouldn't spend time
alone together, well, other than in the plane, of course."

"So the haystack offer has been rescinded?"

She had to be kidding. Please, sweet Lord, let her be joking. "Were you seriously thinking about it?"

Paige scuffed the toe of her tennis shoe through the mud.
"Tough to think about anything else with you around."

"You were actually considering an affair with me while I'm
here? Under this roof? With your brother lurking behind every
corner? Forget the whole damn danger factor of him taking
a shotgun to me, I owe him the common courtesy of not—"
He thumped himself on the forehead. A guy wanted to do the
right thing and then the fates had to twist it all around to bite
him on the butt. "Are you trying to make me crazy?"

"Sheesh, this isn't going the way I planned." Releasing the
droopy branch with a snap that rained leaves on her head, she
perched a hand on her cute round jeans-clad hip—heaven help
him. "No, Bo. I'm not offering a thing other than more of your
theoretical discussion to clear the air. I figured if we talked
about this attraction analytically, it would be easier to laugh
and move on."

"Then you really are nuts." Cold-shower alert.

Without thinking, no surprise around Paige, he swiped a
leaf sticking in her hair. She instinctively backed away, caught
herself and stopped. Still the telling flinch shouted a reminder.

Yeah, she wanted him, but it scared the hell out of her. He was starting to understand the feeling. All the more reason to keep his pants zipped around her. If only he could seal off temptation as securely.

A week later Paige secured the blanket under her daughter's chin, strains of guitar music drifting up through the bedroom window from the front porch. Only seven days since Bo moved in and already his presence filled her life as surely as his music filled the air—country tunes tonight, soft and low enough to soothe a child to sleep.

Or romance a woman.

Her legs folding under her, she sat on the edge of Kirstie's bed, resting back against the antique white iron headboard. Paige nudged tiny glasses to the center of the end table, right beneath the Strawberry Shortcake nightlight, and swung her feet up onto the giving comforter. She patted her daughter's back and allowed herself to listen anonymously.

Kirstie snuffled under the red-and-pink sheets with a shuddering breath that testified to another uneasy journey into sleep. Night terrors had revived over the past week, not that the child seemed to remember anything when she woke. But the mumbled word *Daddy* relayed plenty.

At least it seemed Kurt couldn't be even indirectly blamed for the break-in. An inventory showed missing bottles of Ketamine, indicating a drug-related vandalism. Lightning rarely struck twice. Right? And on the off chance it did, they'd installed a better security system and sturdier locks.

Brushing her fingers over whispery blond curls, Paige studied long lashes resting on a cherub cheek. She could stare at her child for hours like this, amazed at the miracle, awed and humbled by the responsibility of caring for this little life. How could Kurt have taken so lightly what he owed his daughter? Would Kirstie fear trusting men because of how very far her hero father had fallen?

Heaven knew, her own trust had been shaken, enough so she was scared to jump on a sure thing. Sheesh, she had a hot guy under her roof, a guy who actually didn't seem to go for the anorexic, Hollywood type. And anytime he so much as passed the butter—or reached to touch her hair—she scampered back like a scared rabbit.

A scared and very sexually frustrated rabbit.

She'd forgotten there were things far more intimate than a kiss when it came to living in the same house with a nonrelative male. Although Bo slept in a guest room next to her in the rambling old farmhouse, there was something about the way his undeniably masculine footsteps vibrated through the hardwood floors and up through the soles of her bare feet in the morning. Even her delft-blue bedroom reminded her of his eyes, her space no longer a sanctuary.

And the way he pulled a chair out for her at the dinner table stroked at her femininity left pretty much untended these days. The way he also pulled out the chair for Kirstie touched Paige's heart, also left untended of late.

Her daughter had settled into wary acceptance of Bo's presence over the past week. A flight, followed by sing-alongs with his guitar went far in softening up her stubborn daughter until dire predictions of measles, meningitis and ring worm—yuck—slowed.

Life was settling into a near-normal routine. She even found herself looking forward to this time of day when Bo went outside and played the guitar for himself. At first she'd thought he did it to loosen up his hands, then she'd once spied his eyes slide closed as the music took hold of him. Were his eyes closed like that when he kissed her?

A chilly breeze ruffled the curtains and raised goose bumps on her arms. Country ballads gave way to something faster she didn't recognize but found to be no less appealing. Yes, they were settling into a routine with plenty of intimacy—but absolutely *no* kissing. Wise. Safe. She was fine, damn it. She wasn't yearning for unwise and dangerous.

Was she?

Staying upstairs when she desperately wanted to walk down only proved he still had an effect on her. If anyone else played, she would join him on the porch and ask to listen. No more hiding. She wouldn't cower under her quilt like a kid. She would go outside like a grown-up, even risk a little chitchat.

But it would be a cold day in hell before she mentioned kissing again, much less ideas of where those kisses could lead.

Damn, but he was freezing his ass off out here on Paige's wooden porch swing, avoiding the torture of trying to sleep while she snoozed one wall away.

Did she sleep in a nightshirt? Pajamas? Sleep pants and a T-shirt maybe? Or something silky. Or nothing at all with silkier skin to explore. He'd envisioned her in each one and found them all beyond appealing.

Winds kicked up, dropping the temperature another ten degrees or so and rustling the oak tree across the yard. Who'd have thought it could get this cold in May? At least if the lowering temps continued into the night, the freeze would knock out the mosquito population.

"What's that you're playing?" Paige's voice drifted over his shoulder.

Bo glanced back. Hell, he hadn't even heard her coming. He continued to pluck along the strings, waiting for her to join him on the double-seater while Kirstie's swing on the oak twisted in the wind. "I was working on a tune for Cupcake. She seems to like nursery rhymes and poems. I thought she would enjoy hearing one or two of them set to music."

She took her seat beside him, close but not touching, a

stack of paperwork clasped to her generous chest. "That's really thoughtful."

"It's fun." He pulled his eyes off her breasts and back onto the star studded sky. "She's a great kid."

"I think so, but I accept I might be biased." She lowered the folder to her knees. "Do you mind if I hang with you out here while I go through these?"

What was she up to now? He never knew with Paige. "No problem. Do you have a music preference?"

"Whatever you want to play is fine."

His fingers picked up where he'd left off on the tune for Kirstie, night bugs echoing like a quirky back-up band. Paige stayed quiet as he plucked through the piece while the wind carried the scent of fresh-mown grass and Paige's flowery soap. He enjoyed how she just let him play without needing a running commentary. He enjoyed a lot of things about her, which made it tough to keep his no-kissing, no-touching rule for the past week.

Living in the same place crammed more getting-to-know-each-other time into a few days than he would normally have in a month of dates. Along with information he would never find out through dinner and a movie, even dinner and a movie followed by sex.

He'd discovered she refused to share her newspaper with anyone who crinkled the edges or creased the pages in the wrong direction. She was a fastidious neatnik around the house, picking up any crumb she or Kirstie spilled, but would step over Vic's same pair of discarded socks for four days running in an admirable refusal to be anyone's maid.

She needed three alarms ringing successively before she rolled out of bed every morning, a fact that tortured him on a daily basis through the wall as he was forced to wake up early and think about her lying in bed wearing a nightshirt or sleep pants or satin.

Or nothing.

All of that should have made his head explode. Except he knew she overslept because after working all day she often stayed up late curled beside Kirstie to soothe away nightmares. When she read the paper, her eyes filled with sentimental tears over who-knew-what. And while she walked over Vic Jansen's socks, she never said a word about how ratty those socks were. She'd confided to Bo they'd been a present from Vic's daughter shortly before the little girl drowned.

No wonder the guy was overprotective of the females in his life, and this woman with her roughened hands and soft heart more than deserved some pampering.

Bo stopped playing and rested his guitar against the porch railing, then shrugged out of his leather flight jacket. "Here. Wear this. It's cold out tonight."

Teeth chattering, Paige stared at Bo's jacket that would carry his musky-scented heat and reminded herself about the cold-day-in-hell resolve. "I'm fine, thanks."

He skimmed a finger up her chilled arm, raising fresh goose bumps that had nothing to do with the cold now. "Really?"

No, but rejecting the jacket would be a telling move. She'd come out here to prove a point. She set aside her paperwork and slipped her arms into the sleeves. Oh, yeah, definitely still warm and spicy smelling.

Bo tapped the edge of the folders on her lap. "What's that you've got there?"

"Mail. Billing stuff for the clinic. Some paperwork from my attorney in Charleston."

"Attorney?"

"There are so many things to take care of when someone dies, especially when they die in a pile of trouble." She tried to laugh, but it lodged in her throat. "I don't want to think about all of this right now."

She dropped the folders to the porch and weighted them

down with the end table to buy herself time to shake off thoughts of Kurt, which were threatening to chill her faster than the wind.

Paige straightened, forcing her clenched hands to relax. "Make me smile. With something funny, I mean."

"Well, damn." He gave her that bad-boy wink and flash of crooked teeth that made her smile without anything more.

"Thank you."

"Hey, I'm just getting started. When I was six—"

"So you were at the orphanage then?" She settled deeper into the swing and his coat. "St. Elizabeth's, right?"

"Right. You're a good listener." He stretched his legs out in front of him, close to hers without touching, and tapped the swing into gentle motion. "Anyhow, when I was six, I got into some trouble."

"For what?" How much trouble could a six-year-old get into? Her mother-heart clenched at the possibilities.

"I put dish soap in the baptismal font, and when they cranked it up for morning mass…"

"Ohmigod."

"That's what Sister Nic said."

Her mama-heart clenched tighter at the picture of a grieving child no doubt acting out for attention. "What did they do?"

"I had to go to the chapel by myself and say a bunch of Hail Marys. Basically, I got a time-out to think about what I'd done wrong."

The tightness in her chest eased. "Appropriate."

"Yeah, and torture for a kid who really likes attention."

"The very reason you pulled the stunt in the first place."

"Spoken like a seasoned parent."

A parent whose child had nightmares and imagined illnesses. There went that Mother of the Year Award.

She set the swing in motion again with the tap of her toe,

each creak, creak of the chain soothing her back into the moment. "What other stunts did you pull?"

"Released a couple of mice and garden snakes in the convent. Put a bra on a statue of St. Francis."

"A bra?"

"Imagine my surprise when I went through Sister Esther Ann's drawers and found out she was a double-D."

She tried to hold back the snort. No luck.

"Then I poured fertilizer on the lawn so the dead grass spelled out *hellfire*." He continued to count down pranks with scarred fingers. "Spiked the punch with unconsecrated wine at nun-appreciation night so they all got schnookered."

Giggles bubbled up so hard they overflowed, probably much like those font bubbles. "Okay! Okay!" She gasped until tears eeked out and her sides hurt. "I'm laughing. Don't think I can laugh any more without hurting myself."

He extended his arms and let them fall to rest on the back of the porch swing. "My work here is complete."

The heat of his arm scorched right through the leather of his jacket. Still the swing rocked with each nudge of his tennis shoe against the plank porch until the swaying assumed a slow lover's rhythm. Her eyes glided from his feet up his stretched legs. Thigh muscles rippled under well-washed denim.

Gulp.

She wouldn't flinch. Talk. Okay, swallow first, then talk. Paige yanked her gaze up to his. "Did you make all that up?"

"Afraid not."

"You were a handful."

"Some say I still am."

Did he know his fingers toyed with her ponytail?

"Back to the schnookered thing. Right after that, Sister Nic asked me to turn the pages for her when she played the organ during mass." Blue eyes smiled at the memory. "I was such a screwup, I couldn't imagine she really meant me and I didn't know squat about music. I figured she wanted to embarrass me as payback for when she got tipsy off that punch, hiked up her habit and did the electric slide."

She let her head fall back to rest against his arm. "You are so bad."

"You're only just noticing? I must be slipping." He looped a lock of her hair around his finger and tugged. "At any rate, I thought for sure turning those pages would be the worst punishment yet because I'd ruin the whole service. But she said to watch for when she nodded, then turn the page. I did okay. Then I realized that sitting up there, I got plenty of attention from Sister Nic, and the whole congregation."

The vision of a young Bo in need of a mother's love cuddling up next to that wise old nun on a piano bench brought fresh tears to her eyes. "And your love for music was born."

"Pretty much. There were plenty of musical instruments and teachers around. I got free lessons that would have cost a mint anywhere else." He nodded toward his guitar. "By the time I was eight, I could 'Kumbaya' with the best of them."

"That's definitely a story to make me smile. Thank you for sharing it." The man was far more generous with parts of himself than she seemed able to manage. "Sister Nic sounds like a wonderful woman."

"She is."

"Is?" She'd envisioned an ancient nun dispensing that motherly love. "She's still alive?"

"Yeah, alive and kicking at seventy-nine, sneaking her smokes in a retirement home down in Charleston. That's actually why I call her Sister Nic—as in Sister Nicotine, since she used to slip out to the prayer garden for the occasional cigarette. She's really named Sister Mary."

"In Charleston?" She struggled to get the geography of his youth untangled. "St. Elizabeth's was in South Carolina?"

He shifted on the swing, scratching along the back of his neck. Avoiding? "Uh, no. It was up in Chicago."

"So Sister Nic has family in South Carolina?"

"Not exactly."

Which meant she must have moved to be near him. Realization trickled through. She understood enough about retirement setups for nuns and clergy to know money was scarce enough that there wasn't much picking and choosing.

Unless it was privately funded.

By someone like Bo.

Oh, God, surely it was a cold day in hell, after all, because she was about to kiss this generous, funny, bighearted man.

Chapter 9

He saw the kiss in Paige's damp brown eyes even before she swayed toward him. After a week of living together, watching her, smelling her, getting to know this sweet, sexy lady, damned if he could will his sorry ass to move off the porch swing.

Bo cupped the back of her neck and met her halfway. Soft woman and softer breasts gave against his chest until his libido shouted an enthusiastic ooh-rah. Yeah, he was a breast man. Every guy had his preference, even if he was smart enough not to let on, and he liked supple, giving… Hell, he just liked *her*.

She opened to him, moist and warm in contrast to the dry, cold prickling around them. The taste of lemon pie from dessert mingled with something he was coming to recognize as distinctly Paige, mind-blowing Paige, who resurrected every bad-boy inclination he'd worked to stifle for the past week.

"Hey, you," he whispered against her kissed-full lips. "I thought we weren't going to do that again."

"We aren't." She nipped at the corner of his mouth, her hands crawling over his shoulders and up into his hair to urge him back down again.

"We're not?"

She breathed the answer against him. "Nope."

"Then what are we doing?" He had to kiss her once, twice, fast again before he could let her answer.

Her arms looped around his neck as she arched more of that tempting fullness against him. "I don't know about you, but right now most of me is singing."

"I know a lot about singing." And, yeah, every nerve in him was shouting out a chorus while his pulse pounded percussion. He started to reach for her glasses so they could take this kiss to a deeper level…and paused. Things were getting out of hand fast, on her front porch for crying out loud, like he was a teenager.

His forehead fell to rest against hers. "Damn it, I swore to myself I wouldn't do that while I was here."

She stiffened in his arms. "Gee, thanks."

He palmed her back, skimming circles of reassurance even though he knew they couldn't take this any further. "You know why."

"Seems to me there were two of us doing *that*." Her hand slid around to splay against his chest, shadows smudging her eyes in the dim porch light. "Are you playing me?"

What the hell had he done to deserve that comment? He'd been damn near a freaking saint around her until now, all things considered. Well, a saint with mighty devilish thoughts about what she wore to bed each night and how much fun it would be to strip each item off, but he hadn't acted on the fantasies.

Time out.

He forced himself to remember the woman had more emotional baggage than a luggage terminal. "No games, I swear you're—"

"Never mind." She clapped her hand over his mouth. "It's a stupid question. If you are playing me, you wouldn't admit it."

He gripped her wrist and gently lowered her touch away. "I have done more than my fair share of things I'm not proud of over the years, but I'm not a liar." He linked his fingers through hers and held tight. "And I am absolutely telling the truth when I say I've never been as tempted as I am right now. Painfully so."

Her eyes widened right before her gaze fell…to his lap. He fought against the urge to groan until she looked up again, eyes wider. "Oh, my. Ouch."

"Yeah." Ouch about summed it up.

A smile teased along her pretty lips. "Gives total-package-with-bow-and-presents a whole new meaning."

Surprise jolted a short burst of laughter out of him. "The girl next door has a racy sense of humor."

An image of her in a cotton nightshirt with a silky red thong underneath blazed to life. He was *so* toast.

She eased out of his arms and slumped against the porch swing, hugging herself, his jacket swallowing her. "Don't let the glasses and wide eyes fool you. This girl next door has had to learn not to care what other people think. Anything I do these days is for my daughter or for myself."

Her words squeezed his heart tight in his chest. Hooking an elbow on the back of the swing, he stroked a stray hair from her brow, the satin of her skin gliding along his calluses. "You deserved better from life."

"Did I? Maybe. Maybe not." She angled her cheek into his hand. "Couldn't we just have a raging affair?"

God, was he ever tempted, more than he could remember being, but… "You deserve better from *me*."

Rolling her eyes, she sighed, "Heaven protect me from men who think they know what's best for my life." She pressed a kiss into his palm before gripping his wrist to ease his hand away. "Being the girl-next-door type sure does suck sometimes."

"Lady, I meant what I said. You are the hottest damned woman I've ever laid eyes on. But quite frankly, those wide brown eyes of yours scare the crap out of me." And wasn't that more truth than he'd even realized until the words fell out of his mouth? "Do you hear what I'm saying? You're not the kind I would just have an affair with."

More truth than he wanted to admit to himself, but the words were out there in the night air, porch light illuminating her shock. No mistaking it.

"Whoa, wait." She startled upright, rocking the swing. "You're not actually saying you want us to try—"

Was he? Hell, no. This wasn't a woman to mess with on any level if he wanted to look himself in the mirror in the morning with a clear conscience. "I realize that's out of the question. But if things were different, the past, the present, too—yeah, I would want to ask you out on a real date and not some half-assed groping on a porch."

He let himself spin out the fantasy date in the same way he'd spun other fantasies about her, not wise, but a small compensation for painful denial. "I would take you to dinner and talk to you, get to know you better. And sure, I'd start hoping that you would stay over for the night. But if not, that's okay. I could wait because we would be going out again."

She traced a thumb along his neck, gently rasping a fingernail over his late-day beard. "Where would we go?"

"What?" He blinked twice to clear the throbbing need from one innocent touch.

"Where would we go on the second date?" Her hand fell away and she wrapped her arms tighter around her waist again, burrowing her chin into the collar of his jacket as if sinking into the fantasy date along with him.

"For a second date I would ask if it's okay to include your daughter on the outing. If you said yes—"

"—I would."

"—then we would spend the day at the water with my jet ski and some other friends." In Charleston, back where bad memories waited for her. In a world so different from where she'd chosen to rebuild her life. "Not a bar pickup, one-night-stand sort of start."

"No, it's not." Her head rocked along the back of the swing until she looked at him with pensive eyes. "I didn't expect you to be like this."

He wasn't sure what she meant, and thought maybe he didn't recognize himself right now, either. "I'm only trying to make things easier for you."

"And yet somehow everything just gets tougher."

They stared without speaking for…he didn't know how long, until lights clicked on in the clinic, blaring through the windows into the yard and stealing some of their privacy. For the best, because soon he'd be spinning that fantasy date out to more dangerous territory for both of them.

Self-respect and honor were everything to him, especially after the way his father had lived his life. Bo frowned as the thought shuffled in his head. Maybe that was a big part of why he'd chosen the military with its rigid structure and clear-cut rules of behavior to keep his rebel side in check. An odd insight he wouldn't have considered before meeting Paige, who seemed to have a way of clarifying things.

He followed the new notion through and found it fit. Interesting too he'd chosen a career lifestyle not unlike his orphanage upbringing, predominantly male with a tight brotherhood. Which brought him right back to the looming deadline for deciding whether to stay in the Air Force, and still he couldn't form a clean picture of what else he could do with his life.

He did know one thing, clear as day. Hurting this woman would be beyond dishonorable.

Paige glanced over toward the lights streaking across the patchy yard. "I guess that's my brother's not-so-subtle way of announcing he's around." Rising from the swing with a jolt, she shrugged out of his leather jacket and draped it over the back of the swing. "Good night."

"Night," he called, already reaching for his guitar again. No need for the coat, though, since he was far from cold at the moment.

Damn it all, he was doing the right thing. He'd reestablished boundaries while reassuring her of her undeniable appeal. He'd played it letter-perfect, honorably.

So why was he certain her clouded eyes would haunt his dreams now more than ever?

Scanning the sky, Bo gripped the throttle, climbing into the cloudless morning, Vic beside him today for another run out to the Anderson place. At least he wouldn't have to see Anderson drool over Paige.

If she went for the guy someday, would a wedding invitation wing its way to Charleston?

Crap. He needed to get back to work, real work. Even if Paige mystified him, he'd discovered one thing during the past week and a half. He wasn't cut out for tooling around the skies on the equivalent of a tricycle. He needed more action than he was getting in these hops from farm to farm.

He only had a few days left with Paige, then Seth would be back up to speed. The C-17 wasn't ready yet, thanks to the delay of some part, but he would be staying at base, other than a quick trip to Charleston over the weekend for a friend's wedding. He was in the homestretch with hanging tough.

And nowhere near finding his answers or relief. Damn, he would miss her.

He flicked the fuel gauge until the needle moved lower to match his own fuel calculations. He didn't even want to think about what could have happened to Paige with that finicky gauge and the crummy temp pilot.

The sky reclaimed his attention. Maybe if he got out of the service he could be a crop duster. Low level in a Cessna kicked ass, turning a tricycle kind of ride into an edgy risk. He'd earned extra money during college with his private pilot's license by flying advertisement banners over ball games and along beaches. Swoop in near to the ground and fast, hook the banner, scream the plane straight up until it damn near stalled, then haul full-out forward.

Of course he hadn't saved any lives or cows that way, but he'd promoted the hell out of all-u-can-eat buffets and even delivered a marriage proposal once. He'd always assumed he would resurrect that skill when the time came for him to propose. And yet, he'd ended up with a string of broken relationships. For the first time he wondered why a guy so determined to get married someday kept shooting himself in the foot in the dating department.

Vic shifted in the small seat beside him. "I'm not sure how much you know about Paige's husband from when you met her in Charleston."

God, this guy was a broken record. At least things were quiet enough at the clinic now with no repeat intruders. Which gave Jansen more time to worry about somebody hitting on his sister.

Bo started to tell the man to lay off it, already. He was blue from the cold showers and restraint. If he got any more honorable, he'd be up for a freaking Nobel Peace Prize.

Hey, wait.

Apparently Vic didn't know about his role in Haugen's arrest. Interesting that Paige hadn't chosen to tell her brother about the full extent of their Charleston connection—a subject he wasn't all that fond of, either. He settled for a grunt in response.

"I wish I could call him her ex, but the bastard died before she could divorce him."

Now that piqued his interest. "Was she going to?"

"She said she'd married the man and she would stay with him through the trial for her daughter." The big blond guy shifted again in the seat too small for his frame, jeans and boots creaking with each attempt to get comfortable. "But once the trial was over, yeah, she was going to divorce him."

Hearing that shouldn't be so important, but oh, yeah, there came another nudge to his rocky restraint. And why was Vic sharing things guaranteed to make Paige seem more accessible?

Bo eased back on the throttle and leveled at altitude. "He didn't deserve her."

"Damn straight. Sure she made a mistake in marrying Haugen. We all make mistakes." His voice roughened and he cleared his throat before continuing, "She just had to pay for hers *and* his. She says that's the price for trusting him."

He thought of the paperwork and legalities she'd mentioned haunting her even a year later. "What are you trying to tell me?"

"He broke her trust but she got back on her feet, dusted herself off, survived. Barely. I'm not so sure she can get up a second time."

Ah, the real message behind this talk. "She's stronger than you think."

Although *he* was feeling weaker by the day when it came to resisting Paige. Each new revelation about her offered another nudge to his self-control.

"I'd rather she not be put to the test."

"Fair enough." Yeah, he got it. Paige belonged here. She needed her independence. Bo tapped the fuel gauge again, watched it sink, calculated fuel again while the plane droned.

"Look, I've decided you're a good guy—"

Gee, thanks, dude.

"—and if things were different I could probably be okay with you hitting on my sister." His hand shot out. "And don't even insult my intelligence by saying you haven't, because I've got eyes."

Bo chose his words carefully. "What I say or do with your sister is our business. But rest assured, I know she's better off without a guy like me complicating her life."

"Good. I'm not talking as an overprotective brother. I'm speaking as somebody who's been there. A person can look okay on the outside, getting out of bed each morning, facing the day and doing a job, but…"

Only a rock wouldn't feel sorry for the guy who'd lost his kid, then his wife, too, through divorce. "You don't need to say anything more."

"Yeah, well, thanks." Vic scrubbed a hand over his face and stared out the side window without blinking, his pain radiating every bit as strong as Seth's after a long day on his busted ankle.

Ah, hell.

He hated the suspicion crawling through his veins over how those drugs disappeared from the clinic. The guy had every reason to be depressed, a totally normal reaction. Survivor's guilt could be hell. But could he have sought relief from the pain and grief through drugs? He'd discounted Vic earlier, figuring he could get whatever drugs he wanted. However Paige maintained records, too, and would notice discrepancies.

He understood well that guilt was a thousand times worse than a punch. Those first months after the shoot down, most nightmares had focused on Tag taking a boot to the ribs to shield him after his hands had been broken. So where did that leave questions about Vic Jansen?

Hell if he knew anything, except he couldn't see walking away from Paige until he had a few more answers.

Swiping his wrist under his nose, Vic shifted back to all gruff country vet again. "So you can keep your damn hands off my sister for a couple more days?"

Bo thumped the fuel gauge again. "I'm trying, dude, I'm trying."

Problem was, he figured one more nudge from Paige would do him in.

"I'm trying, Mom, but fractions are too hard for first graders, even Uncle Seth says so."

Sitting cross-legged on the blanket soaking up the late-afternoon sun, Paige took two deep breaths—three—then counted to ten for good measure. Doggone that Seth. Kirstie didn't need any help griping about math.

"Well, Uncle Seth also told you that pizza helps, so we'll make a pizza for supper and finish your homework then. Okay?"

"Pizza gives me a stomachache." She inched her glasses up with a prissy sniff. "Last time I ate it, I thought I had a 'pendicitis."

Sighing, Paige glanced skyward for patience with Kirstie and her own very likely unreasonable fears. Bo and Vic were late.

They were only an hour delayed—not that they'd bothered to call—although it probably had more to do with the sick cow and shooting the breeze than anything else. Her nerves were just edgy because of the latest letter from her lawyer, which made her think of Kurt, which made her think of that horrible, horrible night *he'd* been late.

And arrested.

Oh, God. She grabbed her stomach. She was going to hurl, and then Kirstie would be certain her mama was dying of SARS.

Paige tipped her head back farther and gulped in air to dispel the spots dancing in front of her eyes. And yes, yes, yes, one of those dots got bigger until it took the shape of an airplane, coming closer, landing.

Now she really felt dizzy.

Flattening a hand to the blanket, she hung her head in relief for six shaky seconds, then tossed back her hair she'd left down out of silly vanity because Bo's eyes lingered on it one morning when she'd stepped out of her bedroom. "Come on, kiddo. Let's forget about fractions for a while and go say hi to your Uncle Vic."

And Bo.

"No fractions? Wahoo!" Kirstie pitched aside her workbook and sprang to her feet. Sprinting ahead, she turned a clean cartwheel.

Her first in a year. Melancholy tinged happiness a pale blue over all the lost cartwheels and smiles.

Kirstie raced across the field and threw her arms around her uncle's waist until her tiny arms shook from the strain. Was it so much to ask that her daughter feel secure?

Paige met her brother at the nose of the plane. "Where have you been?"

"Whoa." Vic yanked a lock of her hair. "What crawled in your gut and died?"

"You're both late." She glanced over at Bo on the other side of the plane, trying to keep her voice low enough that he wouldn't hear. "A call would have been nice."

"Sorry. I didn't think I needed to check in with my baby sister." He tugged her hair again before swinging Kirstie up on his back and lumbering off toward the kennels.

Paige chewed her bottom lip and wondered why she didn't follow him. She sneaked a reassuring glance at Bo. "I was worried."

He looped a rope through the wing strut. "We had a busted fuel gauge. While your brother worked on Anderson's colicky cow, I borrowed a truck to run into town for a replacement part."

Frazzled nerves frayed even more, thanks to hellish scenarios that all involved something happening to this man. "You're sure it's safe now?"

"Absolutely. Simple problem solved." Bo cinched the knot tight.

"I'm sorry for being a witch."

"You were worried about your brother. That's understandable."

"I was worried about you, too."

He paused midknot. "Run that by me again?"

His stunned expression almost made her laugh. "Hey, I just said I was worried. I didn't declare undying love for you, for Pete's sake."

He strode past, presenting an oh-my nice view. "I'm not used to accounting to people for my whereabouts."

"What about Sister Nic?" She trailed him around the plane.

"She's listed as my next of kin, but she's only to be notified if I die. I don't want her worried with any of the other crap."

Her frazzled nerves gave up the fight altogether. Where were her Tums? "What if you were taken hostage overseas?"

"I wouldn't be a hostage. I would be a POW."

She shivered. "Either way, it's a horrible thing. Someone back here should know."

"Why?"

Could he really be serious? Had no one worried about him on the ground before? And what about when he'd hurt his hands? Surely there'd been someone waiting to console him after surgery. What was with all these men who refused to share burdens? Made it darned hard to lean on someone in return. "So they could worry, pray, wait for you."

"I didn't want to see anyone when I got back."

Got back from where? She watched his hands flex open and closed. A really sick feeling started swelling in her stomach that no amount of Tums would settle.

"Your papers are blowing away."

Huh? She jerked her gaze up from his hands and thoughts they stirred of how he may have been injured. "What are you talking about?"

He pointed past her shoulder. "Over there on the blanket."

Paige spun…to see Kirstie's math book fanning in the wind while her mail skimmed across the lawn. "Ah, jeez."

Her thoughts scattering as fast as Kirstie's homework, Paige dashed toward the closest envelope. Bo raced past to scoop up one, two, then the last of the others before jogging back to pass them to her.

"Thank you," she gasped, as breathless from the run as watching him in motion. She waggled the envelopes in front of her. "More paperwork from the lawyer, something about a safety deposit box I need to open. He says he can handle it for me if I just sign over power of attorney."

"Whose lawyer is this? Yours or Haugen's?"

"The same." Kneeling on the blanket, she unzipped her daughter's backpack.

He tossed Kirstie's workbook and colored pencils inside. "Are you sure this guy's clean?"

"I wouldn't have anything to do with him if I thought otherwise." But of course she'd trusted her husband, too.

Thank goodness Bo was diplomatic enough to stay silent.

"After he—Kurt—was arrested, when it was obvious he'd really done the things they said…" She paused to look up and blink fast. A deep breath later, she met him eye-to-eye again, rock steady. "I told him I wouldn't start divorce proceedings until after the trial, out of respect for the fact we had a child together. But only if he hired another attorney, one with no connections to…" She faltered. "He agreed, even told me to pick."

"And somehow that made things tougher for you."

She nodded, falling back to sit on her legs. "A part of me wonders if a slicker lawyer could have made sure he had better protection inside. I know it's wrong to think that way, but I can't help it."

"He alone is to blame for anything that came his way. He put himself, you, your child in danger."

Even if she couldn't totally absolve herself, it sure felt nice to have a champion. "I don't love him anymore."

She wasn't sure why the words slipped out, but there they were and she wouldn't call them back. He knelt beside her, staring right back with one of those lightning crackle moments. No smiles or laughs, just two people on a blanket with an undeniable tug between them.

He kept his hands on his knee and off her. "I didn't ask."

A dangerously exciting notion niggled at her. "You didn't ask, but you *were* wondering."

He didn't deny it. He just looked her dead in the eye, jaw tight, expression inscrutable and said, "Nudge."

"What?"

He shook his head slowly without taking his gaze off her. "Damned if I haven't been nudged."

"I'm still not following what you're saying."

She thought he was going to…kiss her again?

His pupils dilated in an unmistakable message of arousal—and hunger. Without laying one finger on her, he stroked those smoky blues eyes over her face, her mouth with leisurely precision until her lips parted in anticipation.

Then he blinked, slowly easing back. "I think you should be the one to check out that safety deposit box."

She struggled to keep up with his conversational shift and whatever he had in mind, still stuck back there in the tingly notion that he cared if she'd loved Kurt. She grabbed the blanket and followed. "Oh, uh, I could, I guess, maybe I even should, but—"

"I'll go with you. I have a wedding to attend in Charleston this weekend, and I was going to have to fly there anyway since the C-17's not fixed yet. We can head out late Friday. You could meet up with the lawyer Saturday morning, wedding's not until late afternoon."

A whole weekend alone together? Was this guy crazy? Or brilliant? Paige kept pace alongside, double steps. "I can't just pick up and go. I have a job to consider and a child."

"So bring her with us. She'll only have to miss a day or two of school. She'll probably get a kick out of going to my friend's wedding. It's even on the beach."

And, oh, God, didn't that start to sound like the date scenario he'd spun for her during their late-night porch discussion. "Uh, it sounds nice, but—"

"Great." He slung the Strawberry Shortcake backpack over his shoulder, and why he managed to make that look sexy, she would never know. "It's cheaper for me to fly you than for you to buy a plane ticket."

She strode alongside him in double-time steps, her life rolling out of control faster than the ripple of grain in the fields. "You've got this all planned in seconds."

And what was that about his plane not being fixed so he wasn't leaving Minot yet? Her tummy flipped. His foot thudded on the bottom porch step.

"Bo? Bo, stop damn it." She grabbed his arm, lowering her voice and trying not to pant over the hard play of muscles under her fingers. "We're going to be alone at your place for the weekend? Are you a glutton for punishment or what?"

A hint of his old smile ticced the corner of his mouth. "Apparently so." He sprinted up the steps. "I'll start working on the flight plan and airport clearances."

She grabbed the rail for support as the screen door banged shut after him, his plans rocking her foundation in too many ways. She couldn't handle this. The sexual attraction between them was one thing.

Getting closer to any man—this man—was another matter altogether. Two weeks of intimacy, puppy dog names and shared memories whittled away at her resolve. Who knew what might happen to her heart if they moved onto that date-two scenario?

Kirstie would not be going to Charleston. The visit to her old hometown would upset her daughter, anyway.

Nudge.

Just one little word, but it kept echoing through her head. She'd been letting life drag her along for the past year while she raced to keep up and dodge the next disaster. Right now she wanted to take charge for a change. She would face the lawyer and that safety deposit box herself. And she would quit running from her attraction to Bo.

The time had come to introduce this man to a girl-next-door type in serious need of a fling.

Chapter 10

Bo wanted to fling Paige on her back and just work this crazy attraction out of their systems.

Arriving in Charleston Saturday morning after too many travel delays that crunched them down to the wire on scheduling, he wondered if they would have five free minutes for sex—about all the time he would need, given his current state of frustration.

Except that he wanted hours with her, not some rushed encounter. But then, not much had gone according to plan this weekend. At least they were finally at the base and ready to climb into his Jeep that he'd left parked at the squadron.

His intent to fly her out in the Cessna had shifted, due to an emergency repair on the aging plane. For the best, no doubt, that the problem hadn't occurred midair.

So they'd booked a civilian flight instead, a last-minute

credit-card nightmare that left Paige so pale Bo struggled for a face-saving offer to help. Luckily, Seth had come through with some frequent-flyer miles on a red-eye. Truth or face-saver? At least it put her on the plane.

So much for his hopes of arriving late Friday afternoon and dazzling her with an evening of romance since Kristie was safe and sound with Vic and Seth.

He shuffled his duffel bag from his shoulder onto the Jeep's back seat along with his guitar, marshy Charleston air steaming up off the asphalt. They were both too dragging-ass exhausted to talk and in serious need of a shower. And for some odd reason she ended up looking cute with her hair mussed and glasses skewed, sweat dotting her upper lip until he wanted to kiss it away.

The nudge moment of realization had lowered his defenses, leaving him wide-open to endless more tiny nudges as he finally let himself just watch her and breathe in her new scent. No tropical sunscreen or Skin So Soft today. She wore something distinctly flowery wafting on the humid coastal air. Chosen for him?

She passed over her small carry-on and travel tote. There was no talk of a hotel for her, even if neither of them openly acknowledged how the evening would end—after they met the lawyer at the bank *and* went to a wedding. Damn. Deadly testosterone buildup would level him before they saw the cake cut.

If Paige didn't cut and run first.

The military environment and routine wrapped itself around him with relaxing familiarity, while Paige stiffened more with every second back in the sunny South. Just because of the lawyer's appointment. Right? He didn't want to think overlong about the possibility this base, place, *he* caused those tensing memories.

Time to put the testosterone on hold and help her through the day.

Bo closed the passenger door behind her. "Do you want the Jeep top up or down?"

"Oh, uh…" She smoothed a hand over her hair, then shrugged. "Down is fine. It's not like I'm trying to impress anyone, and the wind sounds nice."

"Fair enough." Stowing the roof, he couldn't keep his eyes from straying to the rows of parked gray planes, waiting, calling, reminding him of decisions to be made.

Later. Paige's problems first.

He settled behind the wheel and guided his Jeep past a blur of military-reg brown buildings, through the security gate. Her head tipped back, she blinked against the bright morning sun then closed her eyes while the wind whipped over them, swirling stronger as they crossed bridges into the water-locked historic region of Charleston.

Was she shutting out the place? Or simply sleeping? He started to question his insistence that she come back to Charleston. Damned arrogant of him, and if he'd screwed up, she would pay the price.

The way Tag and the other crew had taken extra hits when his recklessness cost him broken hands and made him a liability during their capture.

He glanced at her quickly. "You don't have to do this."

Her lashes fluttered open for a quick peek his way. "Now aren't you changing your tune?"

"I want you to do this for you, not because I'm a pushy bastard."

Her eyes closed again as she reached to touch his arm. "I *am* doing this for me. Call me selfish, but this whole trip is about taking control of my life."

She skimmed a finger in a scorching path down his forearm before her hand fell to her lap again.

Well, hell. No mistaking that. How long until they could find a bed?

He navigated the Jeep through a maze of narrow one-way streets lined with squat palmetto trees until he pulled up outside a three-story bank. He backed the Jeep into the tight curbside parking. "Are you ready?"

She rolled her eyes, oak branches rustling overhead, horns honking. "Hell no, but it needs to be done."

"Last chance to make a break for it."

"My running shoes are packed away." She reached for the door. "Let's get this over with."

God, he admired this woman's spunk. He gripped her elbow to stop her. "Hold on a second."

"What for?"

"For this." Leaning, he cupped the back of her head and sealed a kiss to her mouth, firm, intense, full of his restrained ache for her and unwavering drive to see her through this. Safely. He slid his fingers from the thick tangle of her silky hair and angled back into his seat. "Now it's time to go inside."

She blinked, even swayed a little—ooh-rah—before regaining her balance.

Dodging bustling professionals and slow-strolling tourists, Bo ushered Paige through the revolving doors into the ice-chilled lobby. He scanned…and didn't have to look long before finding the man he recognized from Kurt Haugen's case.

The lawyer—Thomas Creech—peeled away from the wall, smoothing his palm-tree tie into a double-breasted suit that fit well, but didn't scream overpriced slick. Creech's startled surprise at seeing Bo attested to the lawyer's memory of him from the early stages of booking Haugen. The distinguished guy might look okay, but no way was Bo leaving her side.

Creech extended his hand and greeted both Paige and Bo. "I could have done this for you, Mrs. Haugen. It would have saved money, time and grief."

Like it mattered now when she was already here? Bo's approval meter for the fellow notched down. Of course that could have had something to do with how long the forty-year-old dude held Paige's hand, complete with a conciliatory pat.

Bo looped an arm around her shoulder. "Closure's important, Mr. Creech."

"Of course." He nodded before gesturing them forward. "Let's get on with it, then."

Bo kept his hand on her shoulder all the way back to the vault, a tomb-silent room lined with drawers. He wasn't sure if she allowed the comfort because she needed it or if she was too numb to notice. With the lawyer standing off to the side, the teller opened the drawer to reveal...

A lone envelope, plain white, with the words "Paige and Kirstie" scrawled on the outside. She shivered under his hand, then stepped forward to take out the letter.

Two deep breaths later, she ran her thumbnail under the seal of the letter, scanned it, her face expressionless, before she carefully folded it and slid it back in, smoothing her hand to close the flap. "That bastard."

"What did he do?" Bo braced for whatever life had thrown Paige's way and ignored the niggling voice in his head telling him that forgetting this woman was no longer an option.

The attorney moved closer. "Is there something important?"

Important? Paige wanted to shout, stomp her foot, dig Kurt up and kick his selfish butt all over again. She'd cut her heart open again by coming back to Charleston for *this?*

Kurt's letter was nothing more than a manipulative ploy, full of justifications for all the horrible things he'd done. No apologies. Just more excuses and meaningless vows of love to his wife and kid.

The narcissistic bastard.

"No. Nothing important at all." She smacked a hand back against the safety deposit boxes. "God, I was hoping he'd left behind evidence to finger every last slime in the operation. But no. He just wanted to let us know—in case something happened to him—how much he loves us. And how he did it all for us, to give us a better life like in the fairy tales and poems he made up for Kirstie. And to remember those if something happened to him. More bull no doubt meant to manipulate our emotions from the grave."

Would she show the letter to Kirstie? Not now. Maybe someday when her daughter was old enough to sort through the nuances of Kurt's amoral mind-set.

She smoothed the letter along the table again as if she could somehow iron out all the wrinkles in her life. "There's nothing concrete about the mess he drew us all into."

Bo's hand fell to her shoulder again, steadying without being overpowering. "You're sure?"

Of course. Wasn't she? "The letter seems straightforward."

"Maybe you should have the cops analyze it for hidden meanings."

A flicker of hope started that maybe something positive could come from this fresh dose of pain after all.

"Of course. We should give it to the police." She would be more than happy to hand over the latest reminder of her past mistakes. She extended her hand to the lawyer. "Thank you for meeting us on a weekend."

"It's not a problem, Mrs. Haugen." He gestured them out of the vault. "Just call me or my paralegal if you need anything further."

She set her jaw and mentally prepped for another trip to the Charleston Police Department instead of an afternoon at Bo's before he left for his friends' wedding.

Her feet slowed along the marble tile. Time to be honest with herself. She hadn't come to Charleston for Kurt or even to read his damn letter. That had merely offered a convenient excuse for what she really wanted.

She'd come to Charleston for a chance to be with Bo, and she wouldn't let Kurt steal anything more from her. But now she had this letter to deal with, and turning it over to the cops would in effect turn over a new leaf for her fresh start.

Paige flattened her hands on the revolving door and pushed—*whoomp, whoomp, whoomp*—until she stepped out on the muggy street, Bo one *whoomp* behind her. She spun to apologize for yet another delay and stumbled against a rushing passerby. "Excuse me—"

Her arm was wrenched in the socket. By instinct, she tugged back even as purse strap bit into her arm. The force increased with her confusion.

"Paige!" Bo's shout sliced through at the same time a knife slashed the strap on her bag.

What the—?

The wiry teen in dark clothes and a ball cap sprinted down the sidewalk, dodging pedestrians with her purse clutched to his stomach. Bo shoved past her, launching himself after the thief, her purse…and the letter.

Screw coincidence. Bo slammed his Jeep door closed outside his three-bedroom rental house. Something was up.

So what if the break-in happened in North Dakota and the purse snatching in Charleston and neither culprit was caught. A pair of attacks in such a short time stretched believing. Which also had him questioning the faulty fuel gauge and more recent malfunction that almost kept them from arriving in Charleston at all.

He wasn't letting Paige out of his sight.

And Kirstie? She apparently still had her secrets, but at least her uncles were watching her 24/7. He might have questions about them, but he didn't doubt for a second that either of them would die for that little girl.

Bo hitched his duffel bag onto his shoulder, passed Paige

her small suitcase and snagged his guitar. At least Paige wasn't dragging anymore. The slight stomp of her feet along the walkway to his one-story brick house telegraphed her anger over the incident—a good sight better than defeat.

The cops had taken their statements, not particularly concerned about a purse-snatcher with more pressing killings, rapes and a campus stalker on their agenda. She'd been firm—go, Paige!—insisting on reconstructing the letters as best she could to be included in her husband's file. She wanted everything available if further incidents were linked to him.

Bo shoved his key into the lock and swung wide the door while she strode by with a hefty exhale. Framed vintage record album covers covered his otherwise bare walls, everything from Abbey Road to Jimi Hendrix to an autograph from his personal idol, Carlos Santana.

Little furniture filled the space, just a cheap-ass sofa long enough to stretch out on when he watched TV, and his perfect chair for jamming, parked next to a filing cabinet packed with sheet music. His largest piece of furniture rested along the opposite wall—a beat-up piano he'd bought at a clearance sale for a high school looking to upgrade their music department. Not fancy, but more than he'd owned growing up and everything he needed now.

Paige slung her sack bag onto the brown leather sofa. "What a long day, and it's not even suppertime."

He finally had her to himself and he didn't dare risk touching her since they had to be back out the door in a half hour. He dumped the two bags on the floor beside the couch. "I'm here if you need to cry uncle again."

"Uncle?" She pivoted in his sparse living room. "How about a battle cry? I'm pissed. Royally, totally pissed."

"Atta girl." He leaned against the sofa and watched her shine in spite of travel grunge and wind-tossed hair that happened to resemble sex-tossed hair to him.

Of course, now that the initial crisis has passed, he found everything reminded him of sex.

"Thanks. It's probably just the adrenaline talking. Well, and all that caffeine from the crummy police station coffee." She circled in his small living room. "This place isn't what I expected."

"How so?"

"Well, first of all I thought you would live in a condo or town house."

He jabbed a thumb toward the scarred piano. "Can't jam in an apartment without the neighbors griping."

"Good point."

"And second of all?"

"What?"

"You said first of all, which implies there's a second."

"Oh, I guess I expected more of a bachelor pad."

"Lava lamps and a trapeze strung from the ceiling?" A fun fantasy image, but not his style. Besides, he had something different in mind for them later.

"A trapeze?" She skimmed a finger along the ivory keyboard without making a sound. "Actually, I imagined a flashier decor, but I should have remembered this whole year has been about learning to look below the surface."

"I believe you just complimented me."

"I did. With all your talk about cool toys, I thought you would drive some brand-new sports car." She sat on the edge of the piano bench, and he thought how strange it was that they were alone in a room and had touched less than they would with a houseful of people around.

"Hey, a Jeep's cool." Damn it all, he was a man comfortable in his skin. Her approval of his lifestyle shouldn't be important.

"Especially one you rebuilt yourself."

Now she sure was full of surprises today. "How'd you know that?"

"Good guess."

He wasn't sure how he felt about her dissecting his personality and surroundings. After years in a communal-style orphanage setting, he valued his privacy.

Jesus. She just wanted to talk about his Jeep. He needed to lighten up.

Shoving away from the couch, he joined her on the piano bench just to prove to himself he could stay in control. "I saw Tag working on his truck at the base auto-hobby shop and asked him to teach me about car maintenance…. I may like my toys, but I grew up too poor not to appreciate the value of a good bargain. And if you like my rebuilt engine, then you're gonna go wild over my used jet ski bought at an estate auction."

A quick laugh jerked her shoulders. She steadied her glasses. "I love how you don't let me stay blue for long."

Love?

His neck kinked, not that she meant anything by the word.

He forged ahead with laid-back in spite of the tempting heat of her thigh burning through her jeans and his. "Who'd have believed a woman would get turned on by a bargain shopper? To think I've been wasting precious bucks on flowers and candy all these years."

"Hey, personally, I'd rather have the lightbulbs changed, since I'm so short. I'll pick out my own flowers if I want them."

They shared an easy laugh in the middle of a tough-as-hell day. He wanted her—here, now, no more waiting, but they had a wedding to attend and damned if he would rush his first time with Paige.

First? Would there be more?

He thrust aside questions guaranteed to kick them both in the teeth and just let himself stroke from her temple to her satiny cheek. She turned her face to press a kiss into his palm, which shot a bolt right to his groin.

"Oh, God, Paige," he groaned. "You're not making this easy. The wedding's in an hour and it's at least a half hour drive."

"That leaves a half hour." She nuzzled his hand again, flicking her tongue along the suddenly hypersensitive pad of his thumb.

The way he felt right now, five minutes would be long enough. But she deserved more than a rushed quickie. He could and would control himself.

He pulled his hand away with regret. "I want to take my time with you. No rushing. No interruptions."

For some reason his words, which others might have taken as a rejection, coaxed a smile and melting sigh from Paige. Already his imagination wrapped fantasies around stirring more sighs from her, louder, fuller, and holy crap if he didn't quit they would both be naked in seconds.

"Come on, lady. We need to haul butt if we're going to make the wedding before the bride walks down the aisle." He rose from the bench and started down the short hall. "Luckily I have two bathrooms. As much as I'd like to shower with you, I think we'd better opt for separates or we'll never get there at all."

He turned to find Paige still on the bench.

"You go ahead." She tapped her glasses. "I'll just use the quiet time to call my daughter and then soak in a bubble bath."

Bubble bath. Was she trying to make him crazy?

A quick hiccup in his horny thoughts gave him a clear second to see… Paige adjusted her glasses again, a sure sign that she was nervous or, worse yet, scared. Of him or lingering emotions from the purse-snatcher?

Either way, she was staying with him. "We're not so pushed for time you can't bathe, and you can call Kirstie on my cell phone during the drive over. Besides, I don't keep bubble bath on hand."

"I brought some."

She'd planned ahead enough to bring bubble bath to his place? He couldn't breathe, much less answer.

"Really, go ahead to the wedding without me. I don't even know these friends of yours."

Air. Yeah. Okay, he could talk now. "They said I could bring a date."

Date.

Now she looked as if the air had left her side of the house, as well. "Thanks, but I wouldn't be comfortable, given what Kurt did." She rubbed along the scrape on her arm from the purse-snatcher's yank. "You're sweet to offer, and I will most definitely be waiting up for you."

Waiting up? Now didn't that distract him from plans for the wedding? Probably exactly what she'd intended. He strode forward, careful to keep his steps slow and unthreatening. He stopped in front of her and tipped her chin. "What *he* did. You didn't do anything."

"That's exactly right. I didn't *do* anything. I'm having to come to peace with the fact that I didn't figure it out and stop him sooner."

He let her words rattle around in his head for a minute until he determined there wasn't a thing he could say to reassure her. Any talk would just lead to more depressing conversation, and hadn't she said often enough she wanted more smiles? Fair enough.

He could deliver.

Bo tapped her nose. "Chicken."

"What?"

"You heard me. You're a big chicken."

Uh-oh. No smile. She steamed, even stomped her foot as she stood—and looked damn cute doing it. "I'm thinking of your friends and not ruining a special day."

"They're good folks. You won't ruin a thing."

She folded her arms over her chest in a last-ditch huff. "I don't have anything to wear. I just brought shorts and a khaki skirt, and that's not nearly formal enough for a wedding."

"Naked sounds good to me, well, except I wouldn't want all those crewdog pals of mine drooling over your fabulous rack."

She blinked twice, fast, startled, then snorted on a laugh. "I'll never understand how you manage to make piggish comments sound funny and complimentary all at once."

"It's a rare gift I have." He winked.

She rolled her eyes. "You're so full of it."

"That I am." A screw-up bad boy to the end. He'd heard it since childhood. "Darcy and Max aren't formal. Their wedding's going to be laid-back, and I do mean *seriously* laid-back. They specifically stated, beach wear and a smile when they called a week ago. Definitely no gold-embossed invitations for the two of them."

"How romantically impulsive."

"Actually, they've been engaged for nearly two years."

"Wow, that's a long time to wait."

Darcy had wanted Max to be sure since he'd been engaged before and the woman was murdered. Darcy's dangerous job as a military pilot didn't offer safe guarantees of a stress-free happily ever after.

How damn strange that it was Max who'd nearly died when the OSI agent had been undercover with them on the mission in Rubistan. Max had been a major player in investigating who on the base was leaking information to Kurt Haugen.

The reunion after they were released had been an odd mix of rejoicing and tense emotions. For once, he'd been glad he didn't have a family to meet him when he'd stepped off the plane. Well, actually, he'd been carried off the C-17 on a litter because he was too drugged up on painkillers to walk.

Maybe he was wrong to take Paige to the wedding….

Nah. He trusted his friends to welcome her if she came with him.

He slid his hands down her arms and let them rest on her hips, increasing the intimacy of their touching boundaries to date. Early foreplay that tormented him, sure, but the payoff would be big. "Come with me, please."

She swayed forward, just enough for their hips to meet, and no way would she miss how much he wanted her.

He stepped back. "Quit trying to sidetrack me, and yeah, I noticed that's what you're doing. I have a tropical shirt you can borrow. All you need is a pair of shorts since it's going to be an oceanside ceremony." He let his eyes speak for him instead of his hands. "I would really like you to be there with me tonight."

"Because you're worried about me?" she asked with unerring insight.

"I have to admit leaving you alone doesn't sit well with me right now." Since he was being truthful, might as well go for broke. Somehow he sensed this woman would find honesty as tempting as any foreplay. "But more than that, I just want to be with you. Time's running out for us, lady."

Chapter 11

Time passed for Paige in a haze of wedding vows, seaside winds and Bo's beautiful music. She hadn't realized until he pulled his guitar from the back of the dusty Jeep that he would be providing the music for the ceremony, a sentimental gift from him to the couple.

And he'd been thoughtful enough to ensure she didn't feel abandoned in the crowd by parking her with a friend of his—instructing that friend not to walk away even if Prickly Paige insisted she was fine. Which of course she would have done.

So now Paige sat beside his friend Nikki Price, a recent college graduate and daughter of one of the crewdogs. They shared a minipack of Kleenex as the bride and groom exchanged pledges of love with waves crashing against the shore. Sunset cast shadows and tequila hues across the sand while tiki torches flickered in the salty breeze, encircling the crowd of about a hundred. How could she not think of her own candlelight wedding? Not to mention her garbled emotions when it came to the new man in her life.

Focus on the moment, doggone it.

The spiky-haired groom sported a tropical shirt and baggy khakis, his long pants the only difference from his shorts-clad friends standing witness in floral shirts of their own. The bride wore a gauzy yellow sundress and no shoes, a beam of casual sunshine in the midst of all the crazy colors.

Snagging another tissue, Paige dabbed more sentimental tears over the love radiating from the two people standing under a floral bower. Even with the beach setting, they hadn't spared expense just because they'd opted for less formal. Sprays of tropical flowers and a spread of food large enough to feed an army waited on the sandy beach beside bowing sea oats. The unconventional ceremony spoke of their personalities and commitment.

A couple of years ago she wouldn't have recognized that, too caught up in appearances and the protocol of engraved invitations to appreciate the importance of the sentiment behind it all. No wonder she hadn't fully recognized her husband's shallow veneer.

And didn't that make her appreciate Bo's surprise frugality and thoughtfulness all the more? She was still working to reconcile her shifting image of him after seeing his house that held his "toys," but bought without extravagance.

Bo's shirt teased her skin with reminders that he would be touching her later. Even Downy-fresh clean, the fabric still carried his spicy scent. Or was he becoming that familiar to her after such a short time? She needed to keep this uncomplicated. She might be ready for sex again, but no way was her battered heart ready to risk more.

She forced her attention back to the present, Nikki pointing out the wedding party with whispered explanations. Matron of honor—the bride's sister who flew fighter planes in

Alaska with her aviator husband. Best man—a longtime friend of the groom who happened to be another pilot in the Charleston squadron, a guy named…huh? Crusty? Sheesh. What a name. Of course the guy did look like a cute but rumpled mess.

The minister raised his arms. "I now present to you, Mr. and Mrs. Maxwell Keagan." The willowy bride gave the minister a gentle tap on the arm. "Oh, uh, Mr. and Captain Keagan."

Laughter rumbled through the crowd while the groom scooped up his bride for a kiss and Bo launched into the final love song.

Where were those darn Kleenex?

The reception started and still Nikki Price stuck to her like glue while Bo helped the band set up. And wasn't that surreal, hanging out with the loadmaster, Tag's, daughter? One of the people hurt by Kurt, since he'd threatened her younger brother and held her parents hostage along with Bo.

How could these people be so forgiving when she couldn't find it within herself to forgive her husband?

A plate of food in hand, Paige plopped into a chair under a palm tree with Nikki. "You don't have to entertain me."

"It's my pleasure. Really." The leggy young woman leaned, silky black hair swinging with the swish of her head. "Besides, everybody's curious about you, so I'm the official spy for the gang."

"Curious? About me?" A chill tightened her skin. She rested her plate on her knees with a shaky hand.

"We've seen Bo with a lot of women—uh, no offense."

"No need to apologize." The chill turned downright icy. "I pretty much guessed his reputation."

"The thing is, we haven't seen him with a woman in almost a year." Nikki popped a sweet-and-sour meatball into her mouth.

"A year?" Icy nerves melted into something… She didn't know what.

God, she was hungry. *Petit four,* pronto.

"Uh-huh. He was dating a flight attendant last May, but that's the last one we can remember."

"I'm sorry to disappoint the rumor mill, but we're not dating." Only planning to have sex. Just liking each other and trying to hold on to objectivity that kept slipping away faster than the waves retreating from the shore.

"Yeah, right. If I believe that one, I'm sure you'd like to sell me a bridge and some swampland."

What could she say to that? Nothing. This woman had made up her mind—and she wasn't far off the mark. Best to change the subject. "So, which of these people crew together?"

"Nice segue. Okay, I can take the hint." The younger woman washed down another meatball with a glass of sparkling water. "They don't have set crews unless they're flying combat. But each of the different squadrons are tight, and certain groupings tend to fly together. Bo crews with Scorch over there whenever he can."

Paige swept her windblown hair from her face, and yeah, she'd left it down for Bo, for herself, too, because Kurt preferred she keep it confined with a fourteen-karat-gold clasp. "Scorch?"

"He once set his mustache on fire in a bar with a flaming Dr. Pepper drink." Shadows crossed her face that seemed to have nothing to do with the setting sun. "The two of them flew with my dad some over in Rubistan."

Nikki shook off the shadows and continued, "My dad also really likes to fly with Cobra. Let's just say his call sign came from the time he dropped his pants once as a joke, and snake references quickly followed. Marriage settled his butt right down, though."

There were so many names she could barely keep them all straight. Like wait, who were Bronco and Rodeo and how come with names like that neither one was a cowboy?

"Where's the commander?" She would have expected him to be at an important event like this, partying right alongside the other crewmembers circling the bonfire.

"He's off picking up his brother-in-law from college, packing up the extra gear and stuff."

"Brother-in-law? I didn't know he's married."

"Oh, he's not anymore. Actually, he's a widower. Most folks don't know, which is a shame because it makes his grouchiness a bit more forgivable."

"I thought everyone knew everything about each other around here." She tipped back her punch cup, pineapple with a definite kick.

"Like I said before, Colonel Quade's a real grouch, so nobody really pries in his business. The brother-in-law went to boarding school. I only know about him because he started at UNC with me this year. We've carpooled a couple of times." She fanned her face with her hand. "The guy's a real hottie, all dark hair and has this fabulously yummy South American accent. Too young for me though."

She started to ask Nikki who she was seeing—

"Bo's a great guy."

Paige froze, wondering if maybe this woman had once been with him or wanted to be. They certainly seemed closer in age.

Nikki laughed. "No. Bo and I are definitely *not* an item, never have been, never will be. He's like a big obnoxious brother. Know what I mean?"

"I have one of those."

"Exactly. He's helped me with some course selections and stuff. I was finishing up my teaching degree at UNC Chapel Hill, where the colonel's brother-in-law goes, too."

"That's nice." She busied herself with more punch to hide her relief while the bonfire flames crackled higher.

"I just thought you would want to know, since other folks have assumed we're more than friends."

"We're just…uh…" She twirled a strand of hair between two fingers.

"Friends? Yeah right. *I'm* his friend, remember? And he doesn't look at me like he wants to peel off my clothes with his teeth and toss them very far away, not to be found for at least a week."

Apparently they weren't hiding their feelings from anyone. Might as well be open then. "If he's such a great guy and you two are friends, how come nothing more came of it?"

"No spark, ya know? There's no explaining what makes that spark happen." Her eyes drifted back over to the cluster of pilots popping peeled shrimp into their mouths. Was she looking for someone in particular or just dreaming of another guy? Tough to tell. But Nikki was still so young, with many years and dreams left to explore.

How morbid was that? Geez, she wasn't exactly 105 herself. Exhaustion and more than a little frustration must be having its way with her. Time to lay off the spiked fruit punch before it ruined the whole night for her.

She'd made her decision to grasp the moment with Bo, and she wouldn't be shaken. She'd come to Charleston to lay her past to rest and that involved facing everything head-on.

Speakers squawked and the canned recorded music shifted to the band warming up. Bo shouldered through the crowd and dropped onto the arm of her lawn chair. "How's it going?"

She clasped her hands around her punch glass to keep from placing her hand on his thigh and further stoking the rumor mill. "Your friend here's just spilling all your secrets."

He blanched paler than the chunks of Swiss cheese on the plate on her lap. She didn't want to think about what nerve that must have struck. Tonight was about putting aside morbid thoughts and concerns.

Pinching up a *petit four,* Nikki pelted him on the forehead. "Nothing particularly juicy, but the night's still young."

Bo set aside Paige's plate and cup with an arousing brush of his fingers. "Then I guess I'd better keep her busy." He tugged Paige's wrist. "Kick off your shoes and dance with me, gorgeous."

Three hours later, by the bonfire, Bo searched the crowd for Paige, who'd been tugged off for more secret sharing with some of the wives and girlfriends apparently determined to see him paired up. A few people avoided her, but in a group this large and with the night to hide subtle emotions, the slight wasn't as obvious.

Good thing because he would hate to kick ass at Darcy and Max's wedding.

Paige seemed to be having fun when they'd danced under the stars, fast, slow, and much like what he had in mind for later, minus the clothes. Hopefully she wasn't pissed with him for making her come along, but after that purse-snatching, he hadn't wanted to risk leaving her alone. Trouble seemed to be following this woman lately with an increasing frequency that made his instincts shout.

And then she was there. Beside him. Smiling. Sliding her soft hand into his.

He gave her fingers a gentle squeeze. "Are you ready to go?"

"I can wait." She flipped her loose hair over her shoulder. "I don't want to take you from your friends. Looks like they still have plenty of party left in them."

"They do. But there's always another party, and I can see them anytime." And soon he wouldn't see Paige anymore.

Her eyes sparked with a similar awareness. "Let's go."

He tugged her hand, weaving them through the press of

people, not a fast trek but he was a determined man. At the edge of the crowd, he bumped smack into Nikki.

"Leaving so soon?" His leggy athlete friend smirked.

"Do you need a ride or anything?" Honor compelled him to ask in thanks for all her help, even as he prayed overtime she would say no.

"No."

Yes! "Well if you're sure."

"I'm good." Nikki waved him on. "I'm actually playing designated driver like a grown-up."

"Cool. I'll catch ya later when I get back in town again."

Nikki fanned a wave. "Night, Paige, great meeting you. Hope we get to see you again."

Paige hmm-ed an answer along with a return wave before tucking her hand back into Bo's. "She's nice."

"Yeah, she is." Tracking up the dunes to the haphazardly parked vehicles, he led her toward his Jeep.

"Why aren't you going off with her instead?"

What? He studied her face for signs of jealousy...and only found confusion. And damn, that tugged at him far more than if she'd been spitting green fire. He released her hand to hook an arm around her shoulders, tucking her closer to his side. "She's more like family."

"That's what she said."

So Paige had asked? Interesting. And how ironic that he had Sister Nic as a mother figure and Nikki for a sister sort. Maybe it was sort of symbolic how they had similar names, like some kind of cosmic family connection to make up for his biological parents. "Besides Nikki's not my type, and even if she was, her father would kill me."

"Like Vic."

"Well, yeah, but I guess *you* are worth the risk." He pivoted her back against his Jeep, liking all over again the way she looked in his shirt.

"She seems perfect for you." She toyed with his top button. "I can't see why she wouldn't be your type."

"Oh, really?" He let his gaze linger on her incredible chest with an obvious leer.

She swatted his shoulder. "You are such an outrageous pig sometimes."

"Made you laugh, though, didn't I?"

"Yes, you did." She stretched up on her toes to press a simple kiss to his mouth.

Simple for about four seconds, and then the heat started again. Next thing he knew a horn was honking and Cobra was heckling the hell out of him.

With more than a little regret, he pulled himself away from Paige and opened the passenger door. "Sorry about that."

"It's okay. Really. We have all night."

Ooh-rah. He closed the door.

She rested her hand on top of his on the open window. "Since we have all night, if you're not too tired, would you mind if we took a drive first?"

A drive? His libido shouted in hoarse frustration at the delay, but if that was what she wanted, patience and foreplay would eventually pay off. He'd learned long ago the best way to romance a woman was to listen. Eventually she made her needs clear.

"A drive sounds great. I got my second wind right about the time they cut the cake." He circled the hood and climbed behind the wheel.

"So you have an extra week in North Dakota and then you're back here for good." She twirled a lock of hair around her finger, threatening his control behind the wheel more than if he'd dipped into the punch.

Which he hadn't. He didn't want anything dulling his senses tonight.

Time was most definitely running out. "That's the schedule."

"How wild that it takes three weeks to fix an engine."

"Bureaucracy." He steered the Jeep onto the road. "Sometimes it takes forever to get the parts. Once, I sat in Spain for six days waiting for them to send a crew chief out to hit something with a rubber mallet."

"What is Mako's job, then?" She gestured for another turn. Why the sudden interest in his military life? Idle curiosity or true desire to learn more about him?

And where the hell was she taking them on this surprise drive? "He's an in-flight mechanic, actually works over in the maintenance squadron. We don't always fly with one. Depends on the mission."

She pointed to the sprawling brick sign illuminated with a spotlight, marking the exclusive subdivision entrance. "Turn left here."

"Not that it really matters to me, but do you have a destination in mind?" He slowed along the quiet street in the sleeping neighborhood.

"Uh, take the first right then left." She kept her head tipped toward the sprawling homes that bordered on mansion size with their manicured lawns. "I've been mulling over what you said earlier."

"Which something?"

"About needing closure." She pointed to the yellow home at the end of the cul-de-sac. "There. Pull over and stop, please."

Realization cold-cocked him. This was *her* old neighborhood, her old house. He pulled alongside the curb and slid the Jeep into neutral.

Holy crap, crime paid well. Even in the dark of night with only the stars and a couple of security lights, he could see she'd lived in one helluva place during her time here as Mrs. Haugen. Two stories, the house was easily four thousand square feet of fairly new construction to go with those columns and wraparound porch.

He would never be able to give a wife anything close to this. Not that he was thinking in those terms about the woman next to him. Sure he wanted to get married someday when the right one came along, but he and Paige had never discussed there being anything beyond next week.

Still, he tried to reconcile his image of the practical woman next to him in that house. He'd seen enough of her brother's faltering business to know she was more than pulling her weight around there, and he'd never heard her complain.

His mind tripped over a question he hadn't considered before. How badly did Vic need money?

"I forgot about the flowers."

Her amazed whisper closed off other thoughts.

"What about the flowers?"

"Kirstie and I planted flowers just like those." She nodded toward the overflowing bed of marigolds shaded by taller daffodils. "And she and I had picnics under that oak tree by the azalea bush. She had little friends here, too, and they raced bikes along the sidewalks."

"All the things kids should do."

"Memories that have nothing to do with Kurt and his damn money." She sagged back in her seat, her thumb toying with the collar of her shirt.

His shirt.

Lust tightened inside him with an urgency to claim her as his, totally separate from this world. "You and Kirstie are well on your way to making more happy memories in a new place."

"I know. But I needed to see this. I needed to know that I didn't screw everything up, that her years here weren't a total mistake."

"She's a good kid. That doesn't happen overnight."

"A good kid who thinks a case of sunburn must be rubella."

"A good kid who's had a rough year, but is putting everything back together just like her mama. I happen to think both you ladies have done a damn fine job."

"Thank you." Her eyes darted as if taking in everything one last time to record each detail. "And thank you for bringing me here so I could remember all those good things Kirstie and I did together."

"What about her father?" He couldn't resist asking.

"He always said he loved her, like in the letter." Shuddering, she skimmed her hands along her bare arms in spite of the eighty-degree evening. "How awful is it to be relieved I never have to show the hypocrisy to Kirstie?"

"Where does he play into those memories you have of this house?"

Yeah, yeah, he knew he had a selfish reason for wondering. Major "duh" moment. He was less than an hour from being with this woman. She'd said she didn't love the scumbag anymore, but she must have at some time. Had that love stopped in the police station? Or earlier, as Vic had hinted?

It mattered to him right now, a helluva lot.

"He was obsessed with getting ahead with his restaurant so he could give us more. We really didn't see him all that often, and if he made it to preschool plays or gymnastic shows, he came late and spent half the time on his cell phone. I used to think if we had more time together, I could figure out what was wrong with him, me, the way I was feeling about him. Or rather, the way I wasn't feeling anymore."

Vic had told him the same thing about her faltering relationship with Haugen, but it felt damn good hearing the words from her mouth. It also gave him a few more ideas on how to romance this woman the way she deserved.

"Silly me, I thought I just had a workaholic husband like most everyone else in the neighborhood. I used to joke he took his cell phone and pager into bed with him."

She tried for a smile. No luck.

Paige glanced down at her lap, tracing a purple flower on the shirt before sucking in a brave breath and meeting him eye-to-eye. "I haven't been with anyone except Kurt."

The conversational shift jolted through him. Then understanding followed about her reasoning for this detour. Listening would definitely work best here because one misstep would cause far more pain than just an end to their evening plans. He stayed silent and let his touch speak reassurance for him by tunneling into her hair to cup her head.

"All I have to go by is sex with a man who had no morals. How *ewww* is that?"

There was no answer he could offer up so he continued a slow stroke of his thumb along her neck, a nonthreatening touch to let her know he was still here. Serious brown eyes stared back at him, brave and determined eyes that made him more than a little sad because making love shouldn't have to be this serious and fearsome.

"Okay, Bo, here it is, straight up. I'm afraid that even as much as I want you, sex could have been ruined for me because it's somehow associated with him, who he was and what he did. I need you to reassure me."

"With sex?" Did she want him as some sort of therapeutic fling? Or did she want *him?*

She crinkled her nose. "Maybe that didn't come out quite right. I didn't mean to sound so…clinical about it all. Let me try again."

It was tough to be insulted when she was being so sweet and earnest. "I'm all ears."

"You are the most honorable, charming and giving man I've ever met. And that's saying a lot considering I think my brother and Seth are really great guys. And of course you're hot as hell and not a relative."

"That last part's definitely a plus." He shrugged off the compliments he wasn't sure fit with a joke.

A smile lit her eyes as much as the stars glinting off her gold glasses. "I need to move forward with my life, and while sex shouldn't be everything, I think the longer I wait to figure this out, the more I'm going to worry and freeze up inside."

She gripped his shirtfront, twisting, her small fist resting against his chest. "And, God, please say something soon, before I absolutely die of embarrassment. I thought men wanted the chance at uncomplicated sex."

"Lady." He paused, shaking his head. "There isn't one thing about you that's uncomplicated. And that's one of the many things I like about you."

"So all my babbling there made sense somehow?"

"Absolutely." Easing back with a quick, tender-as-he-could-make-it kiss, he shifted the Jeep into gear.

Later he would think about the fact that he didn't feel much like the man she described. In spite of his countless flaws he recognized well, he'd always prided himself on never starting a relationship if it didn't stand at least a chance of going somewhere. For the first time, he was about to break his rule.

Because no way in hell could he turn his back on the chance to be with this woman even just once.

Chapter 12

Outside Bo's house, Paige grappled for the Jeep's door handle while chanting in her head that she could do this, she *would* do this. She wanted this, him, all of it, so don't think.

Do *not* think. After a mad dash across town for privacy—a mad dash across the country since they'd left North Dakota, for that matter—finally they were alone.

Bo grazed her arm with his knuckles. "Sit tight. I'll be right around."

To open the door for her? Old-fashioned, but sweet nonetheless. Although, she hoped he would hurry before she thought too much about all the embarrassing things she'd told him while sitting outside her old house. She watched Bo through the windshield as he sprinted around the hood with a speed and obvious urgency that sent a jolt of anticipation through her.

He swept the door open, dropped his keys in her hands and

scooped her out of the front seat, startling a surprised yelp from her as she grabbed his shoulders for balance. "You're crazy."

"For you? Hell, yeah." He charged up the front walk to his house carrying her, stars dancing overhead as she jostled. "Unlock the door, would ya? Use the key with the red-tape marking."

"You could put me down."

"Or you could just open the door so we can get inside sooner."

"Fair enough. One red-tape key coming up."

Once inside, he slid her down along the front of him until there was no mistaking how very much he wanted her. "Finally."

"Finally," she echoed against his mouth.

Looping her arms around his neck, she urged his head down and took the most from the moment as fully as she took his mouth, his kiss, the heat of more dry lightning and want that had been building for weeks. Even longer perhaps, years since she'd indulged in fantasies of a man and a moment just like this.

Bo skimmed more kisses along her cheek, up into her hair until he nuzzled in that way he had of catching her fragrance, which sent a whole new shiver through her. Thank goodness she'd allowed herself the silly vanity of jasmine-scented shampoo and loose hair for the evening.

Her hands climbed inside his shirt to hold him closer, and yes, to feel the warmth of his skin. "I think it's time we test out your sexual peaking theory."

"With any luck," he paused, inhaling along her neck, "there's going to be plenty of peaking going on soon."

"How soon?" She arched to look up at him, which happened to bring her hips closer to his, cradling the hard ridge of his obvious desire against her stomach with delicious intimacy.

"Not too soon, I hope. Although if you keep wriggling like that…" He groaned, backing her toward the hall, his arms linked around her waist guiding her along with him in a sort of tuneless dance toward his bedroom.

She'd showered in the guest bath earlier while he was in his room, so there hadn't been time to see more of where he lived. Although in seconds she would be seeing far more of *him.*

He toed open the door. "Time to live in the moment. No intrusions or interruptions."

They crossed the threshold into his room, the ardent caress of his hands beneath her shirt leaving little rational thought to register much of her surroundings beyond the queen-size bed, a framed Hard Rock Café poster…and yes, yes, yes, a sprawling bed with an inviting red-striped comforter.

And had she mentioned the big bed? "No interruptions?"

"None." He backed from her slowly, hands touching until the very…last…second.

She almost moaned at the loss of his touch. If her knees went this weak over a few kisses, she would be a serious mess soon. She sagged to the edge of his bed, watching with curiosity as he strode across the room and swept aside the miniblinds. Bo jerked open the window, reached to unclip his cell phone and…

Pitched it outside.

"Ohmigod!" She collapsed onto her elbows into the soft give of down filling. "I can't believe you just did that."

"Oh, yeah? Then you probably won't believe this, either." He scooped up the telephone from the bedside table and yanked.

The wire popped from the wall.

A delicious shiver tickled up her spine. Sure it was a macho show and the phone in the next room was still in working order. But, oh, my, it was a wonderfully romantic gesture because it showed he'd listened to her about Kurt's workaholic distance.

Kurt had lavished her with everything from body oils to expensive lingerie, even a roomful of roses and a tray of fresh oysters once, all in an attempt to be good to her. He'd vowed he wanted to shower her with everything, yet always withheld the one thing she craved most, his sole focus.

Her husband could have been seconds away from penetration, and if the phone rang or doorbell chimed, he'd skim a quick kiss while he hiked his pants back up. Now she knew she'd been second to crooks.

Not anymore. She'd made major strides in reconciling her past tonight, and she wouldn't let thoughts of that dead bastard steal even one iota of her attention. Bo deserved a hundred percent of her focus, as well.

And there was no mistaking that she had his complete and undivided attention—the most enticing aphrodisiac of all. Just the two of them. No fancy mood music. No dim lighting or BS extras, and that swiped away any lingering doubts or ridiculous insecurities about the size of her butt.

Rising from the edge of the bed, she kicked her sandals free and shimmied out of her shorts before he could make it across the room. A low whistle of appreciation sounded from Bo, echoed in his eyes, crystal blue deepening to royal hues.

"Now, that's a view to carry a man through the night—you in just my shirt." He sauntered closer, grasping her hips in broad hands and urging her forward until they stood flush against each other again. "Let's slow down so I can enjoy it."

His mouth brushed one corner of her lips, then the other, tormenting until she opened in an unspoken demand that he do the same. And how wonderfully accommodating he was while still taking his slow, sweet time as promised, standing in the middle of the room to neck like two teenagers.

Starting at the strong column of his neck, she unbuttoned, delighting in each inch of toned, tanned chest coming into view. Military dog tags nestled in the dusting of hair across his pecs. Even while his hands moved over her arms, back, teasing along and up the outside of her thighs, his eyes never left hers as if he savored watching her reactions as much as her touch.

Air swirled over her chest in a surprise burst since she couldn't recall him unbuttoning her shirt. She suspected this man could well steal reason and thought. Which happened to be exactly what she wanted right now.

She skimmed his shirt over his shoulders, muscles rippling under her hands. In reaction? Or from restraint? Both equally heady notions.

Her shirt—or rather his *on* her—slithered down and off to pool at her feet, quickly followed by her bra, leaving her in nothing but her panties while he stood in only his khaki shorts. Thank heavens she'd thought to indulge in pink satin after her shower.

She glided her palms along his chest over sun-heated skin taut across muscles, around to his back to pull him against her bare breasts and sighed. She'd forgotten how good skin-to-skin felt.

Or had it ever felt this good?

He danced her backward until the mattress bumped her thighs then—*whoosh*—she fell onto the bed, tugging him with her. He swept aside her glasses, resting them on the bed-side table before stretching along the length of her.

And she'd thought skin-to-skin felt good. The solid press of his weight against her, even propped on his elbows, stirred primal longings that defied description.

She tore at his shorts with frantic hands. "Enough fore-play."

"There's never too much foreplay." He nipped his way down her neck to her breast. He lifted his face to blow cool air over the taut peak of her nipple.

"Says you." She pitched aside his boxers and cradled the

weight of him in her hand until she could see him fight to keep his eyes open.

"Two can play that game." His stroked down her hip, lower until he cupped her damp heat in his palm, the gentle pressure of slow circles threatening to send her leaping out of her skin. "Maybe you're right about enough foreplay for now."

Returning his attention to her breast, he reached into the bedside table, yanked the drawer open, his hand returning between them with a condom—and thank heavens someone was thinking here.

Thick, blunt pressure increased as he filled her, deeper, fuller and definitely more incredible than anything she'd remembered.

"You okay?" He stared down at her with such intensity in those deep blue eyes, she didn't doubt for a second where his attention rested.

"Perfect."

"Yes, ma'am, you are."

His weight braced on his forearms, he loomed over her with sexy restraint, his dog tags dangling to tease between her breasts. Levering on one arm, he swept off the chain and pitched it onto the floor.

Without closing his beautiful eyes, he moved inside her, a long and slow withdrawal that pulled an even longer sigh from her until his thrust shifted her sigh to a moan. Her hands slid over his back, down to grip and learn the feel of him along with discovering a matching rhythm that soon slicked them with sweat.

Whispered urgings grew louder in a rambling litany of need they both responded to even if she couldn't remember what either of them said. Maybe she was too busy relishing the unmistakable heat and want in his expression.

Then she couldn't tell if he closed his eyes or not because her own wouldn't stay open. Her legs glided up of their own will and instinct to hook around his hips, heels hooking together to clamp their bodies closer as she writhed for release. Already? Yes.

"Not going to last much longer if we don't slow down." His words shooshed against her ear in a hot hiss of air.

A year of abstinence. For both of them. Somehow she knew right then it really was true for him, but couldn't wrap her brain around rational thought long enough to figure out why that might be important. "Neither am I."

"Thank heavens."

Each rhythmic glide stroked her higher, pulled nerves into a taut twist until her fingers clenched against the hard planes of his shoulder blades for anchor. Her arms strained from trying to hold him closer, arch and rock her body in time to his in a frantic dance to find completion while somehow extending the pleasure as…long…as…

Her year of abstinence ended with a final crack of thunder and lightning, bathing her in a downpour of sensation that momentarily washed away worries.

He was in a crapload of trouble.

Parked in front of his piano with warm Paige beside him and the scent of sex all around them both, he played through every mellow love song classic he could remember, to offer Paige the romance he should have earlier.

Before he'd pounced on her like an untried horny teenager.

Even now he stifled the urge to tip them both to the floor for round three, and consoled himself with the heat of her thigh pressed to his. Thank goodness his boxers offered a modicum of coverage, because the sight of her in his shirt and nothing more… How about some extra air in this room?

A year without wasn't any excuse for this raging need for more of her. He should have shown some restraint. In the past he'd gone through dry stretches, and afterward had still been in control. Chalk it up to male ego, but he always planned how to ensure the woman walked away fully satisfied.

Any planning with Paige had gone out the window seconds after his telephones.

He also considered himself more of a pragmatist than a romantic on this subject. He figured he would get his big finish regardless, and his chances of being invited back for more "big finishes" were higher if she finished, too. Sure Paige had climaxed…an incredibly beautiful sight he would carry in his mind until the day he died.

But he couldn't remember how the whole process evolved, because he sure as hell hadn't been in control and neither, it seemed, had she. He'd just been…there…with her, in her, touching, caught up in the mind-numbing pleasure and excitement from hearing her gasps, sighs, moans build until they were both so freaking out of control…

He'd told himself he would regain balance for the second go round. Not. And now here he sat at the keyboard looking for order as he'd always done through his music…with no luck.

His fingers stopped along the keys as the last notes faded in the humming piano strings.

Paige's hand fluttered to rest on top of his left. "That was beautiful. Thank you. I can't remember ever having a better concert." She stroked along his hand, the fingers on his left puffy and red, aggravated from hours of guitar playing, followed by his twenty minutes of corny love tunes that somehow didn't feel so sappy with Paige around.

She traced each scar with her lightest of healer touches as if she could somehow erase them. "Should you ice your hand?"

"Probably." Later, when he wouldn't feel like a wuss for admitting he'd pushed too far.

Paige started to swing her legs to the side on the piano bench. "I'll get it for you."

He looped his arm back around her waist and anchored her to his side. "In a minute. I currently have another appendage that's paining me more."

She leaned into his kiss, her fingers still linked with his. Their eyes met and held, her thumb stroking along the ridge of a scar and silently questioning.

As much as he wanted to dodge anyone rooting around in his head, he owed her something in return for all she'd told him. Might as well go for broke since he suspected there was no getting out of this relationship unscathed. "I hurt my hands when things went to crap during a mission overseas in Rubistan."

Horror widened her eyes. "You were injured during a crash?"

"Not exactly. Yes, we were shot down." His brain echoed with the shattering thump, the shriek of warning alarms, the bark of the aircraft commander's voice, Scorch, instructing them all to strap down tight. "You may have heard some of the news reports about terrorists using shoulder-held missile launchers. They popped some planes in Iraq that way, too."

"Why didn't we hear anything about what happened to your crew?" She unfurled her fingers and cradled his hand in both of hers, starting a gentle massage. Did she even realize or was her healer instinct in overdrive?

God, it felt good, though, somehow making words he'd only spoken in the mandatory psych evals easier to spill. "When things are hot in another country, you don't hear much about other things going on in the military. We were a blip in the news, downplayed—a good thing as far as I'm concerned."

"Can you tell me why you were there?" she asked with a rarely found understanding and acceptance that he couldn't share all. So many relationships broke up over just that.

"We were there transporting intelligence equipment that picked up on terrorist chatter and the like." The reason OSI agent Max had been along, although Tag had been forced to destroy all the data before they crash landed, so what the hell had they accomplished? He could almost feel the sun burning the back of his neck as he'd run full-out across the desert, searching low dunes for somewhere to evade and set up a rescue beacon. "Can't say much more than that, but you get the idea."

"I think I do." She blinked hard and brought his hands one at a time to her lips. "If you landed in a country we're not at war with, how did this happen?"

"That doesn't mean everybody likes us there. We were picked up by tribal warlords first—" A ragtag and rabid group in beat-up trucks with plenty of weapons who'd found the crew trying to evade them by lying flat in a dug-out sand pit. "I got a little cocky. Dared look a warlord in the eyes. Had my right hand stomped, the other bashed with the butt of an AK-47 before Tag rolled between me and the next blow."

He shrugged, forcing himself to relax while she continued her subtle massage along one finger at a time as two tears slipped down her cheeks. She didn't sniffle or sob, just kept rubbing even after the tears dripped from her chin onto his wrist.

More determined than ever to shield her, he left out the rest of why they'd been flying over Rubistan. The OSI had been trying to track the link from drug-trafficking terrorists through a military traitor handing shipments over to a U.S. civilian pickup point back in the States. Kurt Haugen. That much information she did not need and he would damn well carry it to his grave.

A fierce protectiveness pounded through him, primitive, irrational and likely unwelcome. But he'd be damned if he would cause Paige one more ounce of heartache.

His sense of honor pinched at his gut. Hard. As much as he told himself he was doing the right thing in keeping this relationship light, he still saw the shadows in her teary eyes he knew would still haunt his dreams. Which gave him all the more incentive to delay sleep as long as possible.

Bo dropped a kiss on her nose, red-tipped from crying tears for him. "Let's go get that ice. Although I have better ideas for using it than on my hands."

Chapter 13

She would never look at an ice cube the same way again.

Paige arched her arms over her head until her knuckles skimmed the headboard, but kept her eyes closed to avoid morning a few seconds longer. A post-sex stretch was without a doubt the best stretch ever. And when that came after the best sex ever? She wanted to keep right on arching as long as possible in case this weekend with Bo was all she would have.

At least she had her body back again after fears her past with Kurt would freeze her forever. She sagged on the mattress and rolled onto her side, clutching the sheet, eager to make more new memories to replace the old. They could stay in bed all afternoon and picnic naked. As soon as she found him.

The scent of coffee and bacon in the air answered her question about the empty space beside her. Gliding her hand along the bare spot as if to capture a remaining hint of the man, she let her mind drift through possibilities of…

A long-distance relationship? Telephone calls and trips cross-country. And he was considering leaving the military. Maybe he would return to teaching, which enabled him to live anywhere….

Yeah, right. Like he would relocate to North Dakota to hang out with a woman he'd known two weeks, and she couldn't even believe she was considering this. Incredible sex must be scrambling her brain. She needed to accept this pocket of happiness and quit thinking about tomorrow.

A rustle sounded outside the window. A squirrel?

Paige wrapped the sheet tighter. The purse-snatcher incident and break-in had her imagining boogey men behind every tree. She snagged her glasses off the bedside table for a clearer view of the window and the overgrown wisteria bush blocking most of the yard from sight.

Had Bo relocked the window after pitching the phones outside?

"Bo?" she called softly, inching to sit up.

The bush rustled, swaying as if swept aside.

"Bo!" She scrambled back toward the edge of the bed, nerves snapping to attention.

A body filled the window. Or rather shoulders and a face. A handsome and hot face.

"Bo." She slumped with relief, staring at her new lover standing outside, a phone in each hand.

He tapped on the pane with his cell phone.

Laughing at her own jitters, she secured the sheet around her and shuffled across the room. A quick look confirmed…yes, he'd locked the window, and his attention to her safety even when they'd been about to jump each other touched her. How could it not, when she'd lived too long with a man who put her and her child at risk?

She flipped the lock and nudged the window up, no easy task while struggling to keep a sheet modestly tucked around her, which elicited a fresh twinkle in Bo's eyes.

"Morning, gorgeous." He leaned inside to drop the phones onto the carpeted floor, the reach placing his face right at her waist for a lingering kiss that tickled as well as aroused.

"Good morning, master of the ice cube."

Fist knotted in the sheet, she threaded the fingers of her other hand through his hair, still damp from his shower. Sheesh, she'd slept deeply not to have heard him. Regret flickered through over the missed opportunity to step inside the spray with him. Before they left tomorrow morning, she would take that memory.

Make the most of every second.

Pulling back, he rested both arms on the ledge and peered up at her. "So is it? A good morning? I didn't mean to lay all that heavy crap from my past on you last night."

"I'm glad you did." She traced along his forehead down to his mouth, which had brought her such pleasure with an ice cube clenched between his teeth. "Makes everything feel more equal since you've had to deal with so much of *my* heavy crap."

And she couldn't help noticing that he'd used sex to dodge further discussion, which also made her realize how little he'd shared about himself that didn't involve a funny story. She might not have noticed before, but now she found herself wanting to know everything about him before he left.

"Fair enough, then." He nodded toward the cell phone. "I thought you might want to call Kirstie this morning."

"She's probably still asleep, with the time difference." Although they would probably be waking soon for church. "I'll check in on her a little later. Thanks for retrieving the phones."

"No problem." He hefted himself up, hooking a knee on the window to propel himself inside.

"Bo?" She startled back a step as he vaulted through and wrapped his arms around her seconds before giving her a toe-curling good-morning kiss.

Holy cow, freshly showered Bo smelled good. He tasted good, too, minty toothpaste and a hint of coffee. She melted into a puddle of hormones again at the stroke of his tongue searching her mouth.

He eased his head up from hers. "Have I told you yet you're gorgeous?"

"Yes, and you're so full of it."

"Not today." He traced her bottom lip with his thumb in an echo caress of some of his ice play the night before. "Being with you was even more mind-blowing than I expected, and let me tell you, I had high expectations."

What did a woman say to that? She had so little experience with morning-after chitchat. None, actually, since she'd never done the affair thing before. He seemed to like her straight-up attitude. She would have to go with that. "I believe it's safe to say you put any of my worries about sex to rest."

Bo winked and dropped another quick kiss on her lips. "My pleasure."

He stepped back and she darn near lost her sheet she'd forgotten to hold because her fingers preferred the feel of his chest. She grappled to secure the wrap. Naked would be fun, but only if he joined in.

For the first time she looked beyond his blue eyes to his clothes—pressed khakis, a button-down shirt and tie, more formal than he'd worn at the wedding.

And so mouthwatering she gripped her sheet tighter to keep from yanking him back into bed with her when he was obviously on his way out the door. "Are you going somewhere?"

"Uh, yeah, for a few hours." Passing her, he strode to his closet and unhooked a dark blue jacket. Avoiding her eyes? "But I'll be back in time to take you out to lunch. I left breakfast on the counter if you're hungry now."

She'd thought they would have breakfast in bed. Where was the great Romeo player she'd expected him to be? Instead she was seeing a man as confused as she felt, which touched her heart more than if he'd showered her with an elaborate meal served up with roses. "Do you mind if I ask where you're going?"

"To see Sister Nic." He shrugged into the sports coat. "We usually catch morning Mass and then have breakfast whenever I'm in town over the weekend."

Ah, now she understood. This man who worked not to share about himself would lose major privacy if she stepped into that part of his world. She waited for the invitation to join him while he gathered up his wallet and change off the dresser. How strange that she would be hurt if he didn't ask her to go along and scared if he did.

He smoothed his jacket and gave his tie a final tightening tug that must have darn near choked him. "Would you like to come with me?"

Nerves pranced in her stomach like one of her four-legged patients. "Yes, I think I would, if you really want me there."

"I do." He nodded, that tie so snug she feared he might pass out before they made it to the Jeep.

Even though he avoided discussing his biological parents, she understood well Sister Mary Nic had been the true mother figure in Bo's life. Was she reading too much into this invitation to join him?

Because, in spite of all her resolutions to simply enjoy a fling with Bo, it sure felt like a meet-the-parents moment.

Everybody else had parents here today except her.

Kirstie hopped out of her Uncle Vic's truck into the parking lot, her white church leathers pinching her feet. She'd asked to wear her tennis shoes with her jean dress, but Uncle Vic made her put on these ugly old things that hurt when she ran.

Scuffing a toe over the sidewalk up to the big brick chapel, she worked to mess up the shoes good while Uncle Vic held her hand on their way. She didn't want to be here with Uncle Vic and Uncle Seth. She wanted her mom, her dad, too. And maybe Bo because he was fun, and if her dad was here, then Bo wouldn't be a boyfriend so it would be okay to have him around.

But her mama was in Charleston. No fair. Kirstie dragged her other shoe, scraping the side along an angel statue with extra oomph. She wanted to go see her old house and her friends and flowers.

And what if Mom didn't come back?

Over by the big steps, she saw him—her stranger friend who told stories about her daddy. The man wasn't wearing his fixer-guy uniform today, just regular clothes like everybody else, but she still recognized him and his bushy eyebrows.

It would be tough to talk to him without Uncle Vic noticing and asking lots of question. He was real good about watching her, holding tight to her hand anytime they went anywhere. Or letting her ride on his shoulders. And when she thought of how nice he was, she felt sort of bad about ditching him. But she would be right back before he knew it.

Still, he was tough to sneak away from, not like Uncle Seth. *Ahhh.* Idea.

She tugged his hand before he could start up the steps. "Uncle Vic? I'm gonna ask Uncle Seth to walk me to Sunday school class so you can get to the doughnuts before all the good ones are gone."

He looked down, a long way 'cause he was so tall. "I'll take you."

She crooked a finger for him to lean toward her, then checked to make sure nobody was listening. "I think Uncle Seth likes my teacher."

Uncle Vic smiled, which made her feel even more guilty because he didn't smile that much. "All right, then, Miss Matchmaker. Have at it."

He let go of her hand.

She would do something nice for him later, like fill the dog bowls with water without being asked. For now she was almost home free.

Kirstie raced across the grass to her Uncle Seth already busy talking to another lady who was wearing a dress Mama would have called "too short for church." A lucky break, since Uncle Seth would want Kirstie out of the way.

She yanked on the bottom of his coat. "Uncle Seth? I'm gonna go to Sunday school with my friend Emily and her mama."

That would be fun except she didn't have friends here. Emily lived back in Charleston.

He pulled his eyes off the short-skirt lady. "Where are Emily and her mom?"

"Uh…" Kirstie looked around the crowd until she found icky Bitsy from her school and pointed. Uncle Seth wouldn't know the difference. "Right there."

"Okay, kiddo. Have fun."

She skipped over toward Bitsy, who told everybody Kirstie's daddy sold drugs so they better not play with his daughter or people would think they were doing drugs, too. She stopped behind Bitsy's mama and glanced over her shoulder at Uncle Seth. He waved once and turned away.

Bingo.

She veered off from icky Bitsy before the meanie could say something nasty. Kirstie ran really fast through a group of people and out the other side, away from where her uncles could see her. Panting, she looked around, searching until she found bushy-eyebrow man. She would have to remember to ask him his name this time.

She folded her hands behind her back and stared up. "Hi."

He jerked, sort of surprised-like and not very nice look-ing, then he smiled and everything was okay again. "Hello, Miss Kirstie Adella. Are you having fun?"

"Not much."

"It's a shame your mama can't be here, too. But at least she's having a good time in Charleston with her new friend."

Her friend. Bo. Kirstie's stomach felt funny, and she hadn't even eaten a doughnut yet.

"Yeah, she is." She held out her hand. "Wanna go for a walk and talk about my daddy?"

"I like your new friend." Sister Nic held an unsmoked cig-arette between two fingers with reverence.

Sitting on the stone bench by a trickling water fountain, Bo studied Paige over by the garden entrance with his cell phone. They would leave for lunch as soon as she finished checking up on Kirstie. "I figured you would. She's a nice lady."

Nice? What a namby-pamby word for an *awesome* lady.

Just looking at that cell phone against her ear made him think of tossing it out the window, which made him think of what came after. And how exciting it would be to peel that khaki skirt and white T-shirt off her later. Then, holy hell, he really needed to quit thinking or he might scorch this garden faster than when he'd poured too much fertilizer on the lawn.

"She obviously cares for her little girl."

He glanced away from Paige and back at the aging nun who'd bandaged his knees far longer than his own mother. They couldn't look any more different, Sister Mary Nic checking in at five feet tall when wearing those clunky nun shoes. She weighed all of eighty pounds soaking wet and could scare the crap out of a roomful of elementary hellions with just a look.

But when she smiled her approval with eyes as dark as her skin, the world was right and he could conquer anything. Which made him wonder what he hoped to accomplish by bringing Paige here? Approval? Maybe. But more than that he needed direction from Sister on what to do next.

"Paige is a good mom." He knew well what a gift that could be for a child. "No surprise Kirstie's a great kid with lots of grit. She's got these big brown eyes behind her glasses that just get to you even when she's cranky or puking on my boots."

He let his eyes linger on Paige while the memories from the air show rolled over him. Seemed like forever ago.

Birds chirped in the magnolias and dogwoods shrouding the garden in privacy. An itch started right between his eyes, as if he'd been targeted by a certain Super Nun's laser look.

Bo snapped his attention off Paige and back to Sister Nic. "Don't go there, Sister."

"Go where?" She brought the cigarette to her nose, but still didn't light it. She must be quitting—again.

"You know what I mean. I realize I'm your best hope for grandbabies but Paige and I are not…" But they were. "She's not…" But she could be. "Hell, I've only known the woman a couple of weeks."

And thought about her nonstop for a year since the first time she'd walked into a police station and into his life. An unforgettable woman.

"She's better than those bimbos you brought around before. And watch your language, please."

"Sure. Sorry. And I don't date bimbos." He felt sixteen again, caught behind the adjoining all-girls' school trying to cop a feel up a junior's uniform blouse. He always had been a breast man.

Sister Nic trailed her fingers through the fountain—and flicked water in his face. "What would you call the others, then, the gigglers who fawned all over you?"

"Hannah was smart." He swiped the droplets off his forehead. "She's a biochemist researcher at the medical university, for crying out loud."

"And you chased her off with that bad attitude when you were recovering from surgery."

Score one for Sister Nic. He'd been an ass to a really nice lady during his recovery. "Who? A charmer like me?"

She placed her cigarette carefully on her lap, a white slash along her dark robes. "You were a pain in the tookus after you returned from wherever it was you went and never told me about—but I found out, anyway."

What? "You found out—"

"I have my sources, but that's beside the point."

Says who? Somebody was going to pay for worrying her, but he'd deal with that person—Tag, no doubt—later. "Then what is the point?"

"Your bimbos, and why you're no longer dating them."

"Ah, of course. And what's the lesson for today, Sister Nicotine?" For once he would welcome someone poking around in his head and offering up a few answers. He trusted her, and he didn't want to hurt Paige.

"No lesson. You're a big boy now, and it looks like you're just about to figure it all out on your own."

No answers. Damn. Stretching his legs in front of him, he crossed his feet at the ankles and tried to pretend this wasn't so important. "I think you give me too much credit."

"And I believe you don't give yourself enough." She tucked her smoke into a pocket for another day. "All this serious talk has me craving a cigarette for real and I've vowed to quit. Again. How about playing me something to take my mind off it."

"Such as?"

"Learned any new Stones tunes lately?"

"I'll see what I can come up with." He swung the guitar up onto his leg and picked through the strings, tuning.

A gasp from under the arbor snapped his attention up. Paige?

Her face paled in the glaring sunlight. Alarms jangled in his head. He shot to his feet and charged across the grass to her side.

"What's wrong?"

She clutched his cell phone to her chest. "Vic thought Kirstie was with Seth, and Seth said Kirstie had gone off with a friend who doesn't remember seeing her." Her hands shook so hard the cell phone slipped from her grasp to thud on the lush grass. "Now they can't find her at all."

Chapter 14

Ten hours later, Paige closed the book to her daughter's favorite bedtime story, so grateful to have her child alive, her hands shook gripping *Goodnight Moon*.

She still couldn't breathe without each gasp slicing icy fear through her. Even holding Kirstie in her arms safe and sound in North Dakota didn't stop the shaking that had started the minute Vic realized he couldn't locate Kirstie to come to the phone.

Everyone reassured her Kirstie had simply wandered off as kids do. Everyone except Bo. He hadn't dished up a single platitude, instead, all action, he'd raced her to the airport. Even when Kirstie had been found a half hour later, nothing would have kept Paige off that plane.

She smoothed a hand over her daughter's cool forehead, stroking back curls still damp from a bubble bath. Kirstie may have seemed unharmed, but Paige's mind kept spinning horrible scenarios of what could happen to a little girl alone during those tension-fraught minutes.

Kirstie's story? She'd been playing with an imaginary friend because Bitsy was icky and mean. Children could be cruel and, God knows, Kurt had given folks more than enough fodder for gossip. Except that didn't explain why Kirstie gave Seth and Vic the slip in the first place.

Perched on the edge of Kirstie's bed while her daughter snuggled under her Strawberry Shortcake quilt, Paige listened to Bo's guitar through the open window. Seeing him so tender with Sister Nic had stolen another little piece of her heart during a weekend that had already made serious inroads on her emotions.

Less than twenty-four hours ago she'd been in his arms, dreaming of ways they could be together again. Something that wouldn't happen tonight when she needed him more than ever.

"I didn't mean to scare you so bad." Kirstie fished under the covers and pulled out her Strawberry Shortcake rag doll.

Parental antennae picked up on the nuance. *So* bad? As in, she'd meant to scare her a little?

Paige studied her daughter's expression for clues while a breeze wafted through the window carrying a hint of fresh-mown grass and an old Rolling Stones tune. She would have to tread warily to keep Kirstie from clamming up altogether as she'd done once Vic found her sitting outside the girls' bathroom as calm as could be. As if she could pretend her uncle wouldn't have already checked that same bathroom when she'd first gone missing. "Tell me more about your new imaginary friend."

"Who says he's new?" Kirstie picked at the yarn hair on her doll.

"He?" More than they'd known before—and frightening as hell. "What's his name?"

Kirstie shrugged.

"If you don't know his name, then he's a stranger."

"His name's Eddie and he wasn't a—" She stopped short.

"What do you mean? He wasn't a stranger?" Her suspicions took root. "And maybe he's not imaginary, either? Kirstie, honey, you have to be honest with me. This is important."

Her tiny knuckles whitened in the doll's red yarn hair. "You're gonna get upset if I tell you."

Like she wasn't already scared to death? What if some pervert... She stroked her daughter's hair in reassurance. She couldn't face what she didn't know. "I promise I won't be mad."

"I know you won't get mad or yell or anything. I mean you'll be sad if I tell you."

"Punkin, you're really scaring me more right now by not telling me."

"He said he knew my daddy."

Breathe. She needed to breathe.

And wow, had Kirstie ever nailed her prediction of her mother's emotions dead-on. She *was* upset, for a myriad of reasons. Top of the list? Kurt and his illegal ties terrified her.

Of course, it could be nothing. Kurt had plenty of old high school friends around here.

"Are you upset?" Kirstie pressed back into her pillow. "I know you don't like it when I talk about him."

Her daughter had been protecting her? Guilt on top of fear, what a toxic mix.

How to approach this? Apparently hiding her feelings had been a bust, so she couldn't lie now. "I am a little upset you didn't feel like you could tell me. And of course I'm sad thinking about your father." And all the potential he'd thrown away for a quick dollar. "When somebody dies, that makes people sad. But you don't ever have to hide how you feel from me. I'm the grown-up, remember? I'm supposed to take care of you."

"Who takes care of you?"

"Grown-ups are supposed to take care of themselves."

"But who's there when you want to cry?"

Bo, who'd held her hand on the plane all the way back from South Carolina while silent tears leaked from her eyes even though they'd already found Kirstie by then.

She couldn't think about him now or she would be a muddle of irrational emotions all over again. "We're talking about the man who spoke to you. What else did he say?"

"That he and Daddy played together when they were kids and he was just checking up on me because Daddy would want him to."

"What did he look like?"

Kirstie scrunched her nose in thought. "Really old. Like you."

Thanks, kid.

"And like Bo."

Okay, she could forgive the "old" comment after all.

"Except he's big and blond and has these really creepy eyebrows." She brought her hands to her forehead and wiggled her fingers. "Like that cartoon cat."

"Garfield?"

"Yeah."

Cute, but not helpful.

"And I think he's a fixer man."

Paige straightened at what promised to be much more significant than Garfield eyebrows. "A what?"

"A fixer-upper man. Um, you know. Somebody who fixes things like when the dishwasher broke and that worker came with his big tool belt."

"A repairman?"

"Yes. The stranger was always wearing those clothes the other times I talked to him."

Other times? Ohmigod. "How often have you spoken to him?"

Kirstie's gaze skittered away.

Paige tipped her daughter's chin. "I'm not mad, but this is important. I need to be able to trust you."

Kirstie fidgeted under her covers before meeting her mother's gaze again. "The first time, I saw him at the air show when I went out the back of the moonwalk."

Paige squelched a shiver at how close danger had been. She'd feared that, but having it confirmed scared the spit out of her.

"And then at the school playground he had on his fixerman clothes and a visitor's pass shaped like an apple so I really thought it was okay if he pushed me on the swing for a while."

This went beyond scary shivers. Her stomach pitched, but she couldn't frighten Kirstie by throwing up. She swallowed back bile.

"And then I saw him again at church."

Think. Think, damn it. She needed answers from Kirstie now while the conversation was flowing. "What did you talk about?"

"Just stuff, like what he and Daddy did when they were kids. He asked me if my daddy made up fairy tales like they used to do as kids, but I didn't want to talk about that. It made me too sad." Her brow furrowed with concentration. "Oh, and he usually asked about everybody here to make sure we're doing okay."

Alarms went off in Paige's head on a number of counts. Could this man have broken into the clinic, using Kirstie to track everyone's whereabouts? She wanted to believe it was still nothing more than a drug-related incident, but she couldn't ignore the possibility that they were being targeted because of Kurt. And how strange was it that somebody wanted to know about the very fairy tales Kurt had mentioned in his letters? This was too weird. So many questions without answers.

However, one thing was certain. She wouldn't be leaving her daughter again, which meant an end to fantasies about sneaking away with Bo. Her daughter needed to be her first priority.

Leaning, Paige pressed a kiss against the baby-soft skin of her daughter's cheek. "You did a great job remembering everything. I'm proud of you for being honest."

Tiny arms wrapped around her neck while the sweet scent of strawberry shampoo and healthy little girl swelled her heart. She would die to protect this child, and make sure anyone who hurt her baby suffered the agonies of the damned along the way.

"Time for you to get some sleep, punkin." Pulling away, Paige clicked off the bedside lamp, night-light plug-in glowing from across the room.

"What did it look like back there?"

Kirstie's question stopped Paige halfway off the bed. "Back where?"

"At home."

A year in North Dakota and Kirstie still didn't call it home. Had it been wrong to leave her daughter behind for the trip? She'd just wanted her child safe and protected, yet somehow things went to hell no matter what decision she chose. "It looked almost exactly the same as when we were there. A new family lives in our old house, and they planted the same kind of flowers we did."

"Merry-golds?"

"Yes, and others, too."

"Daddy and me planted a bush once."

She'd forgotten that. Putting the pain in the past had cost her happy memories, as well. "For Mother's Day, in the side yard, you two planted an azalea as a surprise for me."

"Yep, and Daddy made up one of his stories while we planted it." Her wistful voice mixed with Bo's music echoing up in the dark. "We had lots of fun doing that."

"I bet you did, punkin." She'd been so afraid of upsetting her daughter she hadn't allowed Kirstie to grieve and eventually find happy memories. Another wrong decision she'd made, but one she could rectify. "Would you like to go see that bush and the marigolds sometime?"

"Could we?"

She'd figure out a way to afford it if she had to cure all the cows in North Dakota. "Everyone should have a summer vacation."

"Thanks, Mom." Springing up onto her knees, Kirstie hugged Paige's waist so tight, she struggled not to burst into tears. Kirstie flopped back and under the covers.

"We'll visit the house and all your old friends." And she could see Bo again.

The possibility stirred a flurry of butterflies in her stomach. Other than that brief fantasy about him getting out of the service, she hadn't allowed herself to think beyond sleeping with him, but they'd gone to see Sister Nic. And he hadn't hesitated about returning with her. That didn't sound like a man who was scouting for the door after a one-night stand.

However, even if they had a second night in their future, it wouldn't be now. Call her old-fashioned, but she couldn't see sleeping with him under her brother's roof, with her daughter in the next room. Even if it was half her roof, too, since technically fifty-percent of their parents' home and land belonged to her, as well. But her brother had been footing the bill for the upkeep for so long, she considered it his.

And it wasn't as if she could count on a secret encounter, since she and Bo were so darn noisy.

No sex tonight, and honestly, fear had sapped her. More than anything, she needed to be held, and lucky for her a strong set of arms waited outside on the porch.

* * *

Bo worked his hands across the familiar feel and strings of his guitar, music offering little comfort tonight. As if he wasn't already confused as hell about Paige, now that little girl upstairs had somehow crawled under his skin, too. The flight back to Minot had been the longest of his life. Even knowing Kirstie had been found didn't fully ease the kicked-in-the-gut feeling stronger than any enemy boot.

He kept thinking what could have happened to her. What may have happened to her. Thank God there didn't seem to be any signs of abuse. Still he wanted to wrap her up in his protection.

Except she wasn't his, and if he let himself mull it over too long, he might envision himself as a part of a family. This family. Paige, Kirstie, him—another kid on the way and a dog to greet him at the front door.

A puppy—Honey—curled up alongside his foot, over six weeks old now, soon to go to a new home. Everyone here would move on after he left. Paige would find somebody to settle down with. Kirstie would have a secure life, just as he'd hoped to discover when he'd landed in Minot two weeks ago.

Except, he didn't want them to find someone else. He wanted a chance to explore the possibility that maybe he was that someone in their lives. No more bimbos and pretending to look for a real relationship.

Pretending?

Hell, yeah, pretending, going through the motions of searching for a wife, all the while picking women he would have never fallen for. Sister Nic had been right when she'd said he was close to understanding.

Which left him with a crapload more decisions to make.

The screen door creaked behind him. He glanced back over his shoulder to find…a weary Paige. Her hair had long ago given up on staying inside the rubber band. Her khaki skirt and all-white T-shirt carried travel-wrinkles, along with a coffee stain dribbled right between her breasts from when her hand shook on the plane. And still he wanted her.

Way to go being a sensitive guy. The last thing she needed was him telling her…what? That he wasn't sure how he felt, but he knew he felt more than he ever had before?

Better to keep the conversation safe and light. If ever a woman looked like she needed a laugh…

He set aside his guitar, propping it against the porch railing. "Is Kirstie okay?"

"I hope so. She told me more about those missing minutes and who she was with. She said she's been speaking with this person she calls Eddie for a couple of weeks now and that he claims he knew Kurt." Paige clicked on the intercom beside the door, Kirstie's light snoring snuffle coming through. "This Eddie character was even at the air show."

Bo wished he'd tracked that bastard right then and pummeled answers from him. "The cops will be able to hunt him down."

She settled beside him on the swing. "At least she's sleeping, and how crazy am I, turning on listening monitors like she's a baby again?"

"Not crazy at all. The incident scared a year off my life and she's not even my kid." And Sister Nic wasn't his blood relative, either, but he still thought of her as his mother.

A little *less* understanding tonight would be nice for his sanity.

"Vic's a mess." Paige slumped back on the wooden swing, her legs extended, her toe tracing through the ever-present Dakota dust. "He's up in his room with a bottle of booze. I reminded him this could happen to anyone. The same thing even happened when both you and I were watching her at the air show."

"What did he say to that?"

"Just nodded and said he'd be fine in the morning."

Bo wasn't so sure. He hooked an arm around Paige's shoulder and drew her to his side. She tipped her face up to his with an easy intimacy and familiarity to her kiss that left him longing to race her over to the barn. Something he knew couldn't happen here tonight.

Crooking a finger in the neck of his T-shirt, she stroked along his chest. "I hope you don't mind too much, but we're not going to be able to go off alone. I want to, but…"

"You can't leave Kirstie. Of course I'm sorry we can't be together tonight—" his knuckles grazed along the side of her breast before cradling her face "—but I understand."

"Thank you." She arched up to kiss him again, nothing hot or out of control but so damn sweet and perfect he wanted more just like it.

Although even an idiot would see she needed comfort. "How are *you?*"

"Scared. Mad at myself for being too preoccupied to realize what was going on in her mind." Her head lolled back against his arm while bugs droned in the distance. "I thought she was past the worst of losing her father, but now she's talking to strangers just to feel closer to her dad."

This woman needed so much more from him than a few Kleenex followed by a laugh. "Some things take longer to get over than others."

"You lost both your parents when you were as young as Kirstie. How did you manage?"

Decision time. If he truly wanted to give this thing between them a chance, time to submit to the root-canal telling of a few ugly truths about his past. "Actually, they didn't die at the same time."

A frown pinched her brows together. "They didn't?"

"My mother died when I was five. My folks had already split, but my dad didn't fight for custody then or after she, uh, passed away. He couldn't take care of me on his own—" too expensive, too much trouble, too bratty "—so he turned me over to the good sisters. He had a heart attack when I was fifteen."

While serving twenty-five to life for popping the used-car dealer who'd been taking him for a spin in a three-year-old Mercedes that Jackass Dirtbag had decided he wanted—without the car payments.

Paige's hand fell to rest on his thigh with a soft comfort easier to accept than an emotional display. "How did your mother die?"

"She cut her wrists." He cleared his throat. "Because my father wanted a divorce."

Paige's hand gripped tighter on his knee. In shock? Or reassurance? She stayed quiet, though, thank God.

"A violent death like that—like with Kirstie's father—it's tough for a kid to get over."

He still woke up sometimes smelling the blood. The shrink they'd made him see after the shoot down and capture had told him the dreams were normal, and offered extra insights that had sounded like BS at the time. But what the hell? They might help with Kirstie. "For a while after losing a parent that way, there's a fear that people are going to leave you, which makes a kid do things like run off. She might think she's leaving before being left or testing the grown-ups who are still around."

"By pouring bubbles in a baptismal font and spelling out hellfire with fertilizer on the lawn?"

Or choosing women he couldn't fall for so the pain of rejection would be less if they left. Understanding sure was a bite in the butt tonight. "Something like that."

"And will she get over that feeling?"

"She has you like I had Sister Nic, so yeah, I think she's going to be fine." He hoped.

"I'll take that as an incredible compliment. Thank you."

"It was meant as one, and you're welcome." He let himself play with a lock of her hair, a reward for spilling his bleeding guts at her feet.

"I enjoyed meeting Sister Nic. I'm sorry we didn't have longer to visit."

"So you could wrangle all my secrets out of her?"

She angled a glance his way. "Do you have more secrets?"

"You know more about me than anyone else, more than even Sister Nic since I never fessed up to the fertilizer incident."

Would she realize the importance of how much he'd told her? He'd charmed women for years, but Paige saw through his bull and demanded honest emotions. Scary, and, damn, he hoped she didn't push for more. He'd had enough for one night.

She turned her head to kiss his neck, a perfect mix of soothing and sexy. Kind of like her. Her soft curves melding to his side spiked his temperature.

He couldn't have her tonight, but that didn't mean they couldn't have some fun, and maybe he would luck into one of her smiles along the way. "Tell me what your room looks like."

She grinned against his neck, a sensual caress of full lips he'd felt along more than his neck the night before.

"Surely I've left the door open enough for you to see in since you've been here."

"I didn't dare look because then I'd start walking toward you, and your brother would jam a shotgun between my shoulder blades."

She laughed as he'd hoped, shifting back to safer ground. "It's nothing fancy really, just delft hues."

"Delft?"

"A shade of blue."

"You'll have to be more specific since I have a Y chromosome."

"Very light blue, like your eyes."

"Got it. Blue walls." He tapped the swing back into motion, the chain creaking in response.

"With white trim." She traced the outside seam of his jeans from hip to knee. "I have an old blue-and-white flowered water pitcher of my grandmother's that sparked the look of everything else."

"What about the bed?"

"You've been wondering about my bed?" She skimmed her hand over his knee to the inside seam.

"Wondering about what you look like in your bed." He grazed the side of her breast with his knuckles, painful when it couldn't go anywhere, but more torturous not to touch her at all.

"It's a large four-poster, all white with a white chenille spread."

"Chenille?"

"Y chromosome again?"

"Definitely."

"It has fringe along the edges and kind of a bumpy woven pattern along the top." She worked her way slowly up the inside seam.

"Okay, note to self for future fantasies about a certain hot Dakota babe." He eyed the skyful of stars and fantasized about flying her somewhere deserted and making love out in the open. "Chenille sounds itchy to sensitive places. Toss the spread to the ground before crawling around naked with Paige on the bed."

Much more of this and he wouldn't be able to think. He stopped her trekking hand a scant inch from reaching a destination guaranteed to drain the last of his brain cells. He pressed a kiss to her palm and linked their fingers.

"Sounds like a great fantasy to me." She cuddled closer, her head against his shoulder as she fit to his side. "Thank you."

He didn't have to ask why. Oddly enough he knew she meant thanks for the smile, for holding her shaky hand while tears sneaked past her defenses, for coming back with her—as if he would have even considered otherwise.

Her breathing slowed and evened out until she drifted off to sleep against him as she'd done the night before. Except, life had exhausted her tonight rather than lovemaking.

While she slept warm and soft beside him, Bo stared out at the moonlit dirt and rocks stretching endlessly along the dry plains. What once looked barren to him slowly shifted in his mind, stirring something inside him. No great, startling moment like when he'd realized why he did, in fact, date bimbos. This understanding came to him in a whispering moment as gentle as the caress of Paige's hand along his skin or the subtle scent of her flowery cologne.

She'd taught him to appreciate the understated. The kick he got from watching Kirstie bounce in the passenger seat of the Cessna beat pulling G forces in a T-38. Rock concerts he'd caught in Europe didn't come close to the thrill of hearing the musicality of Paige's laugh. Paige had taught him to appreciate the joy found in a puppy lying across your foot.

He stared out across Paige's front yard that two weeks ago had been nothing more than a dusty stretch of desolate land leading on into monotony. Now he saw the way the wind swayed the branches of the lone tree, tossing a swing that held more than a few memories for him.

The grass was still clumpy and the mosquitoes still chewed his hide, but thanks to Paige he couldn't deny his sense of pride in the heartland of his country. A country he'd sworn to protect with his life. Suddenly his job in the military wasn't about cool toys and adventure, or even about repaying some cosmic debt in honor of those who took him in as a kid.

It was about protecting this patch of stark beauty and the people who walked on it.

He'd come to North Dakota looking for answers from Paige, and he'd found them, just not in the way he expected. And instead of peace, he'd uncovered more problems, since he couldn't figure out how to reconcile his calling to the Air Force with the possibility of stepping into this family.

Chapter 15

Paige sidestepped the puddle left by a dog and swished the mop over the mess on the clinic floor. What a long damn day at work. Only Monday and yet the past weekend with Bo seemed forever away.

She chunked the mop back in the bucket and out again, slapping it against the scarred tile. Certainly there hadn't been a chance to slip away together since she wasn't letting her daughter out of her sight. Through the open window, Paige watched Kirstie corral the puppies back into the kennel with Bo's help—and ever-watchful care.

Cops were searching for a workman named Eddie who might have made repairs at the school and the air show. He hadn't done enough to be arrested, but certainly could be picked up for questioning. And it would help knowing where to look for the threat.

The whole day had been surreal. She'd kept Kirstie home

from school and close by her side at work. Vic was off in the truck on a call. Seth was at the doctor's after putting too much stress on his recently healed foot looking for Kirstie. Which left her manning the office and taking any fly-out calls with Bo and Kirstie. So far the day had been uneventfully exhausting, just routine exams, vaccines and a case of ear mites.

And an overexcited puppy leaving her a "gift" on the tile.

Paige swiped the mop along the floor, ammonia radiating up and watering her eyes. Bo's voice drifted through the window, closer, louder, along with Kirstie's as they finished rounds through the kennels to walk the dogs.

Of its own will, the mop seemed to *swish, swish* over the floor faster toward the open window and screen door. Bo and Kirstie settled on the top step, a lone puppy left out and resting on Kirstie's lap.

The little mutt Paige had asked Bo to name.

Kirstie cuddled the dog up under her chin. "Are you gonna take Honey back with you to Charleston?"

Even though she knew the answer to that question, more popped into Paige's mind. How much longer did they have left together before he went? Would she see him again after? She couldn't envision how, and that made her eyes sting in a way that had nothing to do with ammonia. Her chin dropped to rest on top of her hands propped on the mop handle.

Bo stroked a knuckle over Honey's golden head. "I wish I could, but I can't."

"Mom says I can have one of the puppies. Would you be mad if I kept Honey?"

"I'd be glad to know she had a good home." He angled his head toward Kirstie, late-afternoon sun glinting off the slight curl to his dark hair. "And maybe I could see her sometime if I'm up this way."

"You'll be back?"

"I hope so."

Paige's fingers tightened around the wooden handle. How could she be so thrilled and terrified all at once?

"You still want to be my friend even after I puked on your boots and was kinda cranky when you were around at first?"

"Yes, Kirstie, I'd like to be your friend."

Kirstie hugged the puppy closer, her head dipping to nuzzle his furry softness. "I don't got many friends here."

Paige swallowed down the cotton-wad lump in her throat. Apparently, Kirstie had been holding in a lot of things to keep her mama from being sad.

"Moving can be tough."

"It's not 'cause of the move." She set the puppy back on her knees, flopping long ears back and forth with exaggerated concentration. "My daddy didn't die of the polio."

Paige straightened from her slouch against the mop, the conversation suddenly about far more than future dates. Part of her longed to burst out onto the porch and scoop up her daughter, but she feared an interruption would stop Kirstie cold.

Please, please, Bo, handle my baby with care.

He reached to flop the puppy ears, too, which also happened to bring his scarred hand over Kirstie's smaller one. "I know, Cupcake."

"He, uh," she whispered, clearing her throat and starting again, "he died in jail because he was a bad man."

"So did my dad."

Whoa. Hold on. They'd spoken about his father, and Bo never mentioned this. Why? Something to ask him about later, but right now she needed to focus on her daughter.

"Your daddy died in jail? How come?" Kirstie asked the question hammering in Paige's mind.

"He stole cars." Muscles rippled along his shoulders with tension under the thin cover of his well-washed cotton

T-shirt. "The last time he did it, he killed someone so the police sent him back to jail for good."

"Did somebody shoot him, too?"

"He had a heart attack."

"Oh." In profile, she squinted her brown eyes behind her glasses, canting closer to him. "You don't look like your daddy was a bad guy."

"Neither do you."

"Thanks."

"And thank *you*."

Kirstie went back to flipping Honey's ears with extra focus as if weighting her words. "My mama used to say I got my daddy's nose, back when she used to talk about him. What if I got other parts of him, too?" Her voice went soft again as her hands fell away from the puppy. "The monster parts."

Pain knifed through Paige like a contraction in her midsection where she'd once carried this child close to her heart. She propped the mop against the wall before she dropped it. Her feet pulled her closer to comfort her daughter, even as she knew she should stay back.

"Trust me. You don't." His voice stayed gentle, but surety rang through that even a kid couldn't miss. Paige stopped at the screen door behind them, her hands pressed to the mesh.

"How can you be so sure? Grown-ups tell lies, you know. My daddy said he loved me. But if he really did, then he should have loved me enough not to do stuff that would make him go to jail. He shouldn't have hurt those other people."

"You're right," Bo answered with surprising frankness.

"I am?" Kirstie's cupid mouth dropped open as she looked up at Bo. "You're not going to tell me my daddy really loved me and I shouldn't worry about grown-up stuff?"

Like Paige had said for a year. Her forehead fell to rest against the metal frame of the screen door.

"The way I see it, Cupcake, you already have to deal with

grown-up stuff, so I'm going to explain this to you in a grown-up way. Think you can handle that?"

She nodded, eyes wide and somber. Side by side, Kirstie and Bo sat, looking so much like a father and daughter it hurt Paige's eyes to see their twin shadows stretch down the steps.

"The way I figure it, there are two kinds of love. There's the kind where, sure, people say they love you, and they do. Except, what they want is more important to them than what you need."

How strange that it stabbed, hearing Kurt hadn't the first clue about being a real father. She'd known and understood, but the reality of wasted years and emotions trickled over her like ammonia on an open wound.

"And then there's the other kind of love, the real kind of love, the best kind of love. When you'll do anything to keep from hurting that person, even if means *you* have to hurt. Do you understand what I'm saying?"

Paige most certainly did, because, oh, God, she couldn't ignore much longer what was squeezing her heart.

Kirstie nodded. "I think so."

"Here's an example to help you see it better," he explained with a teacher tone Paige could envision him picking up in his college course work. "I noticed how you realized your mama gets upset when you talk about your father. You kept all that hurt inside you so she wouldn't have to hurt anymore."

Kirstie started nodding faster. "And like how Mama took me to that air show even though airplanes make her sad."

He winced. "Pretty much."

Oh, how easily she could dream of him in a classroom full of kids, entertaining and teaching. He'd talked about getting out of the Air Force, after all, something she hadn't let herself consider for more than a few fleeting seconds. Not that she expected him to move here based on one night of incredible sex, but at least if he left the military, there would be more options. More hope.

Her heart squeezed tighter.

"Sooo—" Kirstie's shoulders straightened with a renewal of her old spunk "—you're saying that on the inside, I love like my mama does. Not like my dad did."

"That's exactly what I'm saying," he said with an insightful patience and understanding that couldn't be taught in any classroom. "There's another cool thing about the real kind of love."

"What's that?"

"It's okay to share the hurts and help each other." He leaned closer. "So if you want to talk to me about your daddy, I'm here to listen."

"Since you understand 'cause your daddy was a bad guy, too?"

"Exactly."

Silence echoed from the two of them while dogs yipped in the kennel, surely as loud as Paige's heart full of budding hope and resurrected dreams.

Kirstie shuffled Honey onto the next lower step. "You know what, Bo?"

"What, Cupcake?"

"I think you love people the way me and my mom do, the real way."

"Why's that?"

"'Cause I bet you don't like to talk about your daddy, but you did it anyway to make me feel better."

Standing in the shadows, Paige watched her daughter throw her arms around Bo's neck while his big hand patted her tiny back with such gentle care. She gave up the fight to hold in tears and let them flow.

Kirstie planted a kiss on his cheek, then rocked back on her heels. "I love you, too. The real kind of way."

A bundle of youthful energy, Kirstie launched to her feet

and down the steps to chase after Honey, turning not just one, but two cartwheels.

Bo stayed on the step keeping watch over her the whole way, his hands clasped between his knees, broad shoulders braced to take on the troubles of the world for others. Even when it hurt him.

She allowed herself more of those whimsical dreams where she envisioned him getting out of the Air Force, moving here, flying for the vet practice or even teaching.

Tears kept right on trucking down her cheeks and she didn't bother wiping them away. For the first time in a long time she didn't question her feelings. She knew. She'd done the very thing she'd sworn never to let happen again.

She'd fallen in love.

Bo heard Paige shuffle behind him. Not that it surprised him, since he'd seen her shadow stretch across about two-thirds of the way through his tough-as-hell conversation with Kirstie. Scrubbing a hand over his face, he considered just walking away without acknowledging her presence. He wasn't sure how much more of the Haugen women his heart could take today. Kirstie's revelations had left him raw.

Which meant Paige must be damned near bleeding out. Guess he was stuck on this porch for a while longer.

He glanced over his shoulder as she swung open the screen door. "You heard?"

"Every word." She sat on the top step beside him, while the sun sank in a swirl of orange and yellows.

"I think she's going to be okay." The kid certainly acted happy enough chasing Honey around the fat tree trunk. Since Paige hadn't interrupted the discussion, he'd figured she wanted him to continue, but he could be wrong. "Are you upset with me? I know she's not my kid, and some of the stuff I said might not have been age appropriate."

She cupped his face in her hands and kissed him with a long, unmoving intensity that wiped away at least some doubts. "You reached my daughter in a way no one has been able to for a year. I'm so grateful to you right now I can hardly contain it."

"I don't want your gratitude." He slid his fingers through her hair and cupped the back of her head so she wouldn't be able to dodge meeting his gaze. "I want us to keep seeing each other."

She blinked fast, and he tried to read her reaction. A little encouragement would be nice here. Instead he found only blind panic.

"Why?"

Her question stumped him. He'd expected a flat-out yes or no. "Uh, because you're hot and I like you?"

"Or because you want to take care of me since I'm a single mother who was married to a criminal—like your mother."

Damn. Paige went straight for the jugular, but he could see where she might draw that conclusion. Paige always did see through his BS, which also left him with no secrets.

Time for more digging deep. "At first when I saw you last year the similar situations crossed my mind. But I can guarantee that when I look at you now, I am *not* thinking of my mother."

Her fists clenched tight in the gesture he was starting to recognize well. She was stiffening her spine and resolve for something difficult. Ah, crap. The door was about to hit him on the ass, and the prospect pressed against his chest. Even his hands went clammy while he waited for her to answer.

"Me, too."

Huh? He exhaled. "Me, too, what?"

"I want to keep seeing you." Her throat moved in a hard swallow, not a smile in sight.

"You do?" Well, hell. Then why the panic? This should be good stuff.

Her fists went downright bloodless. Clenched any tighter, and she would crack bones. "Kirstie and I were already talking about a summer trip to Charleston. She needs to see our old house, too."

"That sounds like a wise idea." He ignored the warning blaring in his head and told himself her nerves were for her daughter, not over spending more time with him. "I'll let you know my travel schedule with work so we can pick a time I'll be in town. I'll wrangle TDYs and weekends here. I've been in Charleston long enough to try for a transfer to McChord Air Force Base, which would at least bring me to the West Coast."

Her head snapped up. "A transfer to McChord? I thought you were considering getting out of the Air Force."

"I was, but you've cleared a lot of things in my head." He cupped the back of her head, needing to touch her. "You've helped me see that, sure, music's important to me, but flying for the Air Force is what I'm called to do."

Her gaze skittered away from his. "So you're not getting out, after all."

Damn. Those warning bells had been there for a reason. He should have listened. Kirstie had even said visiting the military base made her mother sad from memories. "You were willing to keep seeing each other because you expected me to get out and move here."

"I didn't assume you would relocate just for me, but at least there was the possibility, if you decided later there was reason."

He could already see her distancing herself from him, feel the tensing muscles in her neck under his hand.

She plastered on an overbright smile and eased from under his hand. "Forget I said anything. We've only known each other a couple of weeks. We're talking about dating, not getting married."

"Are you sure about that?" Damn it, he'd known better than to push this skittish woman and still the words fell out of his mouth.

She inched back. Much farther and she'd fall off the porch. More panic chased through her eyes, followed by flat-out fear.

How ironic was that? He'd been accused by countless women of having a commitmentphobia and when he'd finally found someone he could consider spending his life with...

She was commitmentphobia personified.

The telephone jangled inside, and Paige sprinted to her feet like a bat out of hell. "I have to take that."

Bo recognized well enough her convenient excuse to run.

Only two weeks, she'd said.

For her maybe, but he hadn't slept with anyone since he first saw her a year ago. He hadn't even *thought* of anyone since setting eyes on her, and now he understood why. Damn straight, feelings happened that fast. He couldn't ignore the truth any longer. He'd fallen for Paige Haugen that fast twelve months ago.

He'd dated at least a hundred women. He should have plenty of practice in playing it cool at a breakup or rejection. But he couldn't think of one word to say when she returned.

Just like when he was a kid, he was out in the cold.

The door swung out from the office again, Paige worrying her lip and keeping her distance. "We'll have to talk about this later. Chuck Anderson's horse that broke his ribs is having trouble breathing. We need to fly out there right away."

Dreams weren't any more substantial than the clouds barely visible in the darkening night sky outside her airplane window.

Paige sat behind her daughter who was up front in the Cessna beside Bo. The hazy green illumination of the instrument panel cast a Halloween glow through the small cockpit. Kirstie babbled on with a million flying questions, filling the awkward silence, thank heavens.

Paige gripped the armrests. God, she was such a coward.

The guy may have hinted at marriage, but he hadn't come right out and said it. And still she'd panicked, not just at the thought of leaving North Dakota, but at the prospect of stepping from behind the safe walls she'd built around her heart.

Could she dare try his date-and-see attitude while her daughter grew more attached to this charming man in their lives? And if their relationship actually took root? She would have to follow him around the world, chance loving again. Plenty of people did it, but her daughter's world had already been rocked more than most adults. Yet Bo had handled Kirstie's fears with more finesse and understanding than her own family had managed.

Unselfish love put the other person's needs first.

All of an hour in love and already she'd flunked the initial test. She'd vowed she loved him and then balked right out of the starting gate. He'd given so much of himself for her, for Kirstie, too.

Who had given back to him? Sister Nic, friends, all of whom he shielded from hearing the difficult parts of his life. He'd admitted to telling Paige more than anyone else, even if he hadn't discussed love.

Her heart bared, her own defensive needs shuffled aside, finally she heard the parts Bo had left unsaid, things perhaps even he didn't know. His mother's suicide and father's abandonment must have left him feeling unworthy of love. Yet instead of wallowing in self-pity—or hiding out as she'd done—he worked his butt off to help others.

Suddenly Bo's charming exterior took on a different shading. He became everyone's friend—without letting anyone get close enough to hurt him, ensuring he wouldn't be left behind again.

This man with such a big-world charm actually had very simple needs. He needed the security of the "real" kind of love. Now it was time for her to find the courage to face wherever that love took them.

The Cessna descended toward the blinking runway lights on the earthen runway. The rear wheels kissed the strip with an end to yet another of Bo's flawless flights that inspired such confidence in his skill.

He slowed, the flared nose of the plane easing down. The plane's landing light stretched forward to reveal…a dead horse.

"What the hell is that—" Bo straightened in his seat and shouted, "Brace yourselves!"

Chapter 16

Damn, damn, *damn it*, they were going to crash.

Bo pulled back on the yoke. Not enough speed to take off. Too much to turn away, which would almost certainly start a tumble. But at least he could get the vulnerable nose gear up again—hopefully. The nose wheel would easily shear off, but the back gear should hold. A jarring way to stop, but a helluva lot safer.

"Come on, come on, come on. Up, damn it," he chanted to the straining Cessna.

Crap. Not going to work. He hammered the brakes. Kirstie's screams bounced through the craft, echoed in his ears.

Denial roared through his veins. But he wouldn't allow emotions to assume control, especially not with Paige's and Kirstie's lives at stake. Training-honed instincts overrode all else, especially too-distracting memories of the shoot down in Rubistan.

Snap. Jolt. The front gear popped off.

Protect Paige and Kirstie. The mantra pulsed through him in time with the teeth-jarring thud of the Cessna against the barrier. The nose slammed over and into the dirt. The seat belt cut into him as his weight pressed forward. The plane shuddered to a halt.

Dust cleared to expose three figures looming beside a large vehicle with headlights streaking ahead. The moon eased from behind a cloud with enough illumination to reveal…

A Suburban. Anderson's. The man stood still and tall, flanked by two men. None of them moving to help or giving any signs of distress over the emergency. Moonbeams glinted off three weapons pointed directly at the plane.

Damn. They'd been lured here. That dead horse on the runway was no accident, although it would surely appear accidental to investigators later, since animals wandered into the road frequently in this area.

He only had a minute at most to speak to Paige and Kirstie away from the others. He needed to make the most of every second and bring Paige up to speed since she was still focused on Kirstie, both pale but seemingly unharmed.

"Paige, you need to look outside. Now."

Her gasp swelled through the Cessna. "Ohmigod."

"Wait and let them come to us." Which would buy him time to think and strategize. "Is everyone okay? Paige? Kirstie?"

He couldn't afford to take his eyes off the men outside again. He reached by touch to snag his cell phone out of his duffel bag full of flight gear, the stench of the smoking engine an acrid reminder they could well be screwed inside the plane, as well.

"I'm fine," Paige answered, her voice shaky but strong considering the hellish situation.

Thank God.

"Me, too," Kirstie whispered. "What's going on? I'm scared."

He allowed himself a quick heartbeat of relief, holding the cell low and out of sight while he thumbed 911. "Paige, no matter what, keep Kirstie close to you."

Kirstie leaned. "Who are you c—"

The side door jerked open. Crap. He inched the cell phone under his seat and prayed someone was on the other end of the line listening. Tough to count on reliable cell tower coverage out here, but he would relay as much as possible on the off chance the cops could hear. "Anderson, put down the gun. We don't want anyone to get hurt, Chuck."

There. He'd gotten both the man's first and last name out in a normal sounding way. He forced himself to think, stay cool. He wouldn't let this be a repeat of his capture in Rubistan where people were hurt because of his recklessness.

"We'll talk outside the plane." The twin beams of the Suburban headlights backlit the beefy farmer, casting his face in shadows. "Now put your hands where I can see them."

Bo leaned to climb out ahead of the others, keeping them inside the safety of the plane as long as possible.

Anderson shook his head. "Nu-uh, Rokowsky. Kirstie comes out first."

Eyes adjusting to the dark while Anderson lifted out the child, Bo studied the other two men—one of Anderson's stable hands in a repairman's uniform shirt holding a Glock. Damned if he didn't look like the fast glimpse of the air show "Eddie" who'd spoken to Kirstie.

Bo checked the third and final gun-toting goon. The crummy substitute pilot? Rusty something-or-another, and he obviously had a connection to Anderson. Rusty wasn't messing around here, either, not with an AR-15 held hip level. That assault rifle carried too much firepower for his peace of mind.

The odds were crap, three men with guns. There wasn't a chance in hell they would let them walk out of this alive, now

that they'd been identified. Hopefully, the 911 call would net
results. Fast. He'd left the phone on for the dispatcher to listen while he stalled and prayed.

If help didn't arrive in time out here in the middle of nowhere? He would have to take them all out. He'd kicked ass
against larger groups than this growing up, and over things
not nearly as important. In fact, there was nothing more important in his world than the woman and child with him.

Bo vaulted to the ground and reached back to grasp
Paige's waist, lifting her out of the plane. Their eyes met and
held in dim starlight. The gentle give of her warmth under his
hands fired more resolve through him. He gave her waist a
light squeeze and hoped it said enough. How he loved her,
admired her. How he wouldn't let her or her child down.

Kirstie sniffled louder, hiccups turning into tears. She
cried, extending her arms, damn near cutting Bo's heart out.
"I want my mama! Eddie, tell these guys to stop."

"Make the brat shut up." Anderson shoved Kirstie toward
her mother, all but dumping her at Paige's feet even while
keeping his weapon level and steady. "We need her calm
enough to talk."

Paige's arms went around Kirstie, tucking her close and
behind.

Kirstie? They needed Kirstie to talk?

He would wager money Vic had been lured away on a
bogus call tonight so Paige would have to come. Given the
recent scare, she was certain to bring Kirstie along.

Anderson circled Paige, Kirstie scurrying in a circle
around her mother's legs to escape. "You could have made
this so easy if only you'd let Rusty here fly for you. Or even
if you'd spent a little time with me, leaned, trusted. I would
have taken care of you and your kid. I've been patient for
damn near a year now."

Logic shuffled the jarring pieces into place. Hadn't Seth's

accident even occurred at the Anderson place when he'd fallen through rotten boards in a nearly new barn? Rusty must have been sent as a plant inside Paige's home for whatever hell this bastard had in mind. Until Bo had ruined that plan by offering to fly instead. Could problems with the plane also have been a frustrated effort to run them out of business so she would need to "lean on him" as the bastard had put it?

Bo stepped between Rusty's AR-15 and Paige. "I don't know what the hell's going on here, but how about we let Kirstie climb into your Suburban—" which would offer more shelter from flying bullets "—and then we can talk."

Anderson's 9 mm never wavered from Kirstie, threatening the person guaranteed to keep them both in line. "I'm afraid we can't do that since apparently she has information good ol' Kurt failed to supply before he died."

What did Anderson and the two goons flanking him have to do with Kurt Haugen's dealings? "That's why you've been speaking to her?"

"Not at first. We just wanted to track her mother's movements in case anything new came to light about Kurt's finances." Angling closer to Paige, Anderson tsk, tsk, tsked. "That damn screwup died without telling us where he'd hidden the money he planned to use when he moved his family out of the country. Stupid fool. There's no getting out of this business once you're in."

Anderson glided his knuckles down Paige's cheek. A hazy red rage threatened to fog Bo's brain as he watched her struggle not to wince. The fighter inside him longed to lash out and end it now, but he wouldn't let impulsive arrogance dictate his actions now as he'd done in Rubistan.

Keep cool. Logical. Be patient and wait.

Paige inched farther in front of her daughter. "You're a part of what he was mixed up in? Drug trafficking?"

"I travel enough to trade shows that no one questions the

movements of my shipments, some of them from Kurt." Anderson shifted his 9 mm to the middle of Paige's chest, stalling any of Bo's plans to jockey into a better position. "Except he held on to the final payment. All the selfish bastard ever said was that he'd hidden the lockbox with the information and we'd never find it."

Watch. Wait. Paige was buying them time with her questions, answers hopefully floating right through the cell phone inside the open plane. He kept his hands loose, ready to act.

"But you had him killed so he wouldn't finger you."

"Not me. Higher-ups who didn't care about his money, small pickings for them. If they'd been a little more patient, we could have had it all. I was almost ready to give up on you and then your lawyer found that safe deposit box."

"How did you—"

"That little break-in put us onto your lawyer. Nice touch with stealing the drugs, don't you think? Anyhow, your lawyer had impeccable credentials—but his paralegal? Not so much. She rolled for a pittance."

"You set up the purse snatcher?"

"I couldn't take the chance you would turn the contents of the box over to the police." Anderson stepped back, nodding to Eddie. "Enough already, for Pete's sake. There's no more time for finesse. Get to it."

The big blond guy with his bushy eyebrows knelt and peered around Paige's leg at the cowering kid. "Miss Kirstie Adella, let's talk some more about the poems and fairy tales your daddy mentioned in his letter. Did any of those include a buried treasure?"

The man tipped a knuckle under her quivering—chin. Kirstie scuttled farther behind her mother.

Bo watched—still logical, still planning, even as he realized rage wasn't red after all. It was a deep purple, darkening his vision into a tunnel.

His world narrowed to the two females beside him. He would die before he let even one of these bastards hurt either Paige or Kirstie.

They were all going to die.

Paige couldn't ignore the obvious reality as clear as the determination in Bo's eyes. They were going to have to fight three armed men while somehow protecting Kirstie if the cops didn't show up very soon. These were heartless criminals who held guns on a child and sacrificed a helpless animal for their own greed. They were beyond reason.

Panic lashed through her even as she accepted there was no other way. But Bo wouldn't be fighting alone. She would claw her way through this for her child—and for him.

Bo had the training, so she waited for his cue to spring. She never once doubted that he would fling himself between them and danger. This man would never risk a hair on her child's head.

Paige gripped her daughter tight against her, fear icing her veins. What the hell had Kurt planted in that letter and in their daughter's memory?

Kirstie turned tearful eyes up, clinging harder. "Mama?"

Rusty vaulted forward, rough hands reaching to grab Paige's arms, twisting and tugging her around by pinning both wrists behind her until they burned in their sockets.

Bo growled. Kirstie whimpered.

Paige went slack in Rusty's grip before either of them suffered from defending her. She shuddered to think of how many trips she'd made out here alone to Chuck Anderson's place, this danger lurking. "It's okay, punkin. I'm all right. Go ahead and talk to him."

"Listen to her." Eddie's smile looked so warm and normal no wonder her child had trusted him. "Nobody wants to hurt your mother, but we need to know about the stories. Be a brave girl and tell us so everyone can go home."

Kirstie's hold stayed tight on Paige's leg. "You mean the princess story?"

"Yes, what about the princess story?"

"The one where the Princess Kirstie marries a king and they get the treasure hidden under the bush."

"What bush?"

"The one with pretty flowers in the side yard that Daddy and I planted for Mama for Mother's Day. The azzy, uh, az-aylee, um—"

"Azalea bush?" Eddie prompted.

"Yeah, that one."

The men exchanged nods.

"You did well, Kirstie Adella." Eddie stood, patting her on the head. "Your daddy would be very proud of you."

Bile burned Paige's throat stronger than the sting of her arms straining against the biting grip. The cops weren't going to make it.

Chuck smiled without it ever reaching his dead eyes. "Nice work, Eddie. How about getting the plane ready now."

The plane? Ready for what? Already Eddie ducked beneath the wing, a toolbox in hand. Was Rusty going to fly them away? But the plane was wrecked, the nose gear sheared off.

"What if Kirstie's wrong?" She struggled to reason with monsters even as she knew it would be hopeless. "If you kill us you'll lose any hope of finding out more. At least keep her alive."

"There's no other choice," Chuck declared. "Once Eddie was stupid enough to tell her his name, we knew it was only a matter of time until they tracked him and she identified him."

"But the police already know about him."

Leaning closer, Chuck whispered against her skin, the sickening spice of his cologne almost gagging her. "And that won't be a problem once I take care of him, too. The poor man will die in the accident with you, and don't bother trying to warn him. He'll never believe you, anyway."

A few feet away Eddie pulled a screwdriver from his tool-box and hammered it through the gas tank. Fuel trickled from the small puncture and tainted the air. The large grill lighter sticking from his back pocket sent a chill of premonition through her.

Chuck stepped back and raised his voice. "I really don't want to scare the child any more than we have to. You two can make this easy and peaceful, or it can be frightening and painful. Your choice. If you fight us, the coroner will simply assume injuries are from the crash. If he can even tell from the charred bodies."

She'd been right not to trust Chuck all those years ago, but she hadn't even begun to realize the depth of this man's immorality.

He turned to Rusty. "Put a gun to the child's head while I tie up the adults."

Her skin turned to ice in the face of such pure evil. Her dead husband may have been a criminal, but never would he have put a gun to a child's head or burned people alive. In that knowledge came at least some peace in the middle of this hell. She hadn't given years of her life to a total monster. Maybe in his own twisted and, yes, selfish way, Kurt had enough humanity in him to love them.

Rusty backed from Paige, hands up, weapon pointing skyward. "I'm not putting a gun to the kid's head. You do it."

The guy was squeamish over which way they died? Good God. At least the arguing might buy some time to angle for a better position.

Eddie tossed his screwdriver in the box and stepped forward. "Fine. I'll do it."

They were out of time. They would have to take their chances with bullets flying.

Paige kept her eyes trained on Bo, love pulsing through her and from him so darn bright she could swear it lit the dark landing strip. Pure love. Just like Bo had said, the real kind of love that empowered. She watched, waited, and saw…

Now.

Bo launched, chopping at Chuck's gun hand while simultaneously booting Rusty in the gut. The traitorous pilot toppled, a shot echoing, going wild as he flailed. His head smacked the side of the Suburban. He crumpled to the ground, unconscious.

Paige kicked the legs out from under Eddie, his head slamming the ground hard for a disorienting second she fully intended to utilize to protect her child.

Crouching, shielding her daughter, Paige shoved Kirstie toward the Suburban. "Crawl under, punkin. Lie flat. Don't watch."

From the corner of her eye, she found Bo and Chuck punching, fighting, each working toward the dropped gun while Eddie struggled to his feet. Rolling away, Paige took cover behind the bumper to gauge her next move.

She scooped up a fist-size rock from beside her tennis shoe. She wasn't the pampered wife of a crooked businessman any longer. The past months had increased the strength of her muscles and resolve.

And this bastard who had stalked her child was heading toward Bo.

Paige sprinted, leaping onto Eddie's back, catching him unaware. Arcing back the rock, she bashed his temple, once, twice. Blood smeared his head while he shouted. He pumped bullets into the air then down again wildly. Pocking the ground near Bo's feet. Then farther.

Toward the plane.

Thwump.

The Cessna exploded. Heat seared her, they fought so close.

The force of the explosion rocked through the ground. Eddie stumbled backward, fell, slamming her to the hard-packed dirt of the runway. Air whooshed from her lungs. She went light-headed. Oh God, she couldn't faint now.

Paige struggled for breath with Eddie's weight still pinning her. Flames licked higher in a circle around the burning craft. A spark from the bullet igniting the leaked gas? Lack of air left her foggy.

Another gunshot sounded. Jolting her out of her daze.

"Bo!" she couldn't stop the scream from ripping through her throat. Adrenaline surged, and she flipped the unconscious man off her and to the side.

A weaving shadow towering in the dark, Anderson pulled the trigger again.

Bo staggered back. Blood bloomed from his right arm, staining white cotton crimson. He dropped flat.

"No! No, no, no, no," she chanted, crawling across the hard-packed earth toward him.

Bo rolled. Alive. He was alive. She scrambled to her feet.

And then Bo was on his side. Rusty's weapon in hand. Blood dripping down his arm, Bo raised the gun and popped two bullets in Chuck's kneecaps.

Shrieking, her old college friend staggered, crashed to ground, gun slipping from his hand. Paige scrambled to scoop up the 9 mm and trained it on the three men while Bo levered up to kneel. Anderson writhed while his two accomplices lay prone and unconscious for now.

Kirstie scampered out from under the Suburban, and Paige didn't even bother reprimanding her for not staying put. Her daughter raced, curls bouncing, and threw herself against Bo.

He flinched, but stayed silent and cupped the back of Kirstie's head in reassurance.

Oh, how she loved him, this incredible man, so much more of a *man* than Kurt could have ever hoped to be. Please,

please, please, let Bo be all right so she would have the chance to reassure him she wouldn't leave him as so many had done before.

Blood trickled down his arm. "Are you okay?"

Gasping, she choked back a mix of laughter and sobs. "I'm fine. Kirstie's fine. I love you. But ohmigod, are you all right? I love you so much. You need to sit down."

He swayed under her hands. "I think maybe you're right about sitting down. And hold that other thought for later because we have some talking to do, lady."

She totally agreed.

Sirens wailed in the distance finally, Bo's cell phone apparently having done its work even though it now melted in flames. He settled back, Kirstie held close. Paige kept her gun steady while she stood firmly planted by Bo's side.

Exactly where she intended to stay.

How long would he have to stay stuck on this damn gurney with a breeze blowing up his hospital gown that left nothing to the imagination?

Bo shifted, winced, paper crackling under him. Son of a bitch, the stitches and IV for antibiotics in his arm hurt.

Once the cops had arrived at Anderson's place, EMS had sped him to a downtown civilian hospital, where a military flight surgeon from the base waited. The bullet had passed through so Doc had only needed to stitch him up with a local anesthetic. He would be transferred to a room soon for observation.

Meanwhile, they could stuff their painkillers until he spoke to Paige.

The battle-ax of a nurse checking his IV antibiotics had sworn Paige was fine. She was next door in another exam room with her daughter—who was also fine, the nurse had rushed to assure him while shoving him back down onto the gurney before he could go find them.

The cop cars—five of North Dakota's finest, had arrested and hauled away Rusty and Eddie. Anderson had made his trip out in an ambulance, but all three were alive to spill their guts. Eddie seemed especially eager to cut a deal—fast—before he met his old friend Kurt Haugen's fate in prison. Authorities in Charleston were no doubt already beginning to work their way through the legalities of digging up some poor homeowner's azalea bush.

Bo had already been on the phone with his commander who'd been remarkably restrained in chewing him out for making him send another pilot to baby-sit the plane with Mako. Now, nothing more held him in North Dakota.

Except two very special people.

A tap sounded on the door before Paige tucked her head around as if his thoughts had called her. "Bo? Are you awake?"

"Totally. Just waiting for you."

And wasn't that the truth? He'd been waiting for this woman for longer than he could remember. He'd certainly waited through dreams of her for a whole year before he'd finally come to claim her, the only woman he would ever want to be Mrs. Rokowsky.

He couldn't wait to hear her repeat the words she'd blurted seconds before the cops arrived.

I love you. A sentiment he returned.

The nurse glanced from one to the other, bustling across the room. "Don't let him walk," she ordered before slipping out into the hall.

Paige leaned back against the closed door. "Kirstie's asleep with three cops watching over her. Gotta love the extra attention from the police department around here."

Exhaustion was stamped across her face, his blood still staining her 4-H T-shirt along with a hefty coating of soot from the burning Cessna. She worried her bottom lip between her teeth as if struggling for words.

Let her keep thinking, because he had two words that needed saying, no more waiting. "Marry me."

Paige's bottom lip slid free from between her teeth, her eyes wide with shock behind her glasses. She blinked fast, then arched away from the door. She tapped his IV pole. "Those must be some incredible drugs you're on there, Captain."

"I'm not on any pain meds. Those are just antibiotics. I told those needle-happy nurses to hold off on the rest until we spoke."

That stalled her feet. "Really?"

"Really. Now come sit here beside me." He'd rather have her on his lap—or under him—but that would have to wait a few days.

She hitched up onto the gurney beside him, flattening a hand to his forehead with a cool, gentle touch. "You feel okay, but—"

"Trust me to know what I am, and right now I'm a man in love with a woman. I'm a man who's finally found the woman he wants to build a life with. And most of all, I'm a man who's damned determined to win her over."

"That's really beautiful, but…" She swayed toward him with a trembly smile that boded well for the rest of what he had to say.

Ooh-rah. The gunshot wound didn't sting nearly as much with Paige's smile to distract him.

"Shush. No more 'but this' or 'but that.'" He pressed a finger to her mouth. "I'm also a guy in a lot of pain. The quicker you let me have my say, the sooner I can have some serious drugs."

That hushed her right up.

"When a man's as close to death as that, priorities line up cleanly. I love you and I love that little girl of yours, who I hope you'll let be my daughter someday. Nothing but the two of you matter."

"I don't want you to be sorry—"

He pressed a finger to her lips again. "Pain meds. Need them soon. Remember?" He circled her lips and dreamed of kissing that luscious mouth for the rest of their lives. "I want to build a family with you and Kirstie, and I want you both to be happy. And yes, that's a marriage proposal, hopefully more articulate than the one I delivered when you walked in. I'd like things to happen fast, but I'm completely cool with a long engagement if you need time."

Pausing, he flinched at the notion of months without her in his home more than from any pull to stitches. "Maybe not totally cool with a wait, but I'll handle it because I realize you have a lot to settle. I can wait as long as you say you love me, too."

Her eyes wide and glinting with tears, she stared back at him. Happy tears? Sad tears? Pissed-off tears? Sheesh, he considered himself good at reading women, but this one—the one who mattered—left him mystified.

He rolled out the plan he'd made somewhere around the time Anderson's bullet nailed his arm, reminding him what a dumb-ass he would be if he lost Paige. "I can move to North Dakota, find a flying job here, or a teaching job, and I can join the reserves. I'll still wear the uniform. I'll still be able to serve."

Moving his finger away from her mouth, he allowed himself the pleasure of a slow stroke that sent her eyes as dazed as he felt before his hand fell onto her soft thigh. Bo waited for her answer, his whole heart on the line.

"No," she whispered.

No?

And he'd thought he was bleeding to death out at the Anderson place. The pain from his gunshot wound didn't come close to this. He forced himself to stop, think, not explode. "Mind if I ask why?"

"Wait." She blinked, the fogged look clearing from her chocolate-brown eyes. Her hands rested against his chest, heating through the thin hospital gown. "You misunderstood. I'm not saying no to you, just to your solution. You don't have to do this for me."

He swallowed down the relief that threatened to choke off words. Way to go, charmer. "I want to—"

"Shush." She laid a finger against his mouth, tracing, teasing. And best of all, smiling. "My turn now, if you want to get those painkillers."

Damn, but he looked forward to climbing out of the hospital bed and crawling into hers. Soon.

"This past year has been more difficult than anything I could have ever expected. I thought everything would heal if I left it all behind. But facing it with you made me realize the problem wasn't from a place, it was inside me. *You* helped me heal and stop hiding." Her smile softened the tired lines around her eyes. "Kirstie and I want to be with you."

"In Charleston?"

"Or at McChord." Paper lining on the gurney crackled as she shifted closer to loop an arm around his uninjured shoulder. "Or wherever you're stationed along the way. As long as we're together. Kirstie's ready for new places and new friends. Even if some of those places and people are familiar, we don't need to seek refuge away from memories anymore."

"What about your brother and the vet practice? What about your work?"

"I'll always be grateful for all Vic's done for me this past year." She smoothed a hand along the back of his neck. "But I'm not so sure having us here is helping him get over his own problems. He can always hire another vet tech, and I can go back to school in Charleston just as easily as here."

"You sound like you've done a lot of thinking while you waited with Kirstie."

"I did a lot of thinking in the airplane earlier. The rest that happened on the ground only made me realize what an idiot I'd been for not telling you right away. I love you, Bo, and I always will. Wherever you go, there's no shaking me."

"You're sure?" His chest went tight and his head swam with a kick of happiness better than any drug to be found around this joint. He didn't deserve her, but intended to work at it.

"Absolutely. I wouldn't change a thing about the incredible man you are." She paused, worrying that bottom lip of hers again before she continued. "Well, there is just one thing."

"And what would that be? I'll make it happen, come hell or high water." After he kissed her.

He slipped off her glasses and damn near fell into her eyes. Dodging his IV, she arched into his kiss, a kiss they'd both more than earned today. Her glasses thudded to the table as he flattened his hand to the small of her back. Her full breasts melded against the wall of his chest, stirring more heat down south than should have been possible, given his recent blood loss. And along with all that heat, the sweet sweep of her tongue stirred a promise of forever.

"About that one thing I intend to change," she whispered against his mouth, lifting his left hand from her back, her thumb brushing over his ring finger. "I want to put a big gold band right here to let the entire female population know that Bo Rokowsky is officially taken."

EPILOGUE

Paige nudged her glasses straight on her nose again, righting her view of the landing cargo plane. Military fire trucks and security police shrieked onto the runway toward the hulking, gray cargo plane touching down, slowing, smoke puffing from the tires and screeching brakes.

All a part of the air-show dramatics at Charleston Air Force Base.

Her husband piloted today, having just flown an aerial demo, dropping a cargo pallet. Now the base fire department was taking a turn strutting their stuff with full gear, despite the sultry heat. Bo had assured her beforehand that it was only an exercise so she wouldn't be stressed—given her delicate condition.

Tilting her face into a magnolia-scented breeze, Paige held firm to the sticky softness of her daughter's fingers, not so little now. All of eight years and nine months, Kirstie proclaimed often enough. Soon to be a big sister in five more months, which she was certain made her seem even older.

She and Kirstie had moved back to Charleston two years ago, planning to live in an apartment while Paige worked at a local vet clinic and started college classes. Three months later she and Bo had eloped. Why wait when they were both certain and everything else had settled out with her husband's mess?

The uprooted azalea bush had proven fruitful in a number of ways—complete with the account number to a bank in the Caymans. The government seized most of the money. But what little remained of Kurt's assets, Paige and Bo had promptly donated to orphanages throughout the U.S. However, the lockbox included a final surprise—an antique ring for Kirstie, one that had belonged to Kurt's grandmother. It didn't hold any substantial financial worth, but sentiment carried a far higher value. Paige had tucked the ring away for her daughter to wear later.

Meanwhile, Bo was the father figure in Kirstie's life these days, a man of honesty, loyalty and, God bless him, frugality. After Kurt's dangerous lust for money, Paige treasured Bo's thriftiness almost as much as she treasured his abundant love and support.

Thanks in part to that encouragement, she now held a B.S. in biology, along with a nursing degree. She still hadn't decided about vet school, but took great satisfaction in having completed college as she'd dreamed of doing for so long.

Life was good and exciting. Paige squeezed Kirstie's hand and savored the happiness, the wonderful sense of normalcy she would never take for granted again.

Fire trucks circled the plane as crew members raced down the steps out of the craft. A final man filled the hatch. The flight-suit-clad aviator, younger than the others, thundered down the steps and made up the distance in seconds, overtaking, passing.

And so wonderfully familiar. Her gaze tracked her sprinting husband abandoning the scene with heart-pounding athleticism. Bo's coal-black hair reflected the sun rays, some of the beams lingering to catch along the hint of curl in his close-cropped cut. Wow, but he turned her on, a feeling she knew would last through their gray and wrinkled years when he would still have those killer blue eyes and that incredible smile with slightly crooked teeth.

Her husband chose that vulnerable moment to glance her way. Dry lightning crackled overhead, her skin prickling, fine hairs rising with an awareness that nature was about to unleash a storm of passion.

How much longer until bedtime?

And speaking of Bo...

He peeled away from his crew and jogged toward her on the tarmac. "Hey, there, gorgeous." He dropped a kiss on her lips along with a hello stroke over her tummy for the baby, then turned to tug Kirstie's ponytail. "Well, hello, Cupcake. Hope you waited for me so we can have one of those steaming turkey legs."

"And hot dogs." Her daughter smiled up, happy, hungry and healthy.

How ironic that with a nurse in the house now, Kirstie no longer suffered disease-of-the-week outbreaks. She'd even made it through a round of school vaccines with barely a wince over the word shots. She was joyful and secure these days.

Bo passed Kirstie folded dollar bills. "Don't forget the cotton candy."

"Got it!" Kirstie sprinted to the nearby booth within eyesight.

Bo stepped behind Paige and looped his arms around her waist, hands folded over their child on the way while they watched Kirstie stand in line. Paige leaned back against him, welcoming the support of a real partnership. "Love you."

He kissed her temple, lingered, his embrace tightening. "Love you, too."

Sighing her contentment, Paige clasped her hands over his on her stomach, still checking on her little girl moving up in the food-stand line—*their* little girl. Paige wasn't sure when they would get past the need to keep Kirstie in view all the time. But for now their daughter didn't seem to mind the extra attention.

Paige tucked her head under his chin. "Do you have to go back in to work?"

"Just for a quick debrief, and then I'm off for the rest of the day." He backed her into the shade of a nearby palm tree, his warm breath along her neck launching tingles all the way to her toes.

"Vic's taking Kirstie to see the latest Disney movie tonight. We will be alone for at least three hours."

"Oh, really?" His voice rang with unmistakable anticipation.

Three cheers for Uncle Vic!

In a strange and wonderful twist of fate, her brother had decided the exploding Cessna was a sign to close his already struggling veterinary practice. He'd sold the family house and moved to Charleston for a fresh start near relatives. He currently worked in a local animal clinic, the stresses lower in a business he didn't own. She hoped that would give him the healing he needed, too.

Seth had taken the insurance money from the burned plane and started a flight school. Last time they'd talked, he planned to fly out for a visit. Kirstie's world was full of family who understood about "real" love—even gaining a grandmother in doting sister Nic.

"Oh, yes, Uncle Vic most definitely is. He even offered to throw in ice cream afterward if we're nice."

Time alone was a real gift, given Bo's frequent TDYs, a kid and two dogs, Honey plus another new puppy just last week.

"Do you want to make dinner plans?" His strong hands

stroked gentle circles over her increasing waistline. "Is there anything in particular our baby's craving?"

"That's sweet." And it really was, given she knew what he really wanted, the same thing she wanted, actually. "But I had something else in mind." She couldn't miss the whispered ooh-rah against her ear. "Did you read that book on pregnancy I gave you?"

"Yeah, I especially liked chapter eight." He sneaked a kiss on her ear that sent fresh shivers of desire through her. "That was the hormone chapter about how some women in their second trimester are particularly, uh, *amorous.*"

"I thought you might enjoy that part." But probably not as much as she was enjoying the slight rocking of his hips against her backside, so subtle no one else would notice, but she couldn't miss.

"Is chapter eight true for you?"

Paige stepped away before she embarrassed them both by dragging him off the flight line right now. She fit her hand in his as they started forward to help Kirstie carry their order. "You're gonna find out the minute Kirstie steps out that door with her uncle, and I can rip your flight suit off."

He flashed a killer crooked-tooth smile her way. "Gotta love that peaking and second trimester all at once. I may need to take some extra naps to keep up."

God, she loved how he made her laugh. She just flat out loved *him.* "As long as we're napping together, that's more than okay by me."

* * * * *

Watch for Catherine Mann's next release,
CODE OF HONOR,
coming from HQN Books in August.

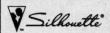
Silhouette®

INTIMATE MOMENTS™

presents a provocative new miniseries by
award-winning author

INGRID WEAVER

PAYBACK

Three rebels were brought back from the brink and
recruited into the shadowy Payback Organization.
In return for this extraordinary second chance, they
must each repay one favor in the future. But if they
renege on their promise, everything that matters
will be ripped away...including love!

Available in March 2005:

The Angel and the Outlaw
(IM #1352)

Hayley Tavistock will do anything to avenge the
murder of her brother—including forming an
uneasy alliance with gruff ex-con Cooper Webb.
With the walls closing in around them, can love
defy the odds?

Watch for Book #2 in June 2005...

Loving the Lone Wolf
(IM #1370)

Available at your favorite retail outlet.

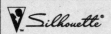

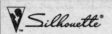

If you enjoyed what you just read,
then we've got an offer you can't resist!

Take 2 bestselling love stories FREE!

Plus get a FREE surprise gift!

Clip this page and mail it to Silhouette Reader Service™

IN U.S.A.	IN CANADA
3010 Walden Ave.	P.O. Box 609
P.O. Box 1867	Fort Erie, Ontario
Buffalo, N.Y. 14240-1867	L2A 5X3

YES! Please send me 2 free Silhouette Intimate Moments® novels and my free surprise gift. After receiving them, if I don't wish to receive anymore, I can return the shipping statement marked cancel. If I don't cancel, I will receive 6 brand-new novels every month, before they're available in stores! In the U.S.A., bill me at the bargain price of $4.24 plus 25¢ shipping and handling per book and applicable sales tax, if any*. In Canada, bill me at the bargain price of $4.99 plus 25¢ shipping and handling per book and applicable taxes**. That's the complete price and a savings of at least 10% off the cover prices—what a great deal! I understand that accepting the 2 free books and gift places me under no obligation ever to buy any books. I can always return a shipment and cancel at any time. Even if I never buy another book from Silhouette, the 2 free books and gift are mine to keep forever.

245 SDN DZ9A
345 SDN DZ9C

Name	(PLEASE PRINT)	
Address	Apt.#	
City	State/Prov.	Zip/Postal Code

Not valid to current Silhouette Intimate Moments® subscribers.

Want to try two free books from another series?
Call 1-800-873-8635 or visit www.morefreebooks.com.

* Terms and prices subject to change without notice. Sales tax applicable in N.Y.
** Canadian residents will be charged applicable provincial taxes and GST.
  All orders subject to approval. Offer limited to one per household].
  ® are registered trademarks owned and used by the trademark owner and or its licensee.

INMOM04R   ©2004 Harlequin Enterprises Limited

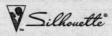

SPECIAL EDITION™

Introducing a brand-new miniseries by
Silhouette Special Edition favorite author
Marie Ferrarella

One special necklace,
three charm-filled romances!

BECAUSE A HUSBAND IS FOREVER

by Marie Ferrarella
Available March 2005
Silhouette Special Edition #1671

Dakota Delany had always wanted a marriage like
the one her parents had, but after she found her
fiancé cheating, she gave up on love. When her
radio talk show came up with the idea of having her
spend two weeks with hunky bodyguard Ian Russell,
she protested—until she discovered she wanted Ian
to continue guarding her body forever!

Available at your favorite retail outlet.

Where love comes alive™

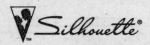
Silhouette®

COMING NEXT MONTH

SIMCNM0205